COLD
LIGHT
OF DAY

COLD
LIGHT
OF DAY

TONI ANDERSON

ALSO BY TONI ANDERSON

For CJMA,
The Light of all my Days.

CHAPTER ONE

"I feel sick," Scarlett Stone warned in a sharp undertone to her lifelong best friend, Angelina LeMay.

"They don't know who you are," Angel responded with a pat on her arm. "Relax and enjoy yourself for a change. I can't believe you actually came with me, but I love you for it."

Her friend wouldn't be quite so understanding if she knew what Scarlett had hidden in her panties. She took a gulp of champagne. This was a stupid idea. Who did she think she was—James Bond?

The thought shot fear through her bloodstream. Too close to home. Too real.

But this wasn't spying on State secrets. She was investigating an old crime, looking for the truth before it was too late. No one would help her. God knew, she'd begged every one of them over the years and they'd all refused. Now it was up to her.

The reception room where the Russian Ambassador to the United States was hosting his annual Christmas party looked like the inside of a palace, with fantastically high ceilings, icy white walls inlaid with gold detail, and two huge chandeliers shining like a galaxy of tiny stars. A grand piano off to one side was being played quietly in the background. The subtle scents of pine mingled with perfume and the spice of mulled wine—the effect cloying, yet oddly nostalgic. The place was crowded. The sense of opulence and history, staggering.

Until 1994, the ambassador's residence had been the Russian Embassy and reeked of a rich clandestine history of secret power struggles. Fitting under the circumstances. Her father had told her the KGB used to operate out of two trailers in the back yard, in the shadow of the huge Washington Post building. She didn't know where the KGB's modern-day equivalent, the SVR, was secreted and she hoped she never found out.

Angel's parents—her father was Congressman Adam LeMay—had received an invitation to tonight's Christmas party but hadn't wanted to attend. Angel had begged Scarlett to take the place of her sister who was hiking in the Mojave Desert. Considering the new ambassador was Andrei Anatoly Dorokhov, Scarlett hadn't been able to refuse, no matter how dangerous and desperate her plan might be. She had no choice.

She took another drink. She needed a little Dutch courage, maybe even a sedative.

"Scar, don't look now," Angel's voice dropped to low and breathless, "but I think my future husband just walked in the door."

Angel LeMay fell in lust on a regular basis.

"I hope you'll be very happy together," Scarlett said without turning.

"Navy dinner dress blues and a gold cummerbund." Her friend fanned herself with her free hand. "I am in love."

"I thought you were only getting married for money?" Scarlett teased.

Angel flashed her dimples. "I'll make an exception for a war hero, and anyway, he might be loaded."

Angel might be her best friend, but it didn't mean Scarlett was blind to her flaws. Her parents indulged her every whim. She "*worked*" on Capitol Hill in her father's office, doing God only knew what—answering the mail if tonight was any indication. Scarlett figured brain atrophy explained most of Angel's poor choice in men. Not that hers was much better. Lab rats and academics were the only guys she dated, and "dated" was an optimistic term. "Grabbed coffee with between experiments" was probably more accurate.

Over Angel's shoulder, Scarlett watched another guy wearing a black tux making his way toward them. His intense coal-eyed gaze never left her friend's butt. Angel was wearing a little black dress, with the emphasis on "little." Few men could resist and fewer tried. He looked up and caught Scarlett watching him. A dimple appeared in one cheek and ebony eyes twinkled. No remorse that she'd caught him ogling her friend's ass. Just that sense of entitlement that if he wanted to stare, no one was going to stop him. Confident and powerful. Somewhere in his late twenties, early thirties, the man had player written all over his handsome face.

He walked up and introduced himself. "Welcome to the home of the Russian Ambassador to the United States. May I say it is a pleasure to welcome such beautiful young ladies. My name is Sergio Raminski, the ambassador's personal assistant." His *W*s sounded vaguely *V*-like, but apart from that his accent was perfect.

He looked more like a bodyguard than any personal assistant she'd ever seen, but maybe she was paranoid. Actually there was no *maybe* about it. A shiver of unease hummed over Scarlett's skin. If ever there was a candidate for foreign intelligence agent, Raminski was it.

According to her dad, a portion of the embassy staff here were actually agents for the Kremlin, the same way some of the Americans in Moscow did more than stamp passports. Angel introduced herself and then introduced Scarlett as her sister, Sarah. Scarlett's nerdy appearance had been overhauled by a pro, something Angel had been doing at every opportunity since kindergarten. She and Sarah looked vaguely alike now that Angel had plastered her with makeup and pulled back her hair. Scarlett had borrowed a strapless, silver gown that shimmered in the candlelight. The skirt had a net petticoat and double layers of gathered silk which flounced around her knees. Four-inch heels meant she was almost chin-level to most of the guys in the room.

Sergio bowed first over Angel's hand, then Scarlett's. When she tried to let go, he surprised her by holding tight for a moment, making her pulse skip a beat, though not in a good way. A blush heated her cheeks and she pulled firmly away.

"Your father was unable to attend?" Sergio asked.

Scarlett's mouth gaped.

Angel stepped in. "After the Vice President's funeral today he felt a little unwell. He sends his apologies."

Scarlett swallowed the knot that had formed in her throat. Her father was the real reason she was here.

"Nothing serious, I hope?" Black eyes were alight with interest.

Insider knowledge is always of interest to Russian officials no matter how seemingly mundane—her father's warnings flashed through her mind.

"Just something he ate at lunch." Angel smiled. She was a pro at lying and manipulation to get what she wanted. From the hard light in his eyes, Scarlett bet money Raminski was better.

"You were lucky you did not all succumb to the sickness." Raminski cranked up the warmth of his smile. "I would have missed out on the best part of the evening—meeting two such lovely, young ladies."

Gag.

It wasn't only Raminski's cheesy lines that made her queasy. She was about to do something that could get her arrested. The idea made her stomach cramp. *Once in a lifetime opportunity*, she reminded herself. And once in a lifetime might be an overstatement. Fate. Serendipity. Seize the moment. *What is the worst that can happen?*

They could lock her up and throw away the key.

Crap.

She swallowed more champagne.

Angel—born flirt—smiled an electric smile and smoothed her hands over her concave stomach, as if more attention needed to be drawn to her goddess-like figure. "I wanted to fit into my dress tonight so I was a good girl at lunch." The expression in her eyes suggested she wasn't normally a good girl.

"Your efforts are much appreciated, Ms. LeMay." Raminski inclined his head courteously to Angel, and then to Scarlett.

He was *so* not her type. She liked men who appreciated a woman's brain at least as much as her body. Not handsome, muscle-bound jerks who only wanted a bout of hot, sweaty, mindless sex.

Gotta get over that, an inner voice complained.

And then it clicked. *This* was her chance. Angel and Sergio Raminski were all distracted and flirty with one another. She just needed ten minutes alone. "Actually," she touched her own stomach, "I don't feel so good. If you'll excuse me for a moment, I need to visit the powder room." She took a step back and jostled the elbow of someone behind her.

"*Fu*...udge," said a deep male voice.

She whirled and came face-to-face with Angel's future husband. She could tell it was him because she'd made him spill champagne down the front of his dress blues.

"I'm so sorry." She grabbed a white, cloth napkin off a nearby waiter and dabbed at the man's white shirt and gold cummerbund. "I'm such a dork."

"That wasn't my first thought." His expression caught her off-guard. It contained a very male look of admiration. She blinked. He took the napkin from her hand and she felt a shiver of something that was definitely not repulsion.

The guy looked...like...Well, he looked fabulous. And hot. Tall enough she had to tilt her head way back even wearing these ridiculous heels. He had military-short, dark blond hair that shone brightly under the chandeliers. A lean face, firm jaw, pale hazel eyes that twinkled with obvious humor and a mouth that tried to suppress it. She resisted the urge to fan herself the way Angel had earlier. Her eyes drifted lower, taking in broad shoulders and a chest-full of medals that jerked her out of her perusal. He was an American hero and not for the likes of her.

Sergio Raminski tried to step in. "Allow me to help."

"Yeah, no thanks." The guy held up his hand firmly as if to ward the Russian off. *Captain America meets the Dark Prince.* "Not a big fan of champagne, anyway."

"You're going to be all sticky." Scarlett grimaced apologetically.

"Sarah Le*May*!" Angel's laugh got dirty and loud and Scarlett flushed with embarrassment.

She opened her mouth to insist she hadn't meant it as a double entendre, but snapped her jaw closed. The sparkle in the sailor's gaze intensified and Raminski's smirk became a full-blown grin. She rolled her eyes. *Great.* Just great.

"If you'd like to get properly cleaned up I can take you to one of the guest suites, or…" Raminski tilted his head to one side and slipped into silky hospitality mode. "Miss LeMay was just going to find the restroom. Perhaps you can accompany one another?"

The American held the other man's gaze so long Scarlett began to feel uncomfortable. Then he turned to her and held out his elbow in a courteous move. "Sure, let me escort you. We can get lost together."

"I know who I'd like to get lost," she muttered quietly, cutting a glance at Raminski as they walked away.

The sailor flashed her a grin. The last thing she wanted was an escort, especially the kind people noticed with good looks and glittering medals, but she needed to get out of here and making a fuss would garner too much attention. Scarlett Stone might run away and hide, but the congressman's daughters had been raised in wealth and privilege. They expected to be treated like society princesses. Outside, in the hallway, a waiter directed them down a long stretch of dimly lit corridor. According to the blueprints she'd studied, this was where she needed to go.

Her heels clicked off the parquet flooring, her footsteps echoing loudly in the relative quiet of the empty hallway.

He moved silently, but she was very aware of the man at her side—his size, his looks, and warm body next to hers. They stopped when they reached the men's room and she quickly disengaged her arm. "I'm really sorry about the champagne."

"Accidents happen." He shrugged easily and held out his hand. "Matt Lazlo."

She shook his hand, his skin warm and dry; grip, strong but not crushing. Her mouth formed her real name for a split-second before she remembered who she was supposed to be. "Sarah LeMay. I'm here with my…sister, Angel." She couldn't hold his gaze, but she could hardly confess the truth just because he had pretty eyes and looked good in uniform. Some secret agent she'd make. She resisted rolling her eyes at herself.

His lips tightened and his expression turned serious. "I'm sorry they made you uncomfortable back there."

Her gaze flashed to his in surprise. She'd spent a lifetime being uncomfortable and few people noticed. She rubbed her bare arms where goose bumps raced over her skin. "It's okay. It was my fault for knocking champagne all over you. I tend to be clumsy unless I'm working." Then her hands were steady as lasers and they needed to be.

"So what is it you do?"

Crap. "Oh, nothing very important," she said vaguely. Sarah worked for an advertising agency but Scarlett didn't want to expand on the lies she'd already told and, under the circumstances, she could hardly tell him she was an expert in solid-state physics.

"Pretty earrings." He tapped one of the sparkling danglies Angel had lent her. Scarlett touched it self-consciously, not used to wearing anything flashy.

She pointed to his medals. "That's some impressive silverware you have there yourself. Thank you for your service." The words made her uncomfortable—not because she wasn't sincere, but because if he knew who she really was, he wouldn't want her thanks. She hunched her shoulders at the thought, folded up a little on herself. America thought her family was the ultimate in treacherous backstabbers and betrayers. Unless she could prove otherwise, they always would.

She noticed a pair of tiny holes in the material where a pin must have sat on his uniform jacket. She reached out and brushed her fingers over the rough edge of the material. "What did you have there?" She raised her eyes to his and watched his pupils flare in surprise.

"Nothing."

She withdrew her hand. "So why'd you take it off?"

One side of his lips kicked up. God, he was pretty. "Take what off?" Sharp intelligence spiked those hazel depths, making them a million times more attractive, sending a jolt right through her system. The timing was a death knell to any possible relationship—and wasn't that the story of her life. She took a step back.

The thought of what she was about to do crowded out the pleasure of meeting a guy who had gorgeous eyes and a keen sense of humor. "I suppose I better hurry up and get back to Angel."

He pulled a face, obviously as keen to return to the party as she was.

"Why did you come tonight?" Scarlett asked, suddenly curious.

"A direct order from my boss. What about you?" He stood with his legs braced apart, watching her as if he had all the time in the world.

She didn't have all the time in the world—she had this one brief moment to try and right a terrible wrong. Even then it might not be enough. "My parents made me," she told him.

It wasn't a lie.

They stood there staring into each other's eyes, and Scarlett forgot to breathe. It was one of those rare moments when you met someone and wanted to spend the whole night getting to know them better. She finally broke the connection. It could never be. She turned and walked to the entrance of the ladies' room, and when she glanced back, Matt Lazlo had disappeared.

Matt Lazlo was not the man for her, no matter how much she might want him to be. His uniform should have served as warning enough.

Scarlett's father's favorite quote had been, "The price of freedom is eternal vigilance," but he'd still ended up in a supermax prison serving multiple life sentences for treason. Now Scarlett was about to take the concept of vigilance to a whole new level and God help her if she got caught.

Inside the restroom, she held the door for a woman who was just leaving. From her position half-hidden behind the large oak door, she spotted the Russian Ambassador coming out of a room across the hall, a room her research suggested was his office. She recognized his face from official photographs— shaggy blond hair and craggy forehead. Short, stocky, but good looking in a blunt, powerful way. Fourteen years ago he'd been the diplomatic attaché here in Washington. He'd returned to Moscow shortly before her father had been arrested.

Coincidence? Scarlett didn't think so.

Her father had always been suspicious of Andrei Dorokhov, but he hadn't found any concrete evidence of espionage. He must have gotten too close, and somehow the Russian had figured out a way to frame him—Scarlett was hoping to discover exactly how and exonerate her father.

The ambassador straightened his fancy white jacket and strode along the hallway in firm strides. Another man left after him, moving in the opposite direction. Scarlett eyed the slowly closing door to the office. Her plan had been to plant her device inside a cleaning supply closet around the corner that shared an inner wall with Dorokhov's office. The technology should be good enough to pick up conversations, but it wasn't ideal. Taking a chance, she dashed across the hall, caught the door just before it latched and darted into the office, closing it gently behind her.

It was dark and she flicked on the overhead light to make sure no one else was in the room. Easier to plead ignorance at the start than to snoop around and find someone sitting in the dark, watching her commit a crime. The room was beautiful in its old-fashioned opulence. A marble fireplace with a large gold-framed mirror above it formed the focal point of the room, and heavy red, velvet curtains shut out the rest of the world. A massive desk made of some dark wood with a satin finish sat to her right.

If she was caught here she didn't know what they'd do to her, but it wouldn't be good.

An ornate brass lamp on the desk was perfect for her needs. She hitched up her skirt and reached inside her panties, removed a small plastic bag. Carefully she laid the lamp on the desk and removed her tiny expandable screwdriver from the bag. It was fiddly, but after only a few seconds she'd removed the base of the lamp and peered inside.

A wave of icy horror swept over her bare shoulders and down her spine. Inside the lamp was another electronic listening device. A sophisticated one. Not a remnant of the Cold War. *Crappity crap.* She wanted to scream but clamped her lips shut. Sweat bloomed on her skin and her palms grew damp. Someone was already spying on Andrei Dorokhov, or his predecessor. And that someone might right now have her under surveillance.

This isn't happening.

She squeezed her eyes tightly shut. Then pulled herself together. It was happening and she needed to get out of there. Fast.

Quickly, she reassembled the lamp and wiped off her prints. There was every chance whoever was spying on the Russians had just witnessed her attempting to do the same thing. Or maybe they only had audio…*Please, only have audio.*

She stuffed the small plastic bag of equipment down her bodice, turned off the light before opening the door a few millimeters. No one was in the corridor so she slipped quickly across the hall into the bathroom. She flushed the transmitter down the toilet and dropped the screwdriver in the garbage.

Her chance was gone. Maybe it had never truly existed—just another fragile hope to keep the illusion alive. She leaned her forehead against the wooden stall door as her heart slammed into her ribs. Adrenaline made her dizzy. Skin clammy. Her body alternated between hot then cold as her reaction shifted from panic to despair. She needed to get out of here. She couldn't believe she'd been so stupid and naïve as to think she could pull this off, but maybe that's how her father had been framed in the first place. Stupid and naïve must run in the family, along with gullible and unlucky.

———

FBI Special Agent Matt Lazlo watched Sarah LeMay hightail it across the plush carpet back to her sister. She intrigued him. Less confident than her sister. Not as obviously beautiful, but certainly more attractive—to him, anyway. Deep thoughts lurking beneath the surface—thoughts he'd like to explore and, come to think of it, a surface he wouldn't mind exploring either. She even smelled good—tangy lemon that was both sweet and fresh.

She wasn't his usual type, all big dark eyes and waif-like figure. He liked lush curves, long hair and a good time smile.

The sister had curves but for some reason it was Sarah who held his attention. They'd shared a connection earlier. He'd have had to be dead not to notice it, and despite many close calls, he wasn't dead yet. He was tempted to ask for her number, though the idea of taking a politician's daughter out for a night on the town did not mesh with his tight budget.

Everyone had to live a little, right?

"A friend of yours?" the Russian Ambassador's wife asked.

Damn. He shouldn't have let his attention wander. She'd cornered him when he walked back into the reception and Matt's survival instincts had kicked in. FBI agents should not hang with beautiful women from the Russian Embassy. If anyone other than Assistant Special Agent in Charge Lincoln Frazer had asked him to do this he'd have wondered about the guy. But Frazer was the rock star of the FBI—he could probably form his own division if he wanted. The guy had received an unexpected invitation to dinner with the President of the United States and had asked Matt to step in at the last minute. Matt would rather be back on his boat drinking beer, but it was hard to refuse Frazer, especially on the day they'd buried the Vice President. The latter had died from a heart-attack at his home in Kentucky. It had followed a series of events that had gotten one of Matt's best friends shot, and the president almost killed. Attending a Christmas reception in Frazer's stead seemed like a small favor under the circumstances.

Matt had joined the FBI for peace and quiet, and a more regular work schedule. The last six weeks had been anything but. He was looking forward to a little R&R over Christmas.

The Ambassador's wife was looking at him expectantly.

"No, ma'am. I only met her earlier when she spilled champagne down my shirt."

Natalie Dorokhov had inky-black hair and ruby-red lips—more Wicked Witch than Snow White. The woman sipped her champagne and eyed him thoughtfully. "She looks about fifteen." Her eyes were pale blue and looked a hell of a lot older than fifteen.

Matt smiled politely. Sarah LeMay was not a little girl. She just had that youthful wholesomeness that defied years. Pointing that out to this woman would go down like a case of VD so he changed the subject. "Are you enjoying Washington, ma'am?"

Natalie smiled smugly. "I enjoy meeting new people. My husband was stationed here years ago, before we met, so he knows the city and has friends here." Her bare shoulders rose and fell. "Though I do dislike being treated like an agent for the Kremlin every time I go to 'tea.'"

"Comes with the territory, I guess." No way was he talking Russian security with her, ever.

Sarah was whispering urgently into her sister's ear before she began physically dragging her toward the door. Sergio Raminski looked pissed. Matt didn't trust the guy and was glad the LeMay women were putting some distance between them and him. Matt had wanted to talk to Sarah again, but she didn't even glance in his direction. So much for the connection he'd imagined.

Too bad. He turned his attention back to Natalie. "Your English is excellent, ma'am."

"Thank you." Her smile grew wider, as if she was hiding a secret. "I had some very good teachers." Her expression changed. "Ah, my husband is trying to get my attention." She put her hand on his bicep and squeezed. It sent a bolt of *get-me-the-fuck-out-of-here* straight through him. "It was nice to meet you, Matthew." Because he introduced himself as Matt, people made assumptions he rarely bothered to correct. "I hope we will meet again sometime soon."

He hoped not.

"Natalie." He inclined his head. First name terms with the Russian Ambassador's wife...? His old buddies on the teams would laugh their asses off, not to mention his colleagues at the FBI. God help him.

Matt checked his watch, figured he'd fulfilled his duty, and handed his glass off to the nearest waiter. He was dog-tired after pulling a series of fifteen-hour days trying to help get monsters off the streets.

Sarah LeMay and her sister were nowhere to be seen. He gave a mental shrug. Not the sort of woman he should be pursuing anyway. Sarah didn't seem like the no-strings, fling type and he was too busy with work and figuring out his mother's care regime to fit in a relationship. He texted Frazer's driver and headed downstairs. The limo was just pulling along the curb when he stepped onto the sidewalk of 16th Street.

There stood Angel and Sarah LeMay arguing on the pavement. Angel was obviously not happy with her sister. He couldn't hear exactly what was being said but she was shaking her finger in Sarah's face and cursing like a senior chief. The urge to step in and protect the slighter woman was almost overwhelming.

Frazer *had* hijacked his evening and told him to enjoy himself. "Can I offer you ladies a ride?"

Angel's furious expression immediately cleared though Sarah grabbed her arm and tried to hold her back.

"You sure can, handsome." Angel shrugged off her sister's grip and sashayed toward him. He almost swallowed his tongue when her coat gaped and he noticed where her hemline hit her thighs. *Holy cow.* The fact he hadn't noticed earlier was astonishing because the woman had *legs.* It pissed him off. He was a trained observer and he'd been distracted. What else had he missed?

Angel slid into the limo and began searching for a bar. Sarah stood on the sidewalk staring at him with haunted eyes. Her chin lifted a notch and her throat rippled. Angel was a flirt but her sister was a different creature entirely.

"Coming?" he questioned.

Emotions raced behind her eyes and she looked like she wanted to bolt.

"Are you okay?" He took a step forward.

She pressed her lips together and nodded quickly. "Yes, thank you." But her voice was small, all laughter gone. Not the same woman who'd teased him earlier. There was something fragile about her. Considering the cynical nature of his job, he was surprised it attracted him so much. He didn't do fragile. He did tough and feisty. Women who gave him shit and knew the score. Women who didn't get upset when he didn't call them the next day, or ever. Sarah LeMay looked like the exact opposite of his usual type and he had no idea why she drew him so completely.

"Want to get in the car?"

Her eyelids closed for a moment and then blinked wide as if afraid to drop her guard. She moved toward him, bunching her skirt to climb in beside her sister.

"Where to?" he asked, getting in beside them.

"A club." Angel looked frustrated by the lack of alcohol in the vehicle. Welcome to the Bureau.

"Home." Sarah's voice trembled. "I'm not feeling well."

It would explain her rapid change in demeanor.

Angel eyed her sister narrowly. "Scar, I swear to God…"

"Scar?" Matt queried.

"Nickname." Sarah said quickly. "Can you drop us at one-forty-five 19th Street, please?"

Matt gave the driver the address while he watched the interaction between the two sisters.

Something was squirrelly. Angel's lips were pressed firmly together, index finger tapping impatiently on her exposed knee. Sarah stared fixedly out the window. The short hairs on the nape of his neck went taut.

None of his business.

Angel turned back to him and broke the tense silence. "So where are you going next, sailor?"

Sarah shot her a glare.

"Home."

17

"And where is home?" She tossed her blonde locks over her left shoulder.

"Virginia."

When he didn't elaborate Angel went back to her impatient tapping.

If Sarah had been the one asking would he have answered differently? Maybe. Would he have offered to bring her home? Definitely maybe. The more he looked at her the prettier he realized she was. Darker brows, dark lashes, perfect lips. Gold streaks amongst mid-brown hair that was pinned messily to her nape. Angel was gorgeous—as was the ambassador's wife—but neither of them had that…what the hell was it? Sweetness? Vulnerability? Smarts?

But the woman was practically vibrating in her seat. He resisted the need to reach out and squeeze her hand in reassurance.

They arrived at the women's house in awkward silence. He got out and held the door. Angel stalked up the stone steps of her parents' home in heels that could be used as lethal weapons. Killer heels, killer dress, killer face. All of which left him cold.

Sarah climbed out of the limo more slowly. "Th-thank you for the ride."

"You're welcome. I hope you feel better soon." Matt stared at her intently, wishing she'd meet his gaze, wanting to ask her out. She turned away and followed her sister up the steps.

Frustrated because cowardice was not something Matt usually tolerated in himself, he climbed back into the limo and the driver pulled away from the curb. He turned to look through the rear windshield. Sarah LeMay was standing on the top step staring after him as if she had regrets of her own.

Dammit.

CHAPTER TWO

Scarlett followed Angel inside the LeMay family row house. The decor was all white walls and pale wood, stylish and appropriate for entertaining bigwigs, as well as being a warm and inviting family home. Scarlett had always felt welcome here. Now she felt like a fraud.

"You're home early." Angel's mother, Valerie, came out of the lounge into the hall to greet them, kissing them both on the cheek. "I thought you were going to a club?"

"Scar wasn't feeling good so we came home early." Angel's voice held an edge her mother thankfully missed. Her best friend was seriously pissed and Scarlett didn't blame her.

Valerie put a cool hand on Scarlett's brow. The woman was even shorter than she was. Concerned brown eyes raked her with affectionate concern. "You don't feel hot but you look pale. You want to stay here tonight?"

"Thanks, Mrs. LeMay." Scarlett always called her 'Mrs. LeMay' even though for years the woman had said to call her Valerie. "I should probably go home. I have work tomorrow."

"On Christmas Eve?" Those brown eyes widened.

Scarlett nodded. "It's a good time to be in the lab. Quiet. Mom's gone for the week to visit Dad…" Silence pressed down like a felled tree. *Crap.*

"You're coming for Christmas dinner, right?" Valerie asked.

Scarlett shook her head. "I have an experiment—"

"Nonsense. You're coming here. I won't hear another word about it." Valerie nodded decisively and that was that.

"Okay, thanks," Scarlett finished lamely. Assuming she hadn't been arrested and stuffed in jail...

"Oh, dear." Valerie reached up to touch her right ear. "You lost an earring."

Scarlett froze as her hand shot up to check. Please don't let it have fallen when she was in Dorokhov's office. Chances were slim. It could have fallen off in the reception room or the bathroom or in the limousine. She'd only been in the office for a couple of minutes, tops.

It was easy to tell yourself not to worry but harder to actually make yourself do it.

"I'll leave you guys to it. Your father and I are watching *It's A Wonderful Life*," Valerie said. "We're at my favorite part where they fall in the pool."

Angel shook her head. "I don't know how you stand the excitement, Mom."

"That's why you have to enjoy yourself when you're young because when you're older you'll just want to stay in and watch old movies with your crusty, old hubby." She kissed her daughter's forehead and walked into the family room, closing the door behind her.

"You're about as exciting as my mother, you know that?" Angel muttered. "Except when she was our age she knew how to party. By the time you hit fifty, we may as well bury you."

Scarlett flinched and crossed her arms. Angel had a Ph.D. in bitchery, which she put to good use when she was mad.

It was easier to ride out the storm than fight. Scarlett followed her friend up the stairs so she could get changed and leave. She needed to be alone.

"I don't know what the hell is wrong with you," Angel continued. "Two of the hottest guys I've seen in *forever* and you drag me away like we're in mortal danger. Do you even like men?"

Scarlett sighed. "I like men just fine."

"I mean the good looking ones, not the dweebs you date." Angel stomped up to the top floor and flung open the door to her bedroom.

Maturity wasn't her strong point. Loyalty was.

Under the circumstances Scarlett hadn't had much choice except to leave the party—not that she could tell Angel her reasons. She couldn't risk involving her in a potential scandal that might get seriously ugly considering who her father was. Angel would go ballistic if she found out the truth and Scarlett didn't want to deal with it right now. Her jaw ached from clenching her teeth. She really hadn't planned this out very well, too excited at the opportunity to plant a listening device to think about the repercussions if things went wrong.

She dropped the remaining earring on Angel's dressing table. "Sorry I lost your earring."

Angel grunted and threw off her heels.

Scarlett would replace the jewelry as soon as she could get to the store.

Angel wasn't done. "How many years have I stood by you? Have I ever asked for anything in return?"

Constantly.

"I'm twenty-five years old and I feel like I'm already trapped inside my boring life. We were supposed to *party*, remember? And that sailor—*oh, my God, Scarlett*, did you even notice the way he looked at you?"

"I spilled champagne down his shirt. He looked at me like I was an idiot."

"He didn't." Angel shook her head. "He was scorching hot and he was into you. You didn't even get his number. You're such a pain in the ass."

Scarlett shed her coat and walked through the adjoining door to Sarah's room to hang it on the back of her door. Yes, she'd noticed how Matt Lazlo had looked at her. It was just another crappy part of another crappy day because she'd desperately wanted a man to look at her like that, and now it had happened…*Hasta la vista, baby.*

In the long run she'd saved herself some major heartache. That wasn't fatalism; it was fourteen long years of experiencing what happened when people found out who her father was.

She found the zipper at the back of the dress and tugged it down, sliding off her heels along with the dress. Sarah was the opposite of her sister in many ways though she liked pretty clothes. She was an outdoor nut. Hiking, climbing, skiing. The only interest Angel had in the outdoors was whether or not she'd get her hair and make-up messed up if she got caught in the rain.

Scarlett wiped off the heavy make-up in the bathroom, then quickly changed back into jeans, black sweater and sneakers. She left her hair pinned at the back of her head, which she covered with a tweed, cloth cap. She grabbed her green, wool jacket off the bed, along with a long scarf, which she wrapped around her neck twice to combat the winter chill.

Angel lay on her bed in her underwear. The woman didn't have a self-conscious bone in her body. She was looking at her phone and smiling.

"I have to go." Scarlett stood awkwardly in the doorway.

Angel's blue eyes cut to her. "You have to get over it, Scar, it's past time. Your dad is in prison. Most people don't even remember what he did—"

"He didn't do it," Scarlett snapped.

Angel lunged to her feet and grabbed Scarlett's arm. Her fingers tightened in a painful grip. "He did it. He got six US intelligence officers killed and sold the United States out to the Russians. You have to accept it and you have to move on. You are not your father."

Scarlett stared into the face of her best friend and said the words she'd been keeping locked down deep inside since her mother had told her last week. "He's dying. Dad's got cancer and he's dying."

Angel's eyes widened and then closed before she pulled Scarlett into a fierce embrace. Scarlett crumpled and they both dropped to the bed. She wrapped her arms around her best friend and tried to hold back the sobs that wanted to escape.

"Why didn't you tell me?" Angel stroked her back, up and down, a warm, calming touch. "Why do you never tell me anything until I yank it from you by being a complete and utter bitch?"

Scarlett wiped her wet cheeks. "You seem to enjoy yourself so…"

"Ha." Angel let her go and Scarlett sat up.

She studied the thick, wool rug at her feet. "I couldn't talk about it, it was just too raw." She looked up. "I'm sorry I didn't give you the chance to get Raminski's phone number."

Angel raised one brow. "What makes you think I didn't get his number?" Her friend's grin was sly and wicked.

Scarlett opened her mouth. "You acted like you were Cinderella dragged from the ball, only you forgot to drop the shoe."

"No way would I leave behind a shoe." Angel's shoes cost more than Scarlett's car. "But more to the point, I also got the sailor's number." Her blue eyes were assessing. "Do you want it?"

Was Angel bluffing? She had to be bluffing.

Scarlett remembered the way he'd looked at her before she got in the limo. Like he cared, which was crazy because he didn't know her, and if he did he'd run a mile. No one wanted to know her when they figured out who she was, and that would go double for an American war hero.

She swallowed to moisten her suddenly arid throat. "No, I don't want it." But the lie abraded her tongue.

———

Matt stretched out in the back of the limo, eyes closed. He'd taken a quick detour to the White House to catch up with his buddy Jed Brennan who he hadn't seen since the guy had been shot. Now Jed was off to sleep in some fancy DC hotel with a very lovely redhead. The guy was so obviously in love with the woman and her cute kid that Matt kind of felt choked. Jed was going to make a great dad, something every child should have, something Matt had missed out on. Still, it had made him a better man in the long run. The asshole who'd fathered him had hardly been a good role-model.

Now Matt was on his way home. One more day until Christmas, and although the wackos never stopped doing their whacked-out shit, even the FBI's behavioral analysts got to chill out in a turkey coma for a few hours. Matt was looking forward to some solid sleep and serious time spent with his mother—not that she'd appreciate it, but it wouldn't stop him being there for her.

His cell rang and he dug it out of his pocket. He frowned when he looked at the screen.

What the hell was ASAC Jon Regan, unit chief of TacOps I, doing calling this late?

"Lazlo," Matt answered.

"You alone?"

Matt glanced at the limo driver but the privacy screen was up. "In a government issue limo."

"You were at the Russian Ambassador's residence?"

Matt swung his legs off the seat and sat up, suddenly wide awake. "You following me?"

"No." Regan laughed but it sounded strained. "Can you tell me why you were there?"

Matt buzzed his fingers through his short hair. TacOps I specialized in covert entry in order to place sophisticated listening and surveillance devices at targeted locations. Basically they were government sanctioned burglars with an array of spy tools that would make James Bond drool.

"ASAC Frazer asked me to take his place at some Christmas party. Pain in the ass." He thought about Sarah LeMay and pressed his lips together. He didn't do regrets— something he'd inherited from his father—but right now he had a few when it came to that woman and her big, brown eyes and lack of phone number. "Why?"

"I'm going to send you a photograph. I want to know if you know this girl."

Matt waited for the image to come through. The picture showed a cute backside encased in a heart-stopping dress with all those crazy petticoats as she leaned over a desk. As distracting as the view was, he concentrated on what she was doing—she looked like she was…dismantling a lamp. *Fuck.*

"Well?" asked Regan.

"Her name is Sarah LeMay—"

"Congressman LeMay's daughter?"

"Yep. She was there with her sister, Angel. Knocked champagne down my front and I walked her to the restroom so I could get cleaned up."

"You think it was an accident?"

Matt thought back to the whole thing. "I did. What's going on?"

"That photo is a still shot of her taking the baseplate off a lamp in Ambassador Dorokhov's office."

Matt's mouth went as dry as a blowtorch. She was an operator? In which case she was beyond a pro. She'd reeled him in with her display of innocent vulnerability. Was *he* a target? Son of a bitch.

Regan cleared his throat. "She was trying to plant a bug in the Ambassador's office only to discover someone beat her to it."

"Someone?" Matt asked dryly.

"That's right." Humor ran through Regan's voice.

"Why the hell would she bug the Russian Ambassador's office?"

"Damned if I know, that's why I called you. You left the same time as she did."

Matt nodded, not surprised that there was surveillance on the street. Watching the comings and goings from foreign embassies must be routine for counterintelligence services. "I gave them both a ride home."

"Give 'em anything else?" The voice was more cautious now.

What's going on?

"If I said 'I wish' do I have to go to sensitivity training?"

"No straight single man on earth would need sensitivity training for telling the God's honest truth. Those women were hot. You should have seen where she hid the screwdriver."

Remembering the lines of her dress, Matt had a good idea. *Shit.* He rubbed his forehead. The idea that he'd been duped did not sit well. "I dropped them at the congressman's house and the driver took me to the White House—"

"You went to the White House?" Regan sounded as if he was choking on his tongue.

"Not inside. Just the rear entrance to meet up with a buddy of mine for a few minutes. It wasn't planned, and I didn't tell her I was going there."

There was a long, tense silence. "Can you meet me at The Center?"

"Now?" Matt virtually passed it on the way to his home. "Do I have a choice?"

"Nope."

"I had a feeling you were going to say that."

"Tis the season to give joy."

"Trust me, if anyone is going to give me joy I don't want it to be you." His mind cut back to the elfin face of Sarah LeMay. An operator who'd nailed him with a pair of big, brown eyes. He'd obviously lost his touch. "I'll be there in ten. Make sure there's plenty of coffee."

———

Andrei Dorokhov opened the door to his office and strode inside. His wife and Sergio followed, arm in arm. Natalie was drunk, but he didn't mind. She flirted with everyone she met, male or female, but she'd never betray him. She wouldn't dare.

Sergio might.

His "assistant" was ruthless and ambitious, but he wasn't stupid. Sergio Raminski wouldn't mess with him unless there was something to gain from it. Andrei understood Sergio better than anyone. He'd once been exactly like him.

Andrei walked to the fireplace and opened a box of Cuban cigars, offered Sergio one and then clipped the end of another before lighting it. The soothing aroma of sweet tobacco eased into his lungs. Natalie poured them each another glass of vodka.

"Here's to a successful evening." She passed him the drink and smiled at him in that way she had, as if he were the only man in the room.

He was lucky to have her. He raised his glass. "*Vashe Zdoroviye, lyubov moya.*"

He took a drink. He wasn't tired. He'd spent most nights of his working life walking the streets of various cities of the world, hiding in dark alleys, passing cash and instructions via dead drops. Running agents. Retrieving information. Passing it on. It was a world where he was comfortable and sure of himself. It was here in this embassy that he worried he wouldn't be what his superiors wanted. He'd pushed for this job. He'd wanted a way to return to the US but to remain untouchable.

A sense of nostalgia uncoiled inside him—it must be the Christmas spirit or one too many toasts to the ladies. For nearly two decades he'd run spy rings around the globe. He missed the thrill of the old days, but he was in DC to make sure the past stayed buried, and certain lies died with the truth. The network of Russian agents had always been more formidable than its American counterpart. Andrei had worked hard and sacrificed much to make sure it stayed that way. Only one man had ever really suspected him, but Andrei had taken care of him the way he took care of everything—with ruthless efficiency.

Sergio wandered over toward the curtains. The younger man was handsome and charming, obviously eager to be off screwing some woman rather than seeing to his master's needs. Sergio had the looks and skills to go a long way in the diplomatic corp—more importantly, he had powerful connections who were all getting richer as Russia expanded its energy empire.

The first hint of a hangover sliced across the backs of his eyes. A sure sign of age and a weakness he wouldn't reveal to anyone. "What do we have planned for tomorrow?" he asked.

"Lunch with the Canadian Ambassador, then an afternoon reception at the embassy for all the diplomats and embassy staff. After that you are free until the twenty-seventh when there is a cocktail party at the Smithsonian."

Russians didn't celebrate Christmas until January 7 and then it was a shadow of the celebrations the Americans indulged in. The only religion that had thrived in Russia for the last century had been Communism. Andrei enjoyed the season, although he saw little relationship between the birth of Christ and shopping. Even so, his wife would have his hide if he didn't get her a generous gift. He planned to take them away for a few days skiing in the mountains, somewhere with a hot tub to soak his aching bones at the end of a day on the slopes.

Sergio continued pacing, then paused, stepped back, bent over and picked something small off the floor that glittered in the light.

Andrei frowned, then strode forward and took it from his assistant's palm. An earring. He raised his brow at his wife. "Do you recognize this?"

Her eyes widened at his tone and she shook her head. "No."

Sergio peered closer into Andrei's palm and pressed his lips together. "It may have been the earring of one of tonight's guests."

"Did you bring her in here?" Andrei asked softly.

Sergio's eyes narrowed. "No, Your Eminence."

"Sweep the room."

"It was swept earlier today, Your Excellency." There was impatience in the man's black eyes.

Andrei gripped Sergio's throat and squeezed. "Sweep. It. Again. Properly this time. Take apart every light-fitting. Every telephone. Examine every cable. No one sleeps until I know the entire building is secure!" Fury ripped through him. He shoved the younger man away and hurled his crystal tumbler at the fireplace where it shattered into a thousand pieces. Clear liquid dripped down the white marble.

He headed for the door.

"Andrei," Natalie called after him. "It's just an earring."

"It's proof someone was in here when they shouldn't have been." He clicked his fingers and though her eyes narrowed, she closed her mouth and followed him out of the room without saying another word. Good. He was not in the mood to control his wife. He was not in the mood to be nice or polite or diplomatic. These people didn't understand the stakes. They might think they did, but they didn't. He would not let the Americans get the better of him. They strode down the stairs, Sergio following closely, past the rooms used for various social functions and administrative purposes, through the kitchens before taking an elevator down to the basement.

Mishka, his head of security, came out the door to meet him. "Do you need something, Your Excellency?"

Andrei held up the earring, which sparkled, in the dim light. "This was on the floor of my office. How did it get there?" He pushed past the man into the security section, straight to the monitors that showed all the cameras within the residence. There were none in his private rooms—above all, he understood the value of privacy. But all the public areas, all the corridors, were monitored.

The uniformed guard scanning the monitors looked at his boss nervously.

"Show me the footage from the corridor outside my office tonight. Start at 7:20 PM." He'd been in his office until just after that.

The security guard scrolled back on the time log and then started playing forward at double speed.

"Stop. Her." Sergio pointed at a woman dressed in a smoky-colored dress, talking to a man wearing a Navy uniform. The guard slowed it down to normal speed.

Andrei watched her closely, noticed she was wearing earrings very like the one he held in his hand.

She and the military man stood close together, as if entranced by one another. *How sweet.* Then she stepped back and walked away. The man went into the men's room and she entered the ladies' room. Another woman came out, and then he saw himself striding out of his office, adjusting his sleeves, eager to get to the party.

He moved out of sight and a few moments later the woman in the pretty, silver dress dashed out of the restroom and across the hall, into his office before the door fully closed.

"Fast forward," Andrei ordered.

Sweat gleamed on the security guard's brow. It didn't take long before the woman exited his office and ran back to the restroom. She looked scared and upset. One of her earrings was missing.

"I don't know how I missed this," the guard said, voice trembling. "I swear I never moved from my post."

The head of security cuffed the man across the back of the head. "*Mudak.*"

"Who is she?" Andrei demanded.

"Sarah LeMay," Sergio answered quickly. "She was here with her sister, Angel."

Everything inside Andrei went cold. "LeMay?"

Sergio nodded.

"The congressman's daughter?"

"They were invited as you requested." Sergio's brows crinkled.

Andrei had sent the invitation in jest—as a warning. He'd never imagined any of them would come. "The man in uniform, who is he?" he demanded. This was bad. This was very, very bad.

Natalie answered. "A young man called Matthew Lazlo."

"He represented FBI Agent Lincoln Frazer," Sergio put in. "A last minute switch."

Andrei had wanted to meet the other federal employee. "So Matthew Lazlo is also FBI?"

Natalie shrugged. Sergio nodded.

Fury moved inside Andrei's veins; cold, precise like razor-sharp ice. He reached inside Sergio's jacket, watching the younger man's pupils flare as he took his gun. Andrei whirled and slammed the guard on the side of the head with the butt of the pistol. The man fell unconscious over the console.

"He's lucky I didn't kill him." He spat on the man. "Send him home. We do not tolerate amateurs." He handed the gun back to Sergio, who took it carefully.

"Do you want to issue an official complaint to the Americans?" Sergio asked in a level voice.

"*Nyet.*" Was the FBI running surveillance on him inside the embassy? Impossible. The stakes were too high, his retribution too potentially damaging. He needed to know what was going on. "Find me the girl, *quietly*," said Andrei. "I want to talk to her." The conversation wouldn't be pretty. "And find out everything you can about the man." He turned to his Security Chief. "No more mistakes, Mishka. Next time I won't be so understanding."

CHAPTER THREE

To all intents and purposes, the top-secret Tactical Operations Center—or "the Center" as agents in the know usually called it—looked like a light industrial manufacturing facility. It was situated off the grounds of the Marine Corps base in Quantico for purposes of safety and secrecy.

Jon Regan held up some sort of wand. Not the magic kind.

Matt raised his arms and kept his mouth shut until the man finished running the thing over his body. *Great.* Another guy examined the limo. What the hell was going on?

"Okay, come with me." Jon strode away.

Matt followed him through one door and then another, into a windowless room within a room. On one of the big screens, Sarah LeMay was displayed in glorious Technicolor as she flicked on a light switch. On another screen was a live-feed of the same room.

"Play the video," Regan ordered, standing with hands on hips, watching the screens. "The team monitoring the surveillance feeds gave us the heads up as soon as they spotted her in there. We patched into the feed after that."

The tech pressed a button and Sarah sprang to life. She entered the fancy office, looked around for a moment, and headed toward the desk. She hitched up her skirts, revealing a pair of shapely legs in those spiky heels. He could just make out the edge of black lace. The atmosphere in the enclosed space got hot and tense as she dipped her fingers into those panties. He could only see lingerie, but it didn't stop his imagination taking it a step further. Sweat burst out from his skin.

He'd never suspected a thing.

She'd been taking the lamp apart with deft dexterity while he'd been wondering if he should ask her out. He'd been played. The expression on her face when she saw the other bug was priceless, as was the realization as she glanced nervously around the room, that there might be a camera hidden somewhere. It made him feel a little better.

"Shit. Here we go." The tech pointed to the live screen. Four men entered the room and started picking up objects and examining them in detail.

"It was only a matter of time," Regan said with his arms crossed. He sounded pissed.

In her video, Sarah reassembled everything, but Matt noticed something small catch the light as it dropped to the floor. "She lost her earring?"

"That is why we don't wear jewelry on an op." Regan nodded. "They already found it."

This explained the henchmen taking the place apart.

Matt watched the woman tuck the small plastic bag into her bodice with a lot more discretion this time. He hadn't noticed her missing earring when he'd seen her afterward—too busy looking deep into her eyes. *Asshole.*

There was a knock on the door. Jon Regan went over and opened it. Assistant Special Agent in Charge Lincoln Frazer walked in wearing a tailored tux. He must have left the White House shortly after Matt.

"I'm starting to feel under-dressed," Regan said dryly. To the tech he said, "Play it again."

This time when Matt watched the video, he kept an eye on her facial expression, on her body language. "She's not acting like a pro."

Frazer leaned back on his heels, considering her. "More like she's being forced to do something she doesn't want to do. Why were you bugging Dorokhov?" he asked the TacOps guy.

"That's need to know," Regan said apologetically.

"I need to know," Frazer argued.

"Yeah." Regan's lips formed a smirk. "I'll get back to you on that one."

"The Russians have a camera set up in that corridor." Matt pointed out. Even blinded by Sarah LeMay's seemingly innocent charm, he'd spotted it in the dim recesses. "Is it active?"

Regan nodded. "When we went in, at night when the big wigs were elsewhere, we hacked into security and played a loop of the place in darkness. It was a piece of cake."

Sarah LeMay had uncanny observational skills. The woman had spotted where he usually wore his Budweiser— the SEAL Trident he'd earned by passing Basic Underwater Demolition/ SEAL training. He'd removed it because he hadn't felt comfortable announcing his special operations background when entering enemy territory. Pity she hadn't noticed the surveillance camera watching the hall. A real operator would have. So, what was she, if she wasn't an operator?

"She didn't do any of that," Frazer said quietly. "So it won't be long before they figure out she was in there. Why would she want to bug Dorokhov?"

"Blackmail? Or maybe she works for another agency or another country?" Regan suggested with a shrug.

"Maybe it's personal," said Matt.

"What was your impression of her?" Regan asked him, "Besides the obvious."

Matt slumped into an empty chair. "She seemed vulnerable. Shy. Uncomfortable."

"You try walking in high heels with a screwdriver in your panties and you'd be uncomfortable," the tech joked.

Matt laughed but inside he felt sick. Duped. "It wasn't that." Jeez, he was gonna sound like a pussy. "She seemed… fragile." He shrugged. "Thinking about it, she seemed okay before she tried to plant the bug, but on the ride home she barely said a word except that she wasn't feeling well."

"Not surprised. She fucked up and she knew it." Regan's tone held no pity.

"She and her sister fought about something." Probably her failed mission. That's why they'd fled so fast, but Angel hadn't wanted to leave…

"You think the sister was a distraction?" Frazer asked.

"Did you see those legs?" Regan snorted.

Matt shook his head. "I don't know. The only person I saw the sister speak to was some asshole called Raminski."

"We checked him out. He's former military, probably GRU or SVR, acts as a PA to the ambassador and bodyguard if the occasion requires. He's good at his job. Has a string of women he loves and leaves on a regular basis. Seems as kosher as any Russian in DC." The assumption was that they all worked for Russian intelligence. It was simpler that way.

"What's Congressman LeMay's connection to Dorokhov?" asked Matt.

"We got nothing." Regan threw up his arms.

"He was invited, so there's something," Matt insisted.

"Hey, Frazer was invited too." Regan eyed the man in question. "What's your connection?"

"I'm a popular guy?" Frazer's expression switched from joking to serious. "Dorokhov sent out dozens of invitations this year. I got the impression he was trawling the waters, trying to make a good impression and some connections. I asked our consultant Alex Parker to see if he could find anything for us between the ambassador and the congressman." Alex Parker was former CIA and co-owned a cyber-security firm in DC. The man was also engaged to the newest member of their team at BAU-4, Mallory Rooney, and from what Matt could see, Frazer was taking full advantage of his expertise and connections.

Whatever worked.

"I heard Parker was good." Regan looked as if he wanted to steal him for TacOps, but was too smart to say anything in front of Frazer. He'd already tried to recruit Matt for his skill set as a former Navy SEAL. Matt liked the Behavioral Analysis Unit, and they kept better hours than TacOps. It was a different sort of job and right now, it suited his needs.

"Ah, shit." The tech threw down his earpiece as the camera and bug both went dark.

Jon Regan swore and turned off his headset. "Whatever LeMay was up to, she just ruined six months of painstaking surveillance work and our chances of getting anything up and running again for at least the next six."

Given the shit going on in the world right now, this wasn't good news.

"Not even Santa will be able to get in that place without a cavity search," the tech remarked.

"Can they track it back to us?" Matt asked, pointing at the video screens.

"Nah. But the Chinese are about to get a lot of pissed off diplomatic calls."

Matt looked at the frozen image of Sarah LeMay, her skirt hitched high up her thigh. He had a feeling every guy in TacOps was going to get a look at that image by Christmas morning. The thought sent a shot of something dark and ugly through his bloodstream. Foolishness. Then he was struck by another thought, something much worse. "Not the Chinese." *Fuck.* "If they found the earring, the first thing the Russians will do is check the surveillance footage from the hallway and go after that girl. And they know exactly where she lives…" His fatigue vanished and a sense of urgency had him on his feet and at the door. "We need to get back to DC ASAP."

———

Gun in hand, Raminski entered the house through the garden doors off the patio at the rear of the property. The TV bleated in the distance. He checked the area before walking swiftly through the utility room, then the spotless kitchen, to the arched doorway. On the right of the hallway, there was a glass-paned door into the family room. A movie played loudly inside. The congressman and his wife were curled up on the couch, backs to the door. Good. He took the darkened stairs, moving silently, hearing another TV upstairs.

On the top floor, there were two doors. One open, lights turned off. He went inside, noted the room was empty. The dress the woman had been wearing earlier hung on the back of the door. He checked the bathroom. No one there.

He went to the connecting door and eased it ajar. The hot blonde—Angel—lay across the bed on her front with her knees bent, feet waving in the air. She wore a short, silky nightgown and matching panties as she watched a movie. He ignored the effect she had on his body, and scanned the room. She was alone.

Where was the other one? It was the other one he needed.

No time to play games. He put his pistol in his holster and pulled the syringe out of his pocket, primed the needle. Two strides took him into the room. A knee across the shoulder blades pinned her down as he shoved her face into the mattress to muffle the screams while he jammed the needle into her ass and pressed the plunger home. He couldn't afford for her to see his face. She struggled wildly, but it didn't take long for the tranquilizer to work. Thirty seconds and she was out. He capped the needle and put the syringe back into his pocket. Searched the room but the woman was alone. He went to her drawers and dragged out yoga pants and a hoodie. Socks and a pair of sneakers. Dressed her, moving her limbs around like she was a rag doll. Found her cell phone and slipped it in his pocket. He hoisted her over his shoulder and retrieved his gun out of the holster as he headed back down the stairs. He paused on the second floor landing and stepped out of sight as someone flushed a toilet on the ground floor. He stayed still until the congressman returned to the family room. The guy didn't close the door fully.

The girl dangled loosely from his shoulder. He eased silently down the stairs. Kept his ears open and eyes on the living room door. The parents never looked away from their movie. His mouth twisted as he recognized the film they were watching. The only Angel getting any wings tonight was their daughter as he spirited her away.

Out of the back door, along the garden path and through the garden gate in the wall that lined the street. The small sedan he'd stolen was still parked there. He opened the trunk and placed the girl carefully inside. He closed the trunk, climbed in the driver's seat, and drove off.

She wasn't the one he wanted, but she was leverage. It wouldn't take long to find the other one.

———

Scarlett decided to walk home rather than take a cab. This part of DC was generally safe and she needed some time and space to get her head together. A part of her knew it was foolish. Another part didn't care. Tonight she'd tried to bug the Russian Ambassador. Everything else seemed irrelevant by comparison. The streets were quiet. Subdued. No one was paying her any attention. Everyone was gearing up for Christmas.

She sank her hands deeper into her jacket pockets, touched another one of the transmitters she'd designed and built. Her sneakers scuffed quietly on the concrete sidewalk. Her breath created a frosty cloud that matched her mood. The snow from a few weeks ago had melted, turning to damp cold that seeped through skin and into marrow. Her teeth chattered. Right now, she didn't think she'd ever be warm again.

She and her mother had decided to split their trips to the prison to maximize the number of visits her father received during his treatment. Plus, her parents deserved some alone time—if being under constant observation counted as alone time. Scarlett could only imagine the pain of watching the person you loved stolen away from you by the very people who were supposed to have his back. It was bad enough losing her father—but losing the love of your life?

Unbearable.

A Christmas tree shone in someone's living room window—multi-colored lights and a gold star on top. A deep, aching sadness washed through her.

On a cold winter's day fourteen years ago, her father had gone to work as usual, and never returned home. That afternoon the feds had banged on the door and searched their small, brick house from rafters to crawlspace. They'd ripped everything apart—including her trust and innocence.

She'd been twelve.

The press had turned a horrendous time into pure torture. They'd camped out on the front lawn. Cameras pointed at every window. Reporters digging through the trash.

Going to school had proven impossible so her mother had home-schooled her. It had been the loneliest time of her life and she'd thrown herself into her studies. Most of their so-called friends had abandoned them. The only person to stand by her had been Angel. The two families had been close for years. Naturally, the congressman had distanced himself after her father's arrest. Who could blame him? But Angel had always been there for her. Scarlett didn't know what she'd have done without her.

There had never been any doubt in the FBI's mind that they had the right guy. The only people who'd believed him innocent were her and her mother. The lawyer had persuaded him to plead guilty to avoid the death penalty, which Scarlett was grateful for in terms of her dad not being executed, but it made proving him innocent a damn sight trickier.

Her mom would have faded away years ago if it wasn't for the fact Scarlett pushed her and prodded her to keep going, to not give up. It wasn't easy, and if her father died, Scarlett didn't think her mother would be far behind. Some days she already felt like an orphan.

A guy in a hoodie walked toward her and an instinctive lick of fear snaked up her spine. Walking alone at night was the only time she wished she was a guy. She watched the man out of the corner of her eye, but he carried on past, not paying her any attention.

Two minutes later, she got to the place where she was housesitting for her boss and let herself in. He was on sabbatical in Scotland until the end of next June. They worked at the cutting edge of technology that controlled how devices communicated with one another—like the fridge telling the Internet it ran out of eggs. Scarlett was tackling vulnerabilities that allowed another device to hijack the system and enable it to start typing malicious code. USB connections were particularly vulnerable. In some ways the research was mundane, in others it was the key to the future of all secure communication.

When housesitting, all she had to do was water her boss's plants and screen his mail for anything important. In the lab, she was also in charge of his grad students and putting out any metaphorical fires. She loved being his Research Fellow and she especially loved it when he wasn't there. Maximum freedom. Minimum interference. It made building and testing her own electronic bugging devices so much easier.

She looked around. It was a gorgeous house in a nice neighborhood, but its silence suddenly struck her as empty. Lonely. Cold. Desolate.

Like her life.

Most of the time she was okay being on her own, preferred it even, but sometimes, just sometimes, she yearned for basic human companionship. Matt Lazlo's face flashed through her mind. There had been something in his eyes. Maybe not anything real or lasting, but definite interest, which would have kept the cold loneliness at bay for at least one night.

It had been an illusion, though. He'd been looking at glamorous Sarah LeMay, not plain boring Scarlett Wilson Stone, daughter of the most notorious spy since the end of the Cold War.

Her cell phone rang. She didn't want to answer, but it was Angel calling. "What's up?"

"If you want to see your friend alive, meet me in the parking lot at Rock Creek Park Trails in thirty minutes, north end of Virginia Avenue. Come alone." The accent was thick Russian. "Do not contact the police."

The phone went dead. *No.* She stood there swaying as the world shifted off its axis. *They had Angel.* The Russians had figured out what she'd tried to do tonight, and her friend was paying the price.

———

Raminski sat in the car in a parking lot on New Hampshire Ave. He dialed Dorokhov on an encrypted phone.

"Did you get her?"

"She wasn't at the house so I took the other girl who was with her earlier. I found out something interesting." He stared at the contact list on Angel LeMay's smartphone, complete with profile photographs. "The girl who broke into your office is not who she said she was. She isn't LeMay's other daughter."

"Who is she?" Dorokhov demanded.

He waited a second. "Richard Stone's daughter."

Malevolence seeped through the night air, thick and pervasive.

"What do you want me to do about her?" More silence. Raminski waited for orders.

"Kill her." Soft. Quiet.

Interesting. "And the congressman's daughter?"

There was another hesitation, this one rife with calculation. "Keep her somewhere safe. I want to talk to her."

"That could prove risky." In too many ways to mention.

"Do it." Dorokhov hung up.

The man started his engine. He called a second number and told the other man the same thing he'd told the ambassador. Interestingly the orders were identical. Richard Stone's daughter died tonight.

CHAPTER FOUR

Matt walked up the steps of the row house where he'd dropped the women earlier, put his finger on the buzzer, and kept it there until he heard footsteps. He'd rather fast-rope onto the roof from a helicopter and break in via an upstairs window than play the lovesick fool.

Congressman Adam LeMay opened the door, thankfully not yet retired to bed. His brows scrunched together and then his gaze dropped down Matt's borrowed black t-shirt, fatigues, and combat boots.

"Congressman LeMay. My name is Matt Lazlo. I need to speak to your daughters, sir."

The man's brows stretched high and wide. He opened his mouth to answer, but someone interrupted.

"Who is it, Adam?" The door opened wider to reveal a woman in her fifties with dark hair and a rounded figure. Her mouth was downcast, clearly expecting bad news from a caller this late at night.

A black SUV with tinted windows idled at the curb. They'd picked up Alex Parker and Mallory Rooney from Parker's DC apartment. They were now inside the car, setting up electronic wire taps on the LeMays' cell phones and landlines to see if they could get a handle on what the women had been up to, and who they might be working with. Frazer had called in a personal favor and got a warrant signed by a federal judge, who also happened to be Agent Rooney's father.

They weren't even case agents, but no way was Matt about to leave Sarah LeMay at the mercy of Russian displeasure. Frazer was worried this was some sort of personal vendetta between the LeMays and Andrei Dorokhov and wanted to act before it morphed into a full-blown diplomatic incident at the worst possible moment given current souring of east-west relationships. Speed was vital; so was secrecy. And, yes, a little personal payback might not be bad for Matt's ego, considering Sarah had made him look like a damn fool.

"I met your daughters earlier tonight. One of them left something in my vehicle."

"Was it an earring?" the woman asked.

She lost so much more than an earring.

"You didn't think it was a little late to drop by?" The woman's eyes sparkled with amusement as she checked her watch. Midnight.

This was why kids shouldn't live with their parents after the age of twenty-one.

"I'm sorry for the inconvenience," he insisted but didn't budge.

The congressman looked baffled. The mother seemed to realize he was serious about seeing them right now. "Okay. Wait here. I'll go upstairs and see if she wants to talk to you."

Matt opened his mouth to insist on talking to both of them, but the congressman stood back as if resigned. "You better come in."

"Angel. Angel?" The mother's voice was getting louder and louder from a few flights up.

"It was actually Sarah I wanted to speak to," said Matt.

"Sarah?" The congressman repeated as if he didn't remember he had a second daughter.

"Adam," Mrs. LeMay shouted down the stairwell. "Check the kitchen, honey, she's not in her room."

Obediently, the congressman went to the back of the house and started calling Angel's name. There was no reply. A prickle of unease slid under Matt's skin. Murphy's Law. Anything that could go wrong would go wrong.

"Is she in Sarah's room, Valerie?" The congressman started up the stairs and Matt followed, leaving the door wide open behind him because he had a feeling the shit was about to hit the fan.

He strode into what was clearly a young woman's bedroom. There were discarded clothes on the floor, including the dress Angel had worn earlier. He walked through the open door into the adjoining room. Spotted the silver dress Sarah had worn hanging on the back of the door. No sign of either woman. He got a bad feeling about this. "Be careful what you touch."

They both gaped at him with matching expressions of shock.

"What do you mean, 'be careful what you touch'?" the congressman blustered, then turned to his wife. "You don't think something bad has happened, do you?"

"Maybe she went home with Scarlett?" Valerie nibbled her lip, then picked up the landline beside the bed and dialed a number.

Who the hell was Scarlett? Matt had a horrible feeling he knew. Angel had called Sarah "Scar" in the limo.

"Scarlett isn't answering. I'm going to try Angel's cell phone." The woman dialed another number. Her face grew very pale. "She's not answering." She looked up. "She always carries her phone."

"It's Sarah I want to speak to," Matt said carefully.

"Sarah?" Congressman LeMay's face was a picture of confusion.

"When did you meet Sarah?" the mother asked.

Matt knew he was missing a whole bunch of pieces from the puzzle and wasn't about to expound on his ignorance until he'd gleaned everything he could from the family.

"I need you both to come downstairs and we can discuss this," he said firmly.

"What's going on?" The mother's eyes honed in on him and narrowed.

"Downstairs. Now." Matt channeled his inner drill instructor and the LeMays finally did as requested.

Frazer stood in the entranceway downstairs.

"Neither woman is here," Matt told his boss.

Frazer nodded and introduced himself to the LeMays. "Where else might your daughters have gone at this time of night, sir?"

"What's this about?" the mother asked. "Angel tells us if she's going out. She knows I don't sleep well if I don't know she's safe."

"And Sarah?" Matt asked quietly.

"*Sarah* is out of town." The congressman glared at him impatiently.

"I was introduced to her tonight at the Residence of the Russian Ambassador to the US."

Valerie's eyes bugged, and her face drained of color. She started to sag, and her husband caught her. "You must be mistaken."

"Pretty sure I was there and not tripping."

"Lazlo," Frazer cautioned.

"Angel took *Scarlett* to the Russian Embassy?" The congressman asked his wife with horror lacing his words. "She wouldn't."

"It appears she did." The woman's lips were bloodless. She pressed them together and inhaled, as if drawing in strength.

"Who is Scarlett?" Matt asked. Obviously, the woman he'd met earlier tonight had lied about her identity.

Valerie's fingers twisted into knots. "Scarlett Stone. I still don't know what that has to do with Angel being missing—"

"Scarlett's a good friend of Angel's," the congressman cut in. "I can't believe they'd go to that party after I expressly told her to decline the invitation. Damn, I need a drink." The guy looked like he was about to pass out.

Scarlett Stone…

"Why do I recognize that name?" asked Matt.

Alex Parker appeared in the doorway. "Because she's the daughter of Richard Stone."

"Richard Stone the *spy*?" Frazer ground out.

Holy motherfucker. That was the sound of shit hitting the fan.

Alex motioned him and Frazer to come closer to the door, and murmured quietly, "Angel's cell phone was just used to call Scarlett Stone. Someone with a Russian accent told Ms. Stone if she wanted to see her friend alive she had to meet them in thirty minutes. Alone."

Matt felt his lip curl. Some bastard was using one woman to threaten the other, which meant Scarlett and her friend were both in very real danger. He checked his watch. The clock was ticking if they wanted to get a handle on this thing.

"You think they have Angel?" asked Frazer.

"They have her cell phone and the woman is missing. It's a safe assumption," said Parker.

Frazer's gaze was compassionate when it landed on the LeMays, but he kept his voice down so they couldn't overhear. "They can't know about this. Not yet. They'll get everyone on the Hill involved and both girls will be dead before morning."

"So you deal with them while I go pick up Miss *Scarlett* and set a trap for whoever has the LeMay girl," Matt urged his boss. "Rooney can come with me."

Frazer was quiet for what seemed like minutes but was just a few seconds. "I need Rooney here. Her political connections might work in our favor."

"Fine. I'll go alone—we don't have time to wait for backup." Matt was itching to move. The clock was ticking.

"I'll go with you. I have some experience." Alex Parker's voice held a trace of irony.

Frazer nodded and checked his watch. "I'm on damage control. I need to make some phone calls to put out as many fires as I can before these people start another war." He pinched the bridge of his nose. "Like we don't have enough going on at the moment."

The country was already on the edge of conflict with half the Middle East after terrorists attacked an American mall two weeks ago. With the VP's death further ramping up tension and general disquiet around the country, this wasn't a good time to start accusing the Russian Ambassador of kidnapping a congressman's daughter. Not without solid proof, and even then the situation would be a political minefield.

Matt headed out the door to the SUV. His priority was finding Angel LeMay and Scarlett Stone alive, and then he was going to make sure they were both very sorry they'd lied to a federal agent.

Mallory Rooney stood on the sidewalk. She sent him a measured smile—one that said she wasn't sure of him yet. She was the daughter of a US senator, and some of their BAU-4 colleagues had been less than welcoming when she'd arrived in the unit in late November, bypassing the usual entry protocols. When the then unit boss had unexpectedly quit and Frazer had been promoted, the other agents in the unit had expected Rooney to receive her transfer orders. Instead, Frazer had given her his full backing. That was good enough for Matt. She was a good agent, if a little inexperienced.

Had *he* been welcoming?

Matt paused. He wasn't sure. He'd been focused on his own issues and his own cases. Still was. He slowed. "Boss needs you inside. Possible kidnap situation but don't tell the parents."

"Thank you, Agent Lazlo," she said coolly.

He slowed further. The woman had recently gone head-to-head with a serial killer who'd kidnapped her identical twin sister eighteen years ago. She was probably more experienced with the work they did than he gave her credit for. "Call me Matt."

Her smile hit her eyes and he figured he hadn't been that friendly. He'd make the effort to do better, but right now, he didn't have time.

His mind moved to the mission ahead. He went to the trunk and pulled on one of the Kevlar vests TacOps kept there—they'd borrowed the vehicle, along with less obvious clothing, from Jon Regan to save time going to the BAU building or home. TacOps had just come off a local job when they'd received the call about Sarah/Scarlett and hadn't had a chance to unload the SUV. The trunk was packed with goodies they might need for a tactical raid, along with city work vests, traffic cones, every lock pick known to man, a small stash of C4, a big bag of dog treats and some tranquilizers for when the dog biscuits didn't work.

The vehicle was probably electronically tagged, which might be a good thing as they didn't have much time to plan this op. At least if they wound up dead TacOps would get their toys back.

Parker joined him and geared up, fast and efficient. That, and the fact Frazer was sending him out with Matt into a dangerous situation, told him the rumors were true. The guy wasn't your typical desk-jockey, computer nerd.

"Where're we going?" Matt asked.

"North end of Virginia Avenue. Near the river. The park near the boat club."

Matt checked his weapon and watched the guy beside him do the same. Loaded his pockets with spare ammo. "Know anything about any of this?"

Parker shook his head. "Stone was before my time."

Fourteen years ago, Matt had been enduring BUD/s. Proudest day of his life when he passed. Afterward, he'd been too busy training to pay much attention to a man selling secrets to Russia, except to despise him on principle.

Matt climbed in the driver's seat. Alex took shotgun.

Matt drove fast, lights on, sirens off. "Pretty bold to kidnap a congressman's daughter."

"The Russians aren't exactly shrinking violets. These guys don't mess around when they're pissed. Dorokhov has a reputation for being hot-tempered and nasty when crossed. Not a great quality in a diplomat, but he's connected. You were a Navy SEAL?"

Matt raised a brow. He didn't talk about his past much. Or ever. "You hack into everyone's file or am I special?"

"Everyone." Parker never took his eyes off the laptop on his knees. "I like to know who I'm working with."

"Who your fiancée is working with, more like." Matt eyed him narrowly out of his side vision.

Parker was busy typing on the computer but Matt knew he had his complete and utter attention. "I protect the people I love," the guy said simply.

Matt wanted to take offense on Rooney's behalf, but he understood the mentality. He'd felt the same way about his brothers on the teams. Been willing to kill and die for every one of them. He had friends in the FBI, but nothing like that forged-in-steel bond. He missed it. "You were Army?"

Parker raised a brow. He wasn't the only one who liked to know who he was working with. Alex Parker was a Distinguished Cross recipient and had seen plenty of action in the sandbox.

"Spotted your lobotomy scar." Matt smirked. "How many Army cadets does it take to screw in a light bulb?"

"One. He just holds the bulb and expects the world to revolve around him." Parker grinned. "Why'd you get out of the teams?" And he obviously liked the hard questions.

"Not something you can do forever." Matt shrugged like he didn't care and didn't miss it. Not that he'd pass a polygraph and doubted he fooled Parker.

"FBI must seem pretty tame after jumping out of airplanes and kicking down doors."

"You tell me." Matt eased back in his seat, making himself relax even as adrenaline drummed hard through his veins. "Rumor has it you were CIA?"

"It isn't like being a soldier. I don't miss it." Parker's expression was implacable, but shadows in his eyes suggested he'd gone to hell and back. The Agency was good at clandestine, but it didn't make them easy to work for.

The glance Parker sent him also told him that he knew exactly what Matt's old career had meant to him. The military family might bitch and squabble, but they were still family. The Agency operated differently. Matt wondered exactly what the man had done, but knew better than to ask.

"Got anything new?" Matt asked, referring to the computer Parker was working on.

"No," Parker said quietly. "But I'm worried about both women."

Matt snorted. "The little witch conned me."

"Scarlett Stone is screwed, whatever happens. If the Russians catch her she's gonna get hurt or dead, but if the US government catches her…The FBI can wave their hands in the air and claim they had nothing to do with any spying on the Russians. A woman like that, caught on tape? She's the ultimate fall guy."

"A woman like what?" Matt bit out. The idea of everyone watching that video drove him crazy, which was stupid.

"Smart, attractive, wearing a fantasy dress and heels, waltzing right into the Russian Ambassador's residence under false pretenses, her father being who he is? They could lock her up and throw away the key. She's the ultimate in deniability."

Matt gritted his teeth. "She never even planted the bug."

"Doesn't matter."

Dammit.

He shouldn't give a fuck. Scarlett was nothing to him. She'd lied to his face and probably caused a major diplomatic incident that might reflect badly on him and his career. Unlike certain society princesses, he needed his damned job. Angel LeMay was missing and God knew what the Russians might do to her if they didn't get what they wanted. Not to mention the congressman who was going to go ballistic if they didn't bring Angel back unharmed and soon. The whole situation was a rubber-stamped goatfuck. But the look he'd seen in her eyes earlier tonight. The spark of something elemental that had buzzed between them…His insides twisted.

He pressed his foot hard on the accelerator and controlled the need to blow through every red light in the city. The lack of intel on the situation bothered him but Scarlett—assuming she turned up to try and save her friend—was in real danger, and for some reason he couldn't stand the idea of her in pain.

There was a quiet ping on the laptop and Parker pulled up a file. Whistled. "She might be terrible at tradecraft, but when I didn't recognize the device she tried to plant—and trust me, if it's patented, I'd be able to ID it—I checked her out in a bit more depth."

"What did you find?" His interest was piqued despite himself. He pulled his weapon from his holster and rested it in his lap. They were almost there. He turned off the cherry lights.

"Scarlett Stone isn't just a pretty face. She's a top research scientist at Georgetown. Has a degree in microelectronics, and a post-graduate degree in solid-state physics, specializing in application-specific integrated circuits. Earned her Ph.D. at twenty-two."

"Are you telling me she built her own listening device? Jesus."

They had a visual on the river. Parker closed the laptop. He flicked the switch on the overhead dome light as Matt doused the headlights. Matt pulled over on the side of the road about twenty yards before the turn for the Rock Creek Park Trails parking lot. Alex Parker tossed him something out of the glove box. NVGs. Might come in handy.

"I'll go north along the river, you go around the eastern side of the park?"

Parker nodded.

"You any good with that SIG?" Matt asked.

Parker's voice held a trace of amusement. "Not bad."

Good. Matt slid out of the car. He'd feel better with more backup but there wasn't time, and a deluge of cops would scatter parties to the four winds. They needed to find both women before someone got hurt. The time for fun and games was over.

———

Scarlett hunched further into her coat as she shivered uncontrollably. She was hidden amongst the trees, not far from the creek that gave the park its name. A bush rustled beside her and her heart exploded in a staccato rhythm that sent a pain shooting along one rib. She gripped her chest. Sighed with relief as something small scampered away. A squirrel.

Tonight had been a lesson in sticking to what she was good at, which in her case was physics. How could she ever have thought she'd get away with this? Sure she could make a listening device, but planting it without anyone knowing? Dream on.

It had taken her nearly the full thirty minutes to get here on foot, running most of the way. Her lungs were burning from the effort. Bare branches clattered overhead, stripped of their leaves by the harsh, winter wind. She had no gun, no one to call for help. The man on the phone had said no cops and the LeMays would definitely involve the police if they found out. The man on the phone hadn't sounded like someone you messed with. He'd sounded like a scary-assed, Russian hit man.

She did not know how to deal with a hit man.

Her fingers hovered over 9-1-1 on her keypad. Her father had taught her to trust the men and women in uniform, but they'd betrayed him, and her personal experiences hadn't been great. Once law enforcement realized Scarlett and her mother believed Richard Stone was innocent despite his guilty plea, cops had little sympathy. However, a congressman's daughter had been kidnapped so rescuing her would be a priority…assuming they believed her story and arrived in the next five minutes.

Dammit.

There was also the minor fact that if the police discovered what she'd tried to do tonight, she would go to jail. With her father's cancer progressing rapidly, she might not get out in time to say goodbye. She might never see him again.

What a fool.

She didn't think the Russians would kill her for trying to plant a bug, especially when she'd messed up so spectacularly. The Cold War was over and she hadn't gleaned any secrets, big or small. Maybe they'd scare her a little. Rough her up. Try and get her to work for them, give them the heads up on a few technological advances not written up in the peer-review journals.

They'd definitely punish her, but she could take it. She shivered harder.

If Angel hadn't been in danger she might have run away for a few days hoping they'd forget about her, but her friend had stood by Scarlett during the worst time of her life. Angel hadn't had a clue as to what Scarlett had tried to do tonight, which made the betrayal worse.

Angel was innocent and Scarlett was stupid—a humbling role reversal.

Maybe everyone was right about letting this go. Her father had been incarcerated for fourteen years. He was going to die in prison. It would take a miracle to prove his innocence and although it might be Christmas, life was a little short on miracles.

Beg forgiveness. Get Angel to safety. Take her punishment. Concentrate on work.

She shivered as the cold wind snuck between her scarf and her skin. Voices echoed from near the ferry terminal. She peered into the darkness but saw nothing.

The parking lot had two empty cars in it and the trails seemed deserted. Maybe she'd come to the wrong place? She bit her lip. She'd checked the sign and this was the place the man had specified. As she peered into the distance, she saw a gang of youths enter the park from the southern entrance near the road. Crap. She slipped further into the shadows and hoped her heart didn't give out from the stress. This cloak and dagger stuff wasn't good for her health. Who in their right mind would want to be a spy?

She didn't think the gang had seen her. With shaking hands, she sank to the base of a tree and hugged herself, wishing she'd obeyed her instincts and never gone near the Russians.

It was up to the kidnapper to make the next move.

———

The quiet rush of the Potomac flowing close-by drowned out any telltale sounds. The boat club was nearby, the Georgetown Ferry terminus due west, but at this time of night this area was quiet and dark. A group of gang-bangers moved further along the trails—if they were looking for trouble they were probably going to find it, but not from him. Matt slipped on the NVGs and stood silently scoping out the area in flattened green monotone. The wind whistled through the branches overhead as he wound his way carefully around sturdy tree trunks. Every sense was on high alert for Scarlett Stone, Angel LeMay, or the kidnapper. Alex Parker should be around the other side of the lot by now. Matt didn't see any sign of the man, though he knew he was there.

He spotted something. A figure huddled at the base of a tree, arms wrapped protectively around itself. He scanned the rest of the area but saw nothing. Two cars sat in the lot but both appeared empty. Carefully he edged closer to the hunched figure. Was it someone involved in Scarlett's mess, or just a homeless person looking for a quiet place out of the bitter wind? He couldn't tell what was in their hands. Were they armed? His hand rested on his SIG Sauer, ready to pull his weapon if they spotted him.

The light of a cell phone revealed the delicate features of a young woman—Scarlett Stone. But in the NVGs, the glare was so bright he had to blink and look away. A second later the sound of a high-power rifle shot tore through the night.

Goddammit.

Scarlett yelped and rolled to the side, then scrambled into a crouched run as another shot scored the trunk where she'd been sitting just a moment earlier. Matt raced flat out toward her and managed to hook an arm and drag her behind a tree just wide enough to shelter them both. She screamed so he clamped a hand over her mouth and hauled her against him. She struggled furiously and he could barely hold on.

"Keep still, dammit. I'm not going to hurt you," he growled in her ear.

She went stiff as a corpse.

Did she recognize his voice from earlier tonight? The idea gave him a strange sense of savage satisfaction. He didn't know why it mattered. She was a job now, nothing more. Her head strained against his hand, trying to look up at his face, but it was too dark for her to see anything and he was wearing goggles.

He shifted, trying to get a view of who was out there. Parker had to be somewhere close-by. Matt held still, giving the other man the opportunity to get into position, knowing he was also giving the shooter time to reposition for a better angle. The idea someone was lining him up in their sights didn't sit easy, but it wasn't the first time he'd been caught in the crossfire.

Time to go. "We're going to run to the right and get deeper into the trees."

"But they—"

He put his hand back over her mouth and carried her. It was faster than arguing. Five yards and they reached a large oak, but Matt wanted to move further out of range so he kept going. The sound of a second shot and sharp scrape of a bullet across his shoulder told him the gunman was good, and he was cutting it close. He piled behind a massive silver birch and dropped Scarlett to her feet, held her tight against him. Then he switched positions so she was pinned to the trunk and he was covering her front. She barely reached his shoulders but every inch felt achingly female.

The scent of her hit him, the sweet citrus of lemons, an unwanted reminder from earlier tonight when he'd been interested in the contents of her underwear for totally different reasons.

Too bad.

He didn't know where the shooter was, but he was guessing across the creek, possibly in one of the condos.

"Matt? Is that you?" she whispered.

"FBI Special Agent Lazlo."

Her gasp of surprise seemed genuine enough. He could see her face clearly in the NVGs. Maybe she hadn't played him from the start.

"How did you know I was here? I-I don't understand." The uncertainty in her voice suggested she thought his attention earlier had been part of a set-up.

He wished that were true. He wished she'd been the dupe in all this.

"Your little stunt at the Russian Ambassador's place was caught on camera." She drew in a shocked breath that pressed her breasts against him and made certain parts of his body pay attention. "You managed to piss off more people than you can possibly imagine with your antics—"

"But how did you find me *here*?" she asked urgently, ignoring his pissed off lecture. "Someone tapped into my cell's GPS?"

He shrugged, not about to admit something that was technically illegal without a warrant.

"Did you know they have Angelina?" She squirmed, trying to gain a little breathing room, but managed to brush more closely against certain areas of his body that didn't understand the difference between a firefight and sex. She froze for a moment and then ignored it. "You have to let me go meet them," she insisted. "He must have seen you and assumed I'd called the cops. If I can just explain—"

A bullet ripped into the trunk just inches from his head. He crowded her closer to the trunk, his body pressed hard into hers, determined to protect her despite the fact she'd put herself in this position. "I don't think this guy came to negotiate, *Scarlett*."

The night got very quiet as they both strained to hear anyone moving around out there.

After thirty seconds of rigid tension, she stretched up on tiptoe and whispered in his ear. "I'm sorry I lied to you."

Her breath was warm against his neck and sent a shiver of reaction over his flesh. The woman did something to him, but he wasn't dumb enough to show it. "I don't care about your name." Another lie, because he hated being deceived, although he was used to it by now. "Why try to bug the Russians. Why Dorokhov?"

Those dark eyes were enormous now. Her mouth opened and closed repeatedly.

Someone was shooting at them and she was holding back? "Spit it out."

"My father is…"

"Richard Stone, the spy."

She shoved against him again, but he wasn't going anywhere. He didn't enjoy physically intimidating women, but he was making an exception in this case. She'd almost gotten killed tonight and she wasn't out of danger yet. He wanted her scared. He wanted her compliant. He wanted her safe.

"My father is innocent."

Matt laughed and a look of hurt flashed across her features. He softened the skepticism in his voice. "He confessed."

"Don't ask questions if you don't want answers." Her eyes narrowed, jaw firmed.

Amused, he said, "Go on."

"My father suspected Dorokhov was involved in espionage activities in the years before he was arrested."

"I'd have thought he'd have known the key players."

She kicked him in the shin.

Dammit. "Assault of a federal officer on top of the spying charges? Looks like your Christmas isn't going to be very merry, sweetheart."

She kicked him again, harder. "In for a penny, in for a pound."

Ouch. Goddammit.

"Shooter's gone," came a voice out of the darkness—Alex Parker, "but don't let me interrupt."

Matt looked over his shoulder and saw the man standing less than ten foot away. "You sure?"

"Drove off in a Ford sedan. I got the plate."

"Nice." Matt stepped away from Scarlett, not liking the way his body protested the distance. She was warm. It was a cold night.

She put her hand in her pocket and he grabbed her wrist.

"Hey!" she cried out.

He retrieved her cell, then checked the other pocket. No weapons.

"I need to try and contact the kidnapper again." Her voice rose with agitation. "I need to get Angel to safety."

Matt tossed the cell to Parker, who caught it in one hand. "You should have thought of that before you got her mixed up in all this." He braced himself to do his job, took out a pair of handcuffs, and pulled one hand behind her back. Her wrists were tiny, fine-boned, and delicate. This was generally the part of the job he liked best and got to do the least.

This time it left a bitter taste in his mouth.

"Scarlett Stone, you have the right to remain silent…"

CHAPTER FIVE

FBI Special Agent Lazlo held her elbow as if she was about to make a run for it. To think she'd found him attractive earlier and mourned the idea of never seeing him again. Now she *hoped* she never saw him again. Being escorted handcuffed into FBI Headquarters in downtown Washington DC reminded her of every humiliation she and her family had ever endured. Was this how her father had felt? Only worse to be hauled in by his colleagues and accused of selling them out for money—of being responsible for the deaths of fellow agents abroad.

Did one get used to the bite of hard metal on soft skin? Of the condemnation and derision on people's faces? Or was each cut and sting a fresh blow? The idea was too much to bear. The thought of her father wasting away in those conditions, without proper treatment, imprisoned for something he hadn't done...

She'd begged him to tell her why he'd confessed, but he'd closed his eyes and refused to speak. He'd avoided the death penalty, but at what cost? Someone must have threatened her mother if he didn't take the fall. Or her.

She wasn't a kid anymore. She'd figured she had nothing to lose except her own freedom by trying to find the truth, but now Angel had been kidnapped and it was all her fault. She tipped her chin higher and choked down the emotions. She needed to fix this. She had to be able to find a way to make this right.

They used the back entrance of the J. Edgar Hoover building. Passing through corridors and metal detectors and security checks, each encounter more humiliating than the last. She caught Alex Parker's eye. He gave her a slight smile. Not reassuring. More apologetic. Sympathetic. It didn't bode well.

They reached an office area and a guy with well-groomed blond hair and the palest blue eyes she'd ever seen, looked up from where he was talking to a pretty agent with short dark hair. The guy wore full black tie and didn't seem to care that he was overdressed for work. She must have ruined his plans for the evening—apparently, it was her night for it. His eyes rested on her cuffed arms and his brows quirked. Out of the corner of her eye, she saw Parker grimace, but her jailer, Matt Lazlo, didn't bat an eyelid. Her foot itched to kick him again.

Good-looking alpha types brimming with too much testosterone surrounded her, making her feel small and insignificant. She didn't remember her dad's colleagues looking like this, but then she'd been a kid. Even the female agent looked like she could kick Scarlett's ass and look cool doing it. If Angel had been here, she'd have been flirting despite the handcuffs. But then if Angel had been here, Scarlett wouldn't feel like someone was carving a hole through her chest with a handsaw.

She swallowed the guilt and remorse. If Angel was hurt, Scarlett would never forgive herself. They *had* to let her fix this. Except she knew from experience they didn't have to do a damn thing they didn't want to. They didn't have to investigate her claims that her father was innocent despite his guilty plea. They didn't have to be lenient when she'd tried to bug a foreign superpower. And they didn't have to give a damn that she just wanted the truth.

She checked the clock on the wall and realized belatedly that this was the office where her father had once worked. They'd updated the decor and installed cubicles and gray carpeting, but the clock on the wall was exactly the same as it had been when she'd been here as a wide-eyed twelve-year-old.

"Where do you want her for interrogation, boss?" Lazlo asked.

A ball of emotion wedged in her throat. It was stupid to feel betrayed by this guy. He didn't owe her anything. She'd lied to him. He'd saved her life. What did she expect?

The feeling was there all the same. So much for finally meeting a man she *connected* with. She wanted to connect all right. She wanted to connect her boot to his shin one last time.

The man in the tux approached carrying a file. "My name is Assistant Special Agent in Charge Lincoln Frazer. Let's go into one of the interview rooms and talk, shall we?"

He was young to be in such a senior position. Definitely the politically ambitious type, which did not bode well for her. Scarlett started toward the room, knowing it would be useless to complain. These people didn't care about her. They didn't care about her father. She was beginning to wonder if they even cared about justice.

"Special Agent Lazlo," ASAC Frazer said as the other man turned to walk away. One of those perfect brows rose in question. "The cuffs, please?"

Reluctantly Lazlo came up behind her and inserted the key. His skin was warm against hers. The scent of his spicy cologne drifted over her, reminding her of the illusion that had beguiled her so completely earlier. His touch was gentle despite the fact she knew he was mad at her for lying to him. Maybe they were even, after all.

"Thank you." She rubbed the soreness from her wrists.

He paused for a moment but didn't reply. She got it. She was the enemy now. FBI agents didn't consort with the enemy. Whatever. Her father had been a straight shooter too, always following the rules. Ironically Matt Lazlo reminded her a little of him. She wondered how far he'd spit if she told him that.

She preceded Frazer into the interview room. Lazlo came too, which surprised her. He looked out of place in his dark t-shirt, black pants, and flak jacket. More military than FBI but then he'd obviously once been in the Navy from the uniform he'd worn earlier—assuming that was real and not some sort of cover. Had he been sent to follow her at the party? That didn't seem possible when she'd told no one of her plans to bug the ambassador.

She sat in an uncomfortable plastic chair across the table from ASAC Frazer. Lazlo positioned himself by the door. Arms crossed, leaning against a wall. The hazel eyes had lost their spark of humor. She doubted he'd ever smile at her that way again. Didn't matter. She turned away.

"Dr. Stone," ASAC Frazer began.

So, he knew her background. She dragged her hat off her head and stuffed it in her pocket. Pushed her hair behind her ear. God, she hoped her boss never found out about this fiasco. Her eyes flicked to the man at the door and her lips tightened. "I need to make a phone call."

"First I need to ask you a few questions about what happened tonight—"

"Look, I get it. I did it." She leaned forward, hands fisted on the tabletop. "But my friend has been kidnapped. You need to get out there and *find* her. She had nothing to do with any of this."

"You didn't tell her your intentions?"

She shook her head.

"And it was pure chance she asked you to go with her to that party and lied to her parents about it?"

"She wanted to go, so she accepted on behalf of her and her sister. Then Sarah went off on some trekking adventure in the desert so she asked me instead. She thought it would be fun and knew they wouldn't let me near the place under normal circumstances—"

"For obvious reasons," Lazlo piped up. *Smartass.*

Scarlett tapped her nails impatiently on the surface of the table. "Angel is always trying to get me to socialize, but I usually say no."

"This time you didn't?"

Scarlett shook her head. "I wish I had, but I knew it might be my one opportunity to find out the truth." She stared down at the table, unable to meet their eyes and witness the cynical judgment gleaming in their depths. Maybe they did believe in the justice system, but that was their problem, not hers. Her belief system had been shattered a long time ago. "Angel was so excited when I said I'd go." And she'd let her down. "She was furious when I dragged her out of there early." She couldn't look at the man she'd flirted with at the party. The man who'd driven her home. Instead, she looked into Frazer's cold, blue eyes. "You have to let me help her. Please." Tears formed, but she blinked them away. Tears made you look weak and that was bullshit. She wasn't weak. Her mother wasn't weak. Anyone who'd gone through what they'd gone through knew all about steel armor and emotional endurance.

Frazer's gaze tracked her features like a human lie detector, but his expression didn't change. "We have people working the case. Hostage negotiators are with the LeMays now."

"He took her phone. Unless he turned off the GPS you should be able to track it within a few meters." Her nails dug into her palms. Shouldn't these guys be *doing* something?

"Her phone was found near the area where someone took a shot at you."

Crap. "They must have seen your agents show up and thought I'd called the cops. Let me try to speak to the person who took her. Tell them that she had nothing to do with any of it."

"Who do you think took her?"

"Who do you think?" She frowned. Surely he wasn't that stupid.

"I'm interested in your thoughts, Dr. Stone."

"Let me talk to the kidnappers, and I'll tell you everything I've been thinking since the day you guys arrested my dad fourteen years ago."

"You think this has something to do with your father's case?"

Scarlett snapped her mouth shut. Them wanting to know her motivation was the only currency she had right now.

"Wouldn't you rather talk to a lawyer?"

She snorted. "I saw how much good lawyers did my father." She got serious fast. "I just want to save my friend. If she's hurt in any way because of what I did…"

"We have professionals who deal with this sort of thing."

"But I'm the person they want and the first few hours are crucial in abductions," she countered. "Give me a phone, and I'll call the person responsible."

Frazer leaned back in his chair, a smile playing around his lips that did nothing to warm his eyes. "So you intend to, what? Call the Russian embassy? Maybe chat with Ambassador Dorokhov himself? Do you really believe he's going to admit to kidnapping a congressman's daughter?"

Scarlett's heart fluttered under her breastbone. Frazer was right, Dorokhov would never talk to her. She dragged her hands over her face. What had she done? She was so stressed she could barely think but there had to be a way to fix this. Problem solving was her forte. "Look. I heard Alex Parker telling Agent Lazlo that he got the license plate of the car of the person shooting at us."

"*You.*" Lazlo interrupted. "The shooter was aiming at *you.*"

For the first time she noticed a tear in the t-shirt he wore. "Were you *hit*?" Her voice rose with concern.

Lazlo exchanged a glance with his boss. "It's a graze." He shrugged as if to emphasize how much it didn't hurt.

Frazer's expression tightened, but he didn't press the issue. *Well, fine.* If they were determined to pretend getting shot was an everyday occurrence, so be it.

"You can find the car though, right?" Otherwise how on earth could they save Angel? "They want to swap her for me. That's all you have to do is hand me over and Angel will be safe. I'd think that would make you very happy." She sent Lazlo a brittle smile.

"They'll kill you. Don't you care about your own survival?" Lazlo bit out.

"Of course I care," she snapped. "But they won't kill me."

His brows rose as if to say "seriously?".

She straightened her spine. "Why would they want to kill me? I didn't *do* anything." Lazlo opened his mouth to argue, but she held up her finger. "Yes, I tried to bug Dorokhov but someone beat me to the punch." Realization dawned. "And the reason you followed me to the park is you already know this. You know what I found when I tried to plant my bug in that office because the FBI already had Dorokhov under surveillance. Why?"

No one answered. Of course no one answered. But then she figured out what they already knew. *Crap.* "Dorokhov doesn't know the bug in the lamp wasn't mine, does he?" She avoided looking at Lazlo, concentrated on Frazer. "The FBI isn't likely to admit they were the ones spying, even to save my skin—" She groaned. "Especially to save *my* skin."

Her eyes swiveled back to Lazlo's. "I think I want that lawyer now."

The tightness of his jaw and the tense set of his shoulders didn't bode well. He straightened away from the wall and opened his mouth.

Frazer beat him to it. "You're free to go."

Scarlett shook her head, certain she'd misheard. "Pardon me?"

"You're free to leave." Frazer repeated and closed the file in front of him with calm finality, all cool, controlled federal official.

"But…" She pointed at Lazlo. "He arrested me."

"A misunderstanding." Frazer smiled, which made him look scary.

73

But so what? It didn't matter. They were going to let her go, and relief made her pulse flutter. She pushed back her chair. She could go home and wait for the kidnapper to contact her again. Maybe the cops would catch the guy this time and find Angel.

"She assaulted a federal agent." Lazlo ground out between teeth that looked fused together.

Frazer swept his eyes over her frame then back to his agent. "You have nearly a foot in height and probably a hundred pounds weight advantage. How assaulted did you get?"

"That isn't the point and you know it." Lazlo's growl deepened. She felt his disapproval all the way down to her marrow.

"Let it go," insisted Frazer.

Lazlo's eyes narrowed. "Sir, I need to talk to you. Now." It didn't sound like a request. She shifted in her seat about to make her escape while she could. He pointed at her. "Stay."

Dammit. "I'm not a dog." But she didn't want to piss him off and sat anxiously on the edge of her seat as the two men went outside to talk. She needed to get out of here before they changed their minds. She needed to figure out how to get her friend to safety because she didn't think the FBI had a handle on this situation. The only decent FBI agent she'd ever known had been locked up while the rest of them threw away the key. No way did she want Angel to become another innocent victim of federal incompetence.

———

Matt didn't know what the hell was going on, but he didn't like it. This wasn't about his ego or the law. In the normal course of events, getting kicked in the shin would rate a two on his reasons-to-get-pissed-off scale. He injured himself worse whenever he did the assault course. This was about keeping Scarlett Stone safe from her own foolishness. He'd rather see her arrested and in jail than running around DC like a grown up version of Veronica Mars.

They crowded around the table where Mallory Rooney was on the phone to the Metropolitan Police Department, trying to track down the shooter's car via traffic cams. Alex Parker was also on the phone. Matt suspected he had the people at his cyber-security firm earning a little overtime doing the exact same thing.

Rooney put down the phone. "No sign of the vehicle yet. They're looking."

A couple of agents from this office sat at their desks and eyed them curiously. The deputy director had given them permission to use the interrogation room and facilities, but expected a full briefing in return.

Parker activated some sort of signal jammer on his key ring and a small red light lit up. He placed it on the desk between them. He kept his voice to a low murmur. "This prevents any electronic listening equipment picking up our conversation within a twenty foot radius. It doesn't stop people physically overhearing what we say. We can talk in confidence, but keep it down."

Matt's brows hiked. What they were discussing was highly sensitive, but who the hell did Parker think was bugging FBI HQ? Maybe the guy was paranoid from being in the security business. Maybe he knew something Matt didn't.

It didn't matter. "You can't seriously be letting her go," Matt said to his boss.

"Direct orders from the chief of the Counterespionage Section in the Counterintelligence Division, Ridley Branson."

Frazer crossed his arms over his chest. He didn't look happy. "Think about it. The Russians aren't going to press charges because it would make them the laughing stock of the entire intelligence community—and one thing the Russians hate is being laughed at by the West. The fact Richard Stone's daughter waltzed in there without them recognizing her? Priceless."

"I'm not interested in the Russians pressing charges." Matt tried to curb his impatience. "I don't want her in some Soviet-era gulag for trying to sneak a look at Dorokhov. Surely we can hold her on something minor?"

"If *we* arrest her, we tip our hand as to the fact it was *us* spying on them, not the Chinese, because how else would we know she was in trouble?"

"Haven't we already tipped our hand by intercepting her at the park tonight?"

Frazer raised his index finger. "Look at it from the Russian point of view. What do they know? A handsome FBI agent is spotted chatting up the daughter of a convicted spy at the Russian Ambassador's residence."

Matt kept his expression carefully neutral.

"Scarlett Stone subsequently enters the ambassador's office uninvited and when they search it they find listening devices. She's shot at in the park and we bring her in for questioning."

"They'll think we were actively surveilling her," suggested Rooney. "They'll think she was Matt's target all along and that we had suspicions about her intentions or activities."

"Won't they think she's working for us?" asked Matt.

"No way." Frazer's facial expression said that was never going to happen. "Her father humiliated this agency and he's still resented by many who now run the Bureau."

Matt exchanged a glance with Alex Parker. His expression remained impassive, but the guy had said Scarlett would make the perfect scapegoat for the FBI's activities. He was right.

"Which puts Scarlett Stone in danger if we let her back on the streets with no protection," Matt argued his point again. "You said yourself the Russians hate being made fools of. They'll wait a few hours and then grab her. She's totally vulnerable." Matt ground his teeth. "*She* shouldn't have to pay for our country's spying activities."

Frazer cocked his head. "She's the one who broke into his office with intent."

"She's the one they caught," Matt corrected.

"Why were we looking at Dorokhov?" Rooney asked the question they'd asked TacOps earlier.

Frazer shrugged, but from the tightening of his mouth, he didn't like the lack of intel any more than Matt did.

"No one knows much about the guy, but the people he makes nervous make me nervous. There was this one thing in Istanbul a few years ago that no one can attribute to him for sure, but…" Parker trailed off.

"What?" Matt asked.

"He found out one of his underlings was screwing his mistress—this was before he was married. Guy was found dead in an alley. Woman ended up in the hospital."

"Beaten?"

"Someone threw acid in her face."

Jesus Christ.

Parker watched him carefully. "That's the story."

Frazer's gaze turned glacial. "Rumor. Gossip. He's the Russian Ambassador, not some Mafia figure." But people in power often abused it. This wasn't news.

There was silence for a moment as everyone processed their thoughts. "The positive thing about letting Scarlett Stone go is that the kidnapper might try to contact her again. In which case Parker should be able to trace the call and we can hopefully locate Angel LeMay before they decide she's more trouble than she's worth."

"Are you fucking kidding me?" Matt didn't lose it often and he never lost it with his boss. "The *positive* thing? They shot at her." Sweet Jesus. The situation was unraveling, and he didn't like what he was seeing here. This was bullshit politics. He trusted his boss but the man seemed to be blind to the danger surrounding the woman in the next room—or uncaring. "What about protective custody?"

"For the daughter of the most notorious spy in US history?" Frazer's lips twisted angrily. "Because she broke into the Russian Ambassador's residence and tried to conduct illegal surveillance? Do you see that request being approved?"

"If we let her go she's dead," Matt stated baldly. He ground his teeth. Russian ambassador or not, the woman was naïve if she believed Dorokhov wouldn't punish her severely for this escapade.

"We can put a tail on her for a few days. Have patrol cars do extra drive-bys past her house. The brass won't act unless they believe she's in mortal danger—"

"She *is*." *Fuck.* "Of course she is."

"Even then…"

Matt put both hands on his head and wished he could rewind his day by six hours and tell Frazer to go to hell when he asked him to go to the Christmas party. Or maybe eight hours so he could get two solid hours of drinking inside him so he wouldn't be in any condition to give a shit. Except

Scarlett would still have tried to bug the Russians, would still have been spotted, and would probably already be dead.

"Fuck."

"She instigated this mess." Frazer's expression betrayed nothing.

"And you're hanging her out to dry." Matt reined in his temper. "Are you really just gonna let them kill her?"

"What if she's right about her father?" Rooney asked quietly.

"He confessed." Matt dismissed the idea.

"The Russians always denied he was their agent," Rooney argued.

"They always do unless there's an exchange in the offing," said Frazer.

Which would never happen for Stone.

"Why else would she go after Dorokhov?" Rooney insisted. She shoved hair off her forehead. There were dark shadows under her eyes and her cheeks were pale. Matt had heard rumors she was pregnant. She didn't complain. She might be a rookie but she was a diligent agent. Smart. "It doesn't make sense unless she believes it is the truth."

"Kids are often delusional about their parents." God knew he'd been delusional about his father.

"She might be working for someone else—corporate or State espionage," Parker suggested. "Or was maybe black-mailed into planting the bug for some other purpose. Her work is on the cutting edge of technology. Maybe it was some sort of test?"

It didn't ring true with Matt. Scarlett was just another kid let down first by her parent and then by the system. It didn't mean she got to take things into her own hands, but a bullet seemed like extreme recourse.

"See what you can find out," Frazer told Parker. "I don't want any more surprises."

Two men Matt didn't recognize walked into the bullpen and Frazer stood a little straighter. "Sir, you didn't have to come in."

Parker palmed his signal jamming gadget.

Ridley Branson cut a stocky figure. Gray haired, lantern jawed with ebony skin. "Not much use being the chief of counterespionage if I don't pay attention to things happening in the intelligence community." His jocular humor set Matt's jaw on lock-down. There was nothing funny about tonight. He stood with his arms folded and tried not to glare at the bastard.

"This is ASAC Guy Clarkson out of the Washington Field Office." Branson introduced another man, medium height, short blond hair. "We worked together on the Stone investigation fourteen years ago." Branson walked over to the mirrored glass where they could all see Scarlett tapping her nails nervously on the plastic veneer of the table. He let out a gusty sigh. "She hasn't changed much since she was a little girl."

"You knew her?" Matt asked.

The chief swept a cold glance over him. Matt hadn't exactly addressed him politely, or even introduced himself.

"I worked with her father, right here in this office. He brought her in with him a couple of times, to pick up files." Branson grimaced as if in hindsight wondering what had been in those files.

Yeah. A little late for those six dead US agents. Someone had dropped the ball. And it hadn't been Matt.

"I have HRT working with the LeMays now. I persuaded them it was in their daughter's best interests to keep this out of the press. I'm expecting she'll be released unharmed in the near future. The Russians aren't going to want a major diplomatic incident."

"I'd like permission to question Richard Stone about his daughter's activities, sir," Frazer asked. "See if he put her up to this."

Deep lines stamped Branson's face with world-weariness. "Put in the paperwork but don't hold your breath." His gaze softened. "Richard is dying. Cancer. Probably won't last more than a few months and the Bureau of Prisons isn't known for its speed or leniency, even in these circumstances."

Shit. Matt turned back to look at where Scarlett was now pacing the small interview room. Compassion pushed past the anger. That's why she'd done it. A last ditch effort to save the man she loved despite his confession. Crazy misplaced loyalty. A small part of him felt a little envious that she loved her father that much. If it had been his, he'd have thrown away the key.

"Cut her loose. The Russians know we're watching her. That's pretty much all we can do for the kid now."

Matt nodded as if he didn't think the guy was an asshole. No way he was leaving her on her own with a target on her back. He hadn't dedicated his life to service in order to sacrifice a defenseless woman for doing the exact same thing their colleagues had done. So what if they had the law on their side? Rules were one thing, but a guy had to be able to look in the mirror and not hate the person staring back. Scarlett Stone was not going to be murdered on his watch. Not tonight.

The FBI didn't have his back, which left him with two options—seduction, or sedation?

CHAPTER SIX

Lincoln Frazer knew something was up with this scenario but didn't give away any hint of doubt with his expression or actions. Espionage and counterintelligence work was a complex dance of move and counter-move, and he didn't pretend to know the characters or ramifications involved.

Matt Lazlo headed into the interview room and jerked his head to indicate Scarlett Stone follow him out. The agent vibrated with tension. He was not happy with this situation and Frazer didn't blame him. The guy might not realize it, but he watched the woman with a mixture of desire and reluctant compassion—and both factors were going to complicate an already tangled mess. Lazlo was a damn fine agent who worked his ass off—smart, dedicated, intuitive. Lazlo was also a former Navy SEAL, which made him function great in a team environment, but also operate well as a creative and independent thinker.

He was also a man. And men made mistakes.

One thing Frazer had learned over the years was while he could tell someone what to do, he couldn't tell them how to think. He could remind them of rules and duty and the letter of the law, he could rebuke them for screwing up. But intelligent people made their own decisions based on individual situations. Circumstances made a difference. Past deeds only went so far in predicting someone's future actions. And desperate situations produced desperate measures. He was living proof of that unfortunate behavioral truth.

When Scarlett Stone got to the doorway, her eyes shot to Branson. She swayed slightly, looking so insubstantial a stiff breeze might knock her over. He understood why she brought out Lazlo's protective instincts but didn't intend to get sucked in. She reached out a hand to steady herself on the jamb. "Agent Branson, I almost didn't recognize you. It's been a long time."

"It's Chief of the Counterespionage Section now, Scarlett," Branson told her sternly. He sat on the corner of a desk, leg swinging as if relaxed and unconcerned. Frazer didn't buy it for a minute.

"Ah, of course, *Chief* Branson." Bitterness rang out, loud and clear. "You haven't been around to visit in a few years so I wasn't up on the Bureau promotions. You've done well for yourself. Your wife and kids must be very proud." Her gaze was unflinching, her chin raised high.

There was an awkward silence. Clarkson kept his gaze glued to the floor. Branson's lips thinned.

"See if you can keep out of trouble, okay, Scarlett? There's a good girl."

Her eyes narrowed at the patronizing tone, but she clamped down on whatever thoughts were running through her mind. *Good choice.* Branson was a powerful man, and powerful men did not like being shown up by young women, even those with genius IQs.

Lazlo took her arm and led her out of the bullpen. Frazer felt a twinge of pity for the girl because she was in serious danger. No doubt she carried a lot of baggage regarding what her father had done, but it wasn't an excuse to go bugging foreign powers. He understood some of what Scarlett Stone was dealing with—taking the law into your own hands was tempting when you felt justified, but it was still wrong.

His superior hooked his thumbs in his pants, one of the boys. "Keep me apprised of any changes in the situation. I've made the safe return of the LeMay girl a Bureau priority. Hopefully she'll be home for Christmas dinner."

"Yes, sir."

"Let's try and keep this amongst ourselves, huh?" Branson looked each of them in the eye, then he and Clarkson turned and walked away.

Speculation was rife in Rooney's gaze. "What do we do now, boss?"

Frazer jolted whenever she called him that. It reminded him how badly he'd messed up and how hard he needed to work to make up for his mistakes. He trusted Rooney and Parker as much, if not more, than he trusted people he'd worked with for years. Their relationship had been forged through blood, death, and necessity, but also in an act of love and mercy. The fact she called him boss was a testament to her dedication to the job. He needed to earn the title.

The correct thing to do in this current situation would be walk away and assume the rest of the FBI could do their jobs without his interference. His role was running Behavioral Analysis Unit-4, helping other law enforcement agencies find killers, traffickers, rapists, and other degenerates. God knew they had enough cases to keep them busy until the next millennia. They analyzed police reports, crime scenes and evidence; they did not run counterintelligence operations or investigations.

But he'd lost faith in the system.

He'd never take anything on blind trust again.

What if Scarlett Stone was right about her father? What if he *had* been set up? Who in this building would consider that possibility? Who would care about a vulnerable young woman's naïve quest for justice? And who might still be dirty?

Frazer checked his watch.

It wasn't his job to question the veracity of old cases. The President of the United States had asked for help with a matter of national importance, and there was a certain assassin who needed to be tracked and caught before she killed again. There were files on his desk that needed urgent attention. It was Christmas Eve. HRT were in charge of the kidnapping investigation so he should just go home and get a few hours' sleep. That's what he should do.

Frazer got out his cell and dialed a number. Lazlo answered. "You're on bodyguard duty until we can find out exactly what's going on. Keep her away from news outlets and tell her Angel has been found safe and sound. That should keep her quiet for the time being. If it doesn't, use your initiative. In the meantime, we'll figure out some way to neutralize the threat to her safety." He hoped he wasn't making promises he couldn't keep or about to make enemies out of every one of his FBI colleagues. But he hadn't joined the Bureau to make friends. He'd joined to protect those who couldn't protect themselves. "Keep a low profile and watch your back."

———

Scarlett could feel Matt Lazlo's disapproving gaze scour her back the entire walk out. They got to a door and he reached past her and opened it, indicating she go ahead of him. The polite gentleman switching out with the ass-kicking FBI agent.

He unnerved her. The whole American hero persona he carried with him like an invisible cloak was the antithesis of her world, where oily doubt and suspicion clung to everything she or her family touched. The fact she was attracted to him on a physical level didn't help. She suspected a lot of women were attracted to Matt Lazlo, even the ones who hadn't seen him in his dress uniform.

"So, what's your next play?" He was trying for nonchalance but didn't fool her. He was still pissed.

As far as the Russians were concerned, she had limited options. One was knocking on the door of the Ambassador's residence and begging for forgiveness, the other was to go home and wait for the kidnapper to contact her. The third was running away—but Angel was in danger. Plus, Scarlett had a life here, a career—assuming her boss didn't find out what she'd been up to in her spare time and fire her from her position, which would make it hellish difficult to get hired on anywhere else. Dammit.

She'd been so stupid to think she could spy on Andrei Dorokhov. Finding out anything useful had been a long shot. She'd planned to nudge a reaction by calling him and then listening in to what he said after he put the phone down. Great idea in theory. Useless if you got busted by both the FBI and the Russian Federation.

Lazlo pressed a warm hand to her back, just above her waist. A shiver ran over her skin and she stumbled.

"Steady."

His touch affected her more than she wanted to admit. Unfortunately, one of the times he'd touched had been to slap on handcuffs. He wasn't her boyfriend. He wasn't her date. He was an FBI agent and she knew the lengths they'd go to get their "man".

"Scarlett?"

"What?"

"Are you okay?" he asked as if he was repeating the question. His voice was soft, gentle even. She didn't trust him or the effect he had on her.

Belatedly she realized she'd stopped moving. "Yes."

"Do you have a plan?"

She jerked away from him. His nearness distracted her, her hyperawareness of him clouded her thought processes. She was a problem solver by nature. Fixing things was what she did, but she couldn't fix this and she couldn't fix her father's situation. Humiliation and anger fought for space on her cheeks. "I need to figure out a way to get Angel to safety."

"FBI assigned a team." He held another door. "If you interfere you might get her killed."

"But it's *me* they want." That much was crystal clear.

"So what? You're going to serve yourself up to them on a platter?"

"Any other ideas?" She was open to alternatives.

Something buzzed in his pocket. He held up his finger to indicate she wait for a moment. Pulled out his cell. Listened intently. She stopped walking even though freedom beckoned within sight. Running away might activate his prey-drive and she was reluctant to show weakness. He'd already rescued her twice tonight. Once with a ride home, the other time from a bullet.

The expression in his eyes shifted but she couldn't read it. "Roger that." There was a long pause, then, "That's good news. Great. Thanks for letting me know." He hung up and met her gaze. "You don't need to sacrifice yourself. They found Angel LeMay wandering near DuPont Circle. She's a little groggy, but basically in one piece."

Her knees wanted to give out, but she locked them. "Can I see her?"

"They've taken her to the hospital." He tilted his head, mouth compressed. Pity filled his eyes. "I doubt the LeMays are gonna want you around for a while."

Oh, crap. She doubted they'd want anything to do with her again. She'd betrayed their trust and gotten Angel abducted. Her hand rose to grip her throat, her voice barely a whisper. "She's okay though, right?"

He gave her a terse nod.

She needed to talk to Angel, to apologize, but a little time to recover and cool down might be a good thing. She hoped the bastards hadn't hurt her. She needed to make this stop. Now. Before anyone else was injured or terrorized. "I guess my plan is to go to the Russian Ambassador's home, beg forgiveness, and hope they decide to leave me alone."

"Seriously? *That's* your plan?" He was looking at her like she was an idiot. "To turn yourself in and beg for mercy?"

"If I go home they'll find me—even if I run away for a few weeks or months they can afford to wait me out. Then I'll be right back where I started, minus a job and most of my savings. I can't abandon my mother and father right now either." She wouldn't be hard to find in Colorado. "The only way I can think of to end this is to apologize and promise I won't do it again. Dad always said the Russians liked people to grovel, so I'll grovel." The idea that her dad was dying was worse than the thought of having to apologize to the man who she believed had a hand putting him in prison. Much worse.

"You are fricking unbelievable."

Her spine stiffened. "Why thank you so much, Special Agent Lazlo. You're fricking unbelievable, too."

She turned on her heel and marched away, pushing through the main doors. Most women probably fell at his feet, blinded by the action hero build and chest full of medals. They hadn't been arrested or insulted by the man.

Outside the frigid air took her breath, but the scent of freedom made up for the chill. The freedom might not last long.

She hunched her shoulders as defeat pressed down on her. Time to pay the piper. "I need to call a cab." She dug into her pocket, searching for her cell phone before remembering she didn't have it. In her rush to escape, she'd left it with the other guy, Alex Parker. No way was she going back inside, just in case they changed their minds about releasing her. She'd have to walk and see if she could flag down a cab.

"I'll give you a ride," Lazlo offered.

She backed away. "You don't have to do that. I've caused you enough trouble for one night."

"Lady, you've caused me enough trouble for a lifetime." A wry smile crossed his features, but there was something in his eyes…a calm patience that told her he was used to getting his own way.

She batted her eyelids dramatically. "You're such a charmer, Special Agent Lazlo. I don't know how the ladies resist you."

"And yet they continue to do so."

"Maybe that's why you were so quick with the handcuffs?" she suggested with an arched look. "To stop the ladies running screaming at the earliest opportunity?"

Amusement lit his eyes. "Hadn't thought of that, but thanks for the tip." Before she had time to refuse, he wrapped his arm around her shoulders and propelled her toward the SUV he'd left in the secure parking lot. *Fine.* He lifted her into the front seat. Gritting her teeth against being manhandled, she drew in a deep breath to calm herself. Getting a ride would be the most expedient way of getting to 16th Street so she should just be grateful.

Sure.

He was eye-level with her. Their faces so close she could see the thickness of his lashes around those mesmerizing eyes. She tried to control the shivers that wracked her body. She didn't know if it was cold, fear, or this man's nearness that affected her. Probably a combination of all three. "Thank you."

His smile turned wolfish. "You're welcome." He slammed her door and she jolted. Next she heard him opening the trunk and unzipping something. He spoke briefly on the phone. By the time he got in the driver's seat, he'd removed his flak jacket and rolled up his sleeves. The thick cords of muscle ran the length of his forearms, and flexed when he gripped the steering wheel. Her eyes flicked over him. He wasn't just good looking, he was perfect.

The scent of clean sweat mingled with his cologne—warm, male, virile. *Dammit.* She fidgeted uneasily. Why couldn't he have a paunch and some flab? Maybe a broken nose or a unibrow, with a severe case of BO?

It's just pheromones, she reminded herself. Basic biology. But her pheromone receptors were doing a happy dance and her breath became tight in her chest as her pulse picked up.

Thank God she was wearing enough clothes to disguise the rest of her body's unwanted arousal, but from the glint in his eyes he knew exactly what he did to her. She looked out the window, but his reflection stared back at her in the glass and her breath caught. Wrong time, wrong place, wrong man.

Definitely, wrong woman.

"I need a coffee, how about you? Might be your last chance?" The words were nonchalant, verging on callous.

Her gaze swung back to his as her mouth dropped open. *What the…?*

"Hey." His shrug was almost jaunty. "I need coffee. You're determined to do this. I've been ordered to stand down. I can't stop you, but at least I can buy you a drink first."

She crossed her arms over her chest. He probably thought she deserved whatever she got and maybe he was right. But she didn't want to go to the Russians, dammit. She didn't want to grovel before Dorokhov. "I don't see that I have any alternative."

"You could run away? Go under the radar?"

"They'll find me. Unlike the FBI, I don't have unlimited resources. Plus, I like my job. I'm good at it."

"Pity you didn't think of that beforehand."

"My dad is *dying*. I know he didn't do all the things he was accused of." Her voice broke. Embarrassed, she looked away.

He started the engine, adjusted the temperature, pulled away, and swung onto 9th Street without making any more snide remarks. It took her a moment to get her emotions under control. She was tired, scared, defeated. She didn't need him to rub her nose in her failings.

After a few minutes he found a coffee shop that was still open and he pulled up outside, leaving the engine running, the heater blasting. "What shall I get you?"

It was the middle of the night, she was tired. Caffeine might help.

"Hot chocolate would be great, thanks." She dug into her wallet for some change but he was already gone. She dropped a five-dollar note into the change holder on the console. She swiveled to see if there were any cars following but, except for the few vehicles that were already here when they arrived, there was no one on the roads.

She doubted the Russians would tail them from FBI HQ. They could afford to be patient. She couldn't.

Lazlo came back a few minutes later and handed her a large cup. "Server gave you whipped cream. Hope that's okay."

She'd drink gasoline as long as it was warm. "That's fine, thank you."

He sank heavily into the leather seat, blowing on his coffee to cool it. "I'm so exhausted I could pass out."

"I'm sorry for keeping you up." *Jeez.* The guy was seriously lacking in tact.

"That was a crazy stunt you pulled back there. You should have just seduced Raminski and bugged his bedroom instead."

The idea sent a shudder through her bones. "I'm not the seductress type. More Angel's forte."

"Oh, I don't know." At first he stared straight ahead. Then he looked her in the eye. "You could have seduced me with very little effort." The flatness of his tone told her it was too late now.

The thought that she'd stood a chance with a guy like him sent a shot of something sharp and aching through her chest. Hot guys like Lazlo didn't date nerd girls like her. But something about his expression, the memory of the way he'd looked at her when she'd stood on the sidewalk outside the embassy, told her it might have been true. And she'd messed it up, along with everything else.

It would have been messed up anyway, as soon as he learned her identity, so the point was moot. But the reminder of that earlier connection was unsettling. *What ifs* and *maybes* rolled through her system like breakers on a beach. To cover her disquiet she took a large swallow of hot chocolate. Wiped her mouth with the back of her hand. "You'd have had a hell of a shock if you'd made it to third base."

He choked on his coffee.

Laughter felt good. It felt honest.

She smiled softly. "I didn't mean to get you involved in my problems, Special Agent Lazlo. I really am sorry."

"Call me Matt and, trust me, I figured that out."

"Matt, short for Matthew?"

Something about her question amused him. His eyes crinkled at the outer corners. "Matthias. My father claimed to be a Bulgarian Roma and named me accordingly."

"You come from gypsy stock?" Her eyes searched his face for some trace but she found none.

He shrugged. "My dad was an asshole of dubious heritage. My mother is a British aristocrat, which pretty much makes me a mongrel. He married her hoping to get his hands on a fortune and dumped her when her parents cut her out of the will." His expression changed. Grew tense.

"Does that make you a lord?" She tried to lighten the atmosphere by teasing him.

"No, but you can call me 'sir' if you like." His grin was wicked before he obviously remembered who he was flirting with. He sobered. "The title probably went to some long lost cousin."

"You don't know?" The heat of the SUV was making her sleepy. Combined with the adrenaline crash, it made her yawn. "Don't you watch *Downton Abby*?"

He raised a quizzical brow as if he didn't know what she was talking about. "Her family disowned her when she married my father. Dad dumped her when she got to the States, but they never reached out to help her. I never felt the urge to look up dear old granny and grampa."

"That's rough."

"Not really. Mom was a fighter." He sipped his coffee. Obviously in no hurry to leave yet. "She did great. She found work in a school and raised me on her own. She resented the hell out of any implication she needed a man to support her."

"Where does she live now?" She'd meant the question as a stall tactic, but realized she honestly wanted to know more about him. She drank more chocolate, grateful for the way it melted the chill inside her bones.

"Near me." He cleared the grit from his throat. "She suffered a brain aneurysm two years ago and never made a proper recovery." *Oh, no.* "She's in a nursing home. Hasn't woken up since the second stroke." He said it in such a controlled manner she knew it affected him greatly.

She knew how hard it was to have a parent who was ill and whom you couldn't help, no matter how desperately you wanted to. She wanted to place her hand over his but didn't have the nerve. "You're looking after her. That's all you can do."

"What else would I do? I'm her son, not some asshole husband," he growled, then sent her a rueful smile. "Sorry."

"Do I sense a little repressed anger? I know a good therapist if you need one."

"Ha. Because you're so balanced? Give me their number I'll make sure they didn't get their license out of a cereal box."

"Funny." A massive yawn stretched her mouth wide. She covered it with her free hand. "Oh, sorry. I'm just so tired all of a sudden."

Matt took the cup from fingers that felt clumsy and wooden. He slipped it into the cup holder. "Close your eyes for a few minutes. I'll wake you when we get there."

"Okay." She tried to keep her eyes open but the harder she tried the heavier her lids became. "I'm sorry about your mother," she mumbled, wanting him to know that she'd heard his pain and she cared despite everything that had happened.

"Just get some rest." His voice was rough.

A five-minute catnap was all she needed. She clenched her fingers in her lap and prayed Dorokhov didn't want any grisly mementos. She wasn't a brave person. She tended to retreat in the face of danger. Everything about tonight had been out of character and look what it had gained her? Trouble. Great big heaps of trouble. No way was she ever trying anything like this ever again. Hopefully Dorokhov would embrace a little Christmas spirit and maybe let her clean floors for a week. Whatever it took to go back to her normal, boring life.

———

It was two AM and Andrei Dorokhov sat staring at the fire, sipping expensive brandy. Natalie had gone to bed an hour ago, irritated by his bad mood. She didn't understand.

He hoped she never understood. The cell phone in his pants' pocket rang. He shifted and pulled it out. He didn't know the caller, but answered it anyway.

A man's voice. Easily recognizable even after fourteen years of aggravated silence. "Last time we spoke I held a knife to your throat and made you promise never to return to the States. Did you forget so easily, Andrei?"

"I forget nothing, *blyat.*"

"You've caused quite the shit storm. You just couldn't leave it alone, could you? Your goddamn Russian ego couldn't take some perceived slight to your manliness. She's just a kid looking for answers and you try to take her out? What did you think she'd discover if she bugged you?"

"Why don't you tell me?" Andrei suggested slyly.

There was a long pause. "It was over and done with. Why did you have to come back?"

"Are you losing your nerve, old friend?" Andrei taunted the other man.

"I'm no friend of yours, asshole."

He wasn't sure which of them had more to lose should the truth come out, but neither wanted it to happen. "You forget all the fun we had spinning those tales."

"It was never *fun,*" the man gritted out.

"The photographs suggested otherwise." Andrei slid in the reminder like a knife, but instantly regretted it.

"You're not the only one with photographs, Andrei."

Sweat formed on his back. "Those were staged and you know it." He'd been drugged and disgusting things had been done to him. It made him feel ill to even think about it. One day he was going to gut the man on the end of the line, and enjoy doing it.

"Didn't look staged from where I was sitting. Obviously there are some hellish good actors out there because even asleep you looked like you were enjoying it."

Andrei felt gore rise up inside him.

"Anyway," the voice was cheerful now, "we all know how homophobic the politburo was. I don't figure the Russians have progressed much in that area, but maybe I'm wrong. Hey, you'll probably find a lot of friends in—"

"*Ya nei goluboy!*"

"Seriously, Andrei, it's your business."

Andrei wanted to smash the phone in his rage but that would be a mistake. He calmed himself and understood the man was getting his revenge. He'd earned it. However, there were more important issues at stake. Pride would need to wait. "Enough about ancient history. We both have things that we don't want to become public knowledge. It's time to clean up those loose ends before they strangle us both."

"Nothing can be traced back to either of us," he warned.

"No mistakes," Andrei agreed. "You deal with the old problem, I'll deal with the new."

"You screw this up, next time it'll be a bullet, not a knife."

"I think you've lost your sense of humor, Marlon."

"Don't call me that—"

Andrei hung up. He didn't like being threatened, but the idea of those photographs going public pleased him even less. He'd come back to America to figure out a way to get them from his former asset. Scarlett Stone had slowed his mission and got in his way. Worse, she'd taken him for a fool. She was about to learn what happened to those who crossed those powerful within the Russian Federation.

Little girls who meddled with fire got burnt.

CHAPTER SEVEN

A glint of the moon's silver skimmed the horizon. The sea looked moody, as if it hadn't decided between calm or stormy; a bit like the way he felt about the woman he carried in his arms. Smart or stupid? Loyal or delusional? His instincts said the former on both counts but the attraction was clouding the waters. He needed his job. Couldn't afford any dumb-ass mistakes.

Matt adjusted his grip, grateful she wasn't some six-foot Amazon and hoping she didn't want to press charges when she woke up. Kidnapping wasn't part of his normal repertoire, but Matt was nothing if not adaptable. It was as illegal as hell, not to mention immoral—pity he didn't give a damn under the current circumstances.

The tide nudged the boats in the Quantico marina against the dock and the wind whistled through the rigging. Ice, sharp on the breeze, scraped across his bare skin. The twenty-seven foot yacht he called home had several advantages over standard accommodations. First, berth rental was cheap—he needed every cent he could get to pay for his mother's care. Second, he was close to work. Disadvantages were the cramped living quarters—and he was close to work.

He walked around the outer pier to berth number seventeen and climbed awkwardly aboard, careful not to bump

Scarlett's head on the railing. She was going to be furious with him when she woke up, but better that than dead or brutalized. If anyone saw him they'd think he was a goddamn serial killer—exactly the sort of sick bastard he hunted on a daily basis.

He unlocked the cabin door and turned on the lights, cranked up the heat. Then he took Scarlett through to the main stateroom and laid her on the bed. Took off her sneakers and drew the comforter up to her chin. Her features were softer in sleep, and without make-up, she looked even younger than she had at the party. Twenty-six. He was ten years older and it felt more like one hundred. War did that to a guy. War and seeing victims of crime on a daily basis. Not that he regretted his career choices, both had allowed him to make a positive difference to society, something he valued after having a deadbeat father. He'd made his mother proud and that was good enough for him.

Scarlett whimpered in her sleep and the sound did something to his insides. She was going to freak when she woke up. Go apeshit, especially when she discovered he'd lied about Angel. But Frazer had said to sit on her and frankly, he hadn't seen much alternative to knocking her out until he could persuade her not to present herself as a sacrifice to the altar of the Russian Ambassador.

He smoothed a stray lock of hair off her forehead and then pulled back. Too creepy. Too reminiscent of what some perps did when they had others under their control. He strode to the galley and put on the gas burners to boil water for tea. He needed sleep, but first he needed to warm up and decompress.

He stripped off his t-shirt and ran a paper towel under the warm tap, wiping away the blood that had dried on his skin from the bullet that had kissed him earlier. It stung a little but was no big deal. He dug out the antiseptic solution and cleaned the wound. He'd spent years dodging bullets as a SEAL and he didn't let the whole near-death thing bother him. When your time was up, it was up. No point worrying about it. His mother would be well taken care of for as long as needed and the one good thing about her condition was she'd never know she'd lost him.

Yeah, maybe it wasn't such a great bonus point, but it was all he had so he'd take it.

Her condition was gut churning, having survived the initial aneurysm she'd suffered a secondary stroke a few days later. At least he'd been with her at the time, holding her hand through the pain. The doctors told him it was doubtful she'd survive. A few weeks later when she had shown no sign of improvement, they'd wanted to pull the plug. Matt knew she wouldn't have wanted to be kept alive on a ventilator so he'd gone with their decision. When they'd taken her off life support his mom had started breathing on her own. She wasn't brain dead. She was in a deep coma, one he doubted she'd ever come out of, but she was inside there somewhere. The doctors couldn't tell him the extent of the brain damage and the likelihood of recovery was minimal. So he did what he could for her. Hoped she knew, somewhere deep down, that she was cherished and protected.

She was in a good care facility. The best. They saw to her every need and she was safe, secure. He visited every day he wasn't on the road. And every day her condition reminded him no one lived forever.

No one.

So better make damn sure what you did in life counted.

He dug around for milk in the fridge, poured boiling water over a tea bag and let it brew for a few moments before digging the bag out and throwing it in the garbage. Downing a couple of beers was tempting, but he needed to warm up first. Winter made living on a boat a little more testing, but summer made up for it.

His cell phone rang. He glanced at the display. His boss. He weighed the idea of pretending to be in the head versus getting this over with. Duty won.

"You have her," Frazer said without preamble.

"Yeah."

"She complain?"

Matt laughed. "Not yet, but she will."

Frazer paused. "I probably don't want to know."

Good call.

"MPD got a lead on that car the shooter used. Found it dumped near the observatory."

"Any sign of the LeMay girl?" He kept his voice down on the off chance Scarlett heard him. Not likely considering the small dose of tranquilizer he'd given her to make her sleep, but he liked to be careful.

"Nothing. Parker is monitoring cell phone communications and I'm in touch with the head of HRT who's an old friend of mine. Until the kidnappers make contact, they have nothing to go on. There are case agents assigned to try to find Angel, but…let's just say I think Parker's chances are better. I'm hoping the fact she's a congressman's daughter will go a long way toward keeping her unharmed. They want Scarlett, not Angel. Rooney and Parker are still looking for a link between LeMay and Dorokhov, but there might not be anything except the fact LeMay is a congressman who got an invite, and Scarlett used their connection to get to the ambassador. Dorokhov sent out hundreds of invites to his Christmas party this year."

Which left Matt stuck here babysitting a woman against her will while others did all the work. "What do I do with her tomorrow?" He rubbed his eyes. "Is it take-your-kid-to-work day?"

"She didn't look much like a kid when I saw her. You need your eyes checked?"

Had Frazer guessed he was attracted to her? "My vision is 20/20 and you know it."

"We'll monitor the situation and talk in the morning. Get some sleep."

"While everyone else works around the clock?" *Great.*

"Your job is to keep her safely out of sight until someone figures out where Angel LeMay is being held, and while I see what I can use to get Dorokhov to back off. That mission should be a piece of cake for a man of your experience."

Matt grunted. "You hoping to find a carrot, or a stick to use on Dorokhov?"

"At this stage I'll take anything I can get. A stick might be more satisfying but harder to wield. Even if we find evidence of him committing a crime, his diplomatic immunity makes it almost impossible to touch him unless Russia waives his rights. However we can make it difficult for him to do his job if he decides to threaten American socialites and research scientists."

"Scarlett said her father suspected Dorokhov was a Russian spy. Could he have been working with him?"

"I don't know. I'm getting on a plane to Colorado in a few hours, I'll be sure to ask him. I managed to get hold of a copy of the Stone investigation case file. I'll send you a copy before I leave. Just keep Scarlett occupied until we retrieve the LeMay girl."

Sounded easy enough. He could work from home.

"Just one thing." His boss's voice became low and soft. "Don't let those big, brown eyes fool you. Scarlett Stone graduated with a Ph.D. in solid-state physics at the age of twenty-two. She's no fool. Don't let your guard down."

Matt pulled a face at the phone. "Have you ever known my work to be influenced by a pretty face?"

"No, I haven't," Frazer said quietly. "But some women learn how to profile men like us in the womb. We're all vulnerable under the right circumstances to the right woman. We all have an Achilles heel."

"Even you?"

Frazer stayed silent.

"Don't worry boss. I'm immune to the allure of beauty. Give me honesty and integrity any day."

"So the blonde you met at the Christmas party with the long legs and big—"

"Hey."

"—hair, was full of honesty and integrity?"

"Well, at least she didn't build her own electronic surveillance from scratch and gain access to the Russian Embassy under false pretenses," Matt argued.

"Yeah, but do you remember her name?"

Shit. "Sure I do."

"Liar." Frazer called him on it. "But women like Scarlett Stone—we remember their names. Don't get attached. She's in a bad place and doesn't have any friends. Women like that…they can bring you to your knees."

The guy was nuts. Matt had spent years of his life literally bleeding for his country and that was before he joined the FBI. He wasn't about to sell out, or fall for someone as intrinsically compromised as Scarlett Stone, no matter how pretty her face or how soft her lips. Frazer had a reputation for being good at reading people—obviously even super-agents had off days.

"Just figure out how the hell we can send her home without a target on her forehead. I want my life back." But he was talking to dead air.

————

Raminski had been forced to call in reinforcements because the idea of hitting the woman turned his stomach.

"Where is she?" asked Mikhail Churnokov, head of the Russian Ambassador's personal security detail. Former KGB, the man used old school tactics with the subtlety of a T-72 tank sneaking down the Mall.

"In there." Raminski nodded to a door. It was three AM and he had no leads on where Scarlett Stone had gone since she'd left FBI HQ. The feds in the park had ruined his carefully laid plans, requiring him to make rapid adjustments to his strategy. He hadn't expected Stone to call the feds for help.

But no one knew where she'd gone. She hadn't gone home. She hadn't gone to her office.

They were in a warehouse. It was a rough area, squalid. This facility was secure though. Few were dumb enough to trespass on these grounds. None repeated the error.

Mikhail thrust the door open and it banged off the inner wall. Angel LeMay lay on a filthy mattress with her hands tied behind her back, gagged and blindfolded. She appeared to be asleep, but Sergio wasn't fooled.

Mikhail marched over and lifted her by the hair. She cried out. Certainly not asleep anymore. The man dragged her to her feet and she stood there sobbing in pain and terror. There wasn't much to her. Raminski doubted she weighed a hundred pounds wet.

He dampened his feeling of regret. She and her "sister" had played them for fools and threatened his very existence. He needed to know what she knew. He needed to find the other woman before anyone else did.

"Where is your little friend, *sooka*?"

Angel made a high-pitched squeal as the man twisted her elbow. Raminski couldn't make out any of the words with the gag in her mouth.

"Give her the chance to answer the question." He ordered in Russian. Speaking in his native language was probably the best way of concealing his identity while still being in the room and making sure the other man didn't kill her with his enthusiasm for the job.

They needed Angel alive. Otherwise their *leverage* would turn into a reason for retribution.

Mikhail glared, then let go of Angel's hair, and tried to untie the gag, his thick fingers struggling with the knot. Finally, he tore it downward and left it dangling around her neck. It was clear the man didn't care much for him. The feeling was mutual.

As long as they were on the same side it didn't matter.

Mikhail grabbed her hair and pulled her head back, exposing her throat. The blindfold remained in place. "Where is your little friend, Scarlett Stone?"

Angel LeMay licked her lips, then spat in Mikhail's face. Sergio winced as Mikhail backhanded her. She went down to her knees on the mattress and Mikhail kicked her, catching her high on the thigh.

Sergio held back the impulse to intervene. He couldn't give away his position. Couldn't afford to look like anything but a loyal servant to mother Russia.

"Where is she, *vlagalische*?"

"How the hell should I know?" Angel snapped, trying to defend herself by curling into a fetal position.

"Stop." Sergio raised his hand to get Mikhail's attention. The guy was breathing hard. He suspected he got off beating others. "Ask her did she plant any other bugs, or just the ones in the ambassador's office?"

Mikhail repeated his questions in English.

"I don't know what you're talking about." Angel spoke rapidly, voice full of fear and anger. Raminski hadn't expected her to put up a fight. "I don't know who you are or what you think I've done but—"

Mikhail hit her again and Raminski's stomach lurched when blood flowed from her nose and dripped onto the dirty, concrete floor.

"Tell her we know she lied to get Scarlett Stone into the building."

Angel spat out blood and lifted her chin. "What does Scarlett have to do with any of this?" She was hurting but not cowed. His admiration for her grew. He hoped she survived this ordeal. He hoped they both did.

"Wait." She tried to sit up on the mattress. He'd expected her to do nothing but cry after the beating Mikhail was dealing out, but she was tougher than she looked. "I *made* Scarlett come with me. She didn't want to, but I forced her into it. Mom and Dad didn't know anything about it, either." Blood smeared her chin. The skin on her cheekbone was split.

"Then she must know that her friend Scarlett planted listening bugs in the ambassador's office. Tell her."

Mikhail repeated his statement in thick, guttural English.

Angel's mouth opened and closed. "No. No! I don't believe it. You're making a mistake because of who her father is. Scarlett would never have done anything that...*insane*. You're making a mistake." Her voice rose as she repeated herself. "My father will freak out—"

Mikhail hit her again, a hard slap this time that must have stung because she stopped talking. "Where is she?"

Angel jerked away from her attacker and fell to the mattress. "I don't know! We fought because she wanted to leave the party early—" She cut herself off as if realizing what she'd said.

"She wanted to leave because she'd planted a bug."

"No. No." Angel shook her head and Mikhail kicked her in the stomach, thankfully not connecting properly.

Raminski winced. Shit. He needed to find the other woman, but this one had to still be alive in the morning. He steeled himself against her cries as Mikhail used his fists again.

The cries turned to grunts then begging. "Please, I'll tell you where she is. Please don't hurt me." She was crying now. "She was housesitting for her boss. I don't have the address. It's on the 1800 block of California, near the corner of 24th Street. It has a dark green front door." Tears poured down her cheeks and she sobbed into the mattress.

"Enough," Raminski ordered. He believed her. Even if he didn't, there was only so much violence he could stomach. Mikhail backed away slowly.

107

Raminski's phone buzzed in his pocket and he answered it. The voice on the other end said they had another lead on Scarlett Stone. Good. He walked over and squatted beside where Angel LeMay lay shivering. Blood streaked her face. Thankfully the blindfold hid her eyes.

He lowered his voice to a gruff whisper and spoke in English. "If you're telling the truth and we find her, you will be home by Christmas morning." He let that image linger for a moment. He touched her cheek gently. She flinched and jerked back. "But if you're lying, my friend here gets to open his presents early and he can decide exactly what he wants to do to you. Then we let the rest of the men take turns until they've had their fill. Then you spend a lifetime taking strangers between your legs until you're too used up to care. No one will want you after that. Not even your parents." He slid his hand under her top and cupped her breast. She cried out and tried to twist away but he pinched her nipple, controlling her with focused pain, forcing her to nod, to submit to him. Proving he could do what he damned well pleased with her body and her opinion was of no consequence.

"Be a good girl and things will go easy for you. Misbehave and things will start to get ugly." He released her, regretting things had to be this way when a few hours ago he'd been keen to beguile and seduce. She turned her face into the filthy mattress and sobbed.

Scarlett Stone had done this. It was her fault.

His threats weren't real. They didn't run a sex ring, although he could easily find someone who did. But he needed her to believe he was serious. He needed her to be scared out of her wits and stay obedient and quiet while he found the other girl. Angel LeMay might survive this ordeal if she behaved. Scarlett Stone didn't stand a chance.

———

Scarlett felt groggy as she inched her eyes open. Her head pounded, not so much with pain, more a thin veil of fog that clouded her thoughts. A small porthole showed it was still dark outside. Her eyes stretched wider. Porthole?

How could she be on a boat?

A hairpin dug into her scalp, reminding her of last night's party. She reached up and pulled out the clips that remained, placing them on a cupboard attached to the side of the boat.

Boat.

Where was she? The last thing she remembered was going for coffee with Matt Lazlo. *Crap.* He must have drugged her, which meant he'd planned the whole thing before he'd offered her a ride. But why? She threw the covers off, relieved to find she was fully dressed. He didn't seem like the date-rape type, but who knew? What did a rapist actually look like?

The door opened and there was the man himself.

"What did you do?" she asked angrily. "You better have a good reason for drugging me and bringing me here. This time you're the one who committed a crime and you owe *me* an apology."

A smile creased his cheeks. "I apologize." Despite everything, he was way too attractive for her well-being. He held up a mug in one hand. "Peace offering."

He was wearing worn jeans and a black t-shirt. She could just make out the graze where the bullet had taken off the top layer of skin along the top of his bicep. It hit her how close they'd both been to death. She hadn't even thought about it last night, she'd been too shocked, too focused on trying to make restitution and get out of the situation she'd so foolishly got herself into. Matt Lazlo had saved her life and she was so grateful it was hard to be angry with him. Still, she didn't know what was really going on, or what he wanted from her.

She looked at the mug in his hand. Her throat was parched, limbs heavy. "How do I know that's not drugged, too?"

"I didn't put anything in it." He took a sip to prove it, and she couldn't help noticing he had to bend his head to fit in the room properly. He passed her the mug and she took it, surprised to smell fragrant tea rather than the coffee she'd expected.

"I could lie and say you fell asleep and I decided to bring you home so you could get a few hours' sleep before handing yourself over to the Russians."

"But I'm not that stupid."

He cocked a brow to suggest he wasn't about to comment on that.

"What did you give me?"

"Something a friend of mine uses on guard dogs."

"You gave me dog drugs?" Good God. "How did you know what dose to use?"

"I called an expert for advice. We decided to double up the usual Jack Russell dosage."

She looked away, suppressing the desire to grin. Even after everything that had happened last night, he amused her.

Was she a prisoner here, or had he really given her the chance to sleep on her decision about turning herself over to the uncertain mercy of Andrei Dorokhov? Even now, she didn't see what other choice she had.

She spotted a trident pin on the cramped dressing table beside the door. The holes in his uniform suddenly made sense.

"You were a Navy SEAL?" She pointed. "Why did you take it off last night?"

"I didn't want to advertise everything about myself to the people at the embassy."

"A bit like me, then." She pulled a false smile and batted her eyelashes.

"Not quite like you, Dr. Stone. I didn't have anything electronic in my underwear."

"Huh. So you say."

He raised a brow.

Her cheeks heated. She was perilously close to flirting with the guy. He'd arrested her. Kidnapped her. *He also saved your life.* She blew on the tea to cool it so she could drink it faster. She was starting to feel really stupid about everything that happened, but it didn't change the reality that she was in big trouble with few options. She eased out of the sheets and pushed her feet into sneakers, the vulnerability of her situation striking her afresh. "Did you hear from Angel?"

He shook his head. "But she's fine." His lips tightened as he watched her tie her laces.

"Am I your prisoner, Special Agent Lazlo?" she asked straight out.

"Not exactly." He crossed his arms over his chest, showing off those muscles again. She hadn't realized arms could be so attractive. Maybe he did it on purpose. Navy SEAL distraction tactics. "I've been asked to watch you while my colleagues at the Bureau see if they can wrangle a deal that ensures your safety."

"Really?" She bit her lip. That was more help than she'd expected and certainly more than she deserved. "Like a bodyguard?"

"Child-minder was the term that popped into my head." The smile didn't hit his eyes.

Her chin rose a notch and she held his gaze. He hadn't thought she was a child last night and they both knew it. He looked away, conceding the point. Neither wanted to remember the fact they'd both been so obviously attracted to one another.

"What do you do with the Bureau? HRT?" she asked.

"Behavioral analyst."

She blinked in surprise. "Seems like an odd decision to put an elite soldier in a desk job."

His smile dimmed. Lip curled.

She backtracked quickly. "I mean I can tell you're a smart guy. It's just that you look like the hands-on hero-type rescuing damsels in distress, rather than the desk-jockey type answering the phone and assimilating data." Her hands flexed in agitation. That's exactly what he'd done for her last night— rescued her distressed damsel.

"Heroes come in all shapes and sizes, Scarlett. There is no 'type.'"

"I know that." Did he really think she was stupid? "My father always said not to ignore the class nerds and quiet ones, just because the captain of the football team asked me out."

"Did you take his advice?"

Humiliation crawled up her face. "No one ever asked me out, Special Agent Lazlo. After Dad was arrested, I was home-schooled." She didn't want to be in this enclosed space with another guy she found attractive but who thought of her with contempt. Been there. Done that. "I didn't date. I poured myself into my studies and found something I was good at—something that didn't lie about how the world really worked."

She stood, uncomfortable opening herself up like this. No one liked pathetic, least of all her. "Why did you join the FBI after the SEALs? You could have made a fortune as a private contractor."

"I was needed in the States."

"Your mother?"

His eyes sharpened on her. "You have a good memory."

"Even when sedated, apparently." She nodded. She put her hand in her pocket and brushed against the other listening device. "It's what got me where I am today."

"I thought that was your unrelenting quest for justice and naïve belief in a man who should have known better."

She drew in a breath to defend her father.

There was a soft thump on the side of the boat. Matt frowned and tilted his head for a fraction of a second. When she opened her mouth to argue he held his up in such a way she remained quiet. He listened intently. Then he moved so fast she almost fell back onto the bed. He grabbed her hand, snatched the trident off the dresser and stuffed it in his pocket and went into the main cabin. He shrugged into his jacket, pocketed his wallet, creds, phone and keys. Caught her hand again.

"What…?" Scarlett didn't get the chance to ask. He dragged her out onto the back deck.

"Keep low," he whispered, a weapon materializing out of nowhere in his left hand.

It was still dark, but the faint blush of dawn edged the western horizon. He helped her off the gangplank, sprinted to the seawall, and threw himself over. She was somehow carried along with him, the rough stone scraping her skin. They were on the outer side of the seawall on a lip that was about two feet wide and ran the whole length of the pier. Cold wind buffeted her warm skin, clearing her mind of the last vestige of sleep. He pulled her along the ledge, just a few feet above waves that washed gently against the rock. They crouched low, staying out of sight. Once they got to the end of the pier, closest to land, Matt stopped running and sat down, pulled her tight against him, his big body crowding her against the rock.

"What are we doing here?" she whispered against his chest, trying to ignore the way his heat and strength made her want to lean closer, take a little bite.

"Quiet."

Great.

She inhaled his warm, male scent as his heart thumped strongly against her cheek. As nice as it was to be held by such a seriously gorgeous man, she was beginning to think he was a lunatic. Certifiable.

She tried again. "Matt—"

BOOM!

The explosion shook the rock beneath them, and for a couple of seconds Scarlett couldn't hear anything. The blast wave of heat shot above their heads. Fire rained from the sky, bits of canvas and rope thrown fifty feet into the air, coming down to pepper the sea and harbor with flames.

CHAPTER EIGHT

Oh, my God. Scarlett's jaw dropped. "Did someone just blow up your boat?"

"Yeah. Hush." He pressed a finger to her lips and she stared at him stupidly. She must have been shouting but was too deafened to know it. His heart thudded reassuringly strong against her chest as he kept her pressed tight against him.

"How did you know we had to get out of there?" She tried to keep her voice to a whisper as the pressure equalized in her ears.

"I've laid a thousand charges on a thousand hulls—I recognized the sound but I'd never heard it on my boat before." He shrugged as if his instinctive reaction hadn't just saved both their lives. "Underwater demolition is a SEAL specialty, remember?"

She gaped at him. He was taking this so calmly, "But someone just blew up your *boat*." Her eyes bugged. "They were trying to kill me, weren't they?"

Matt nodded. "That's twice in twelve hours. Didn't figure they'd include me and my damn boat though."

"Former boat." *Oh, my God.* "Do you have insurance?"

He frowned, but amusement lit the depths of his hazel eyes. "Not sure it covers this, but yeah, I have insurance."

This was all her fault. "I'll buy you a new boat, Special Agent Lazlo." The man had just saved her life *again*. "How much do they cost?" She had no idea. "I'll probably need to get a loan."

"We'll worry about that later." He took her hand, still keeping low as they jumped down onto the shoreline and then cut up behind some trees.

"I told you you had a hero complex," she said shakily.

His eyes were cataloguing her features. Looking to see how she was holding up. Not very well, as it happened. "One damsel-in-distress rescued. Check." The edge of his mouth kicked up. "Keeping up my daily quota."

The guy had just lost his home, but he was joking with her even though it was her fault. He was nuts. She came to a standstill. Put her hand over her mouth as the enormity of what had happened hit her. "This is awful. I don't know what to do."

He put a hand on each shoulder. "You know what they say in the teams, Scarlett?" It was the first time he'd said her name with anything but derision.

She shook her head.

"The only easy day was yesterday."

"Yesterday *sucked*," she reminded him.

"You survived, didn't you? And today's already off to a great start."

"Yay?" she whispered uncertainly.

He urged her to keep moving. "We made it through another attempt on your life and, assuming we stay out of sight, it'll be a while until they know they failed." They were walking fast along a back road. He tucked her under his arm and urged her to move faster. They looked like young lovers out for an early morning stroll—obviously the illusion he was going for. It felt nice to be held like this, protected and cherished, in a way she'd never experienced. She couldn't afford to get used to it.

"Still want to turn yourself in to Dorokhov?"

The Russian seriously wanted her dead and she had no idea why—well, aside from breaking into his office and trying to spy on him. There was that word again. *Spy*. It made her brain hurt.

The man had kidnapped her best friend and tried to kill her *twice*. Damn. "I don't think he's going to accept my apology, is he?"

"No, I don't think he's going to accept your apology, Scarlett." Matt agreed.

Her life was over.

She had no clue if she was even going to make it to Christmas Day. She kept that thought to herself. No point sharing her pity-fest with a man who'd give her a pep talk about sucking it up. She'd suck it up until she fell apart or died—that didn't mean that inside she wasn't self-destructing with terror.

An idea took hold. "Do you think he thinks I found something to incriminate him and absolve my father?"

Matt gave her an exasperated look and his arm tightened across her shoulders. "I think you pissed him off and the crazy bastard thinks he's powerful enough to get away with murder."

"So what do you think I should do?" She was asking for advice from a man who'd arrested her and then had his home destroyed. Logically he might not be impartial, but logic had disappeared ever since she'd slipped into that party under an assumed name.

"You need to disappear for a while."

She thought of her work. Her job was all she had and now she'd put it in jeopardy. Despair expanded inside her. "That's not going to be easy."

"Hey, it could be worse." He gave her a squeeze, which felt so natural and so right, it sent a bolt of regret through her.

"How?"

"You could be in jail." His smile was half-hearted. "Actually you might be better off locked up."

"If I kick you, will you slap on the cuffs again, Agent Lazlo?"

"Don't tempt me, Dr. Stone. Don't tempt me." But the twinkle in his eye was gone, and he was obviously thinking about the fact someone had just tried to kill her and hadn't minded taking him and all his worldly goods along with her. Nothing like a dose of reality to bring you back down to earth with a bang.

———

Raminski bent and tugged the zip on his drysuit, enjoying the pull as it worked its way across his shoulders. He whistled soundlessly as he stripped off the neoprene, black pants and shirt underneath, both slightly damp after his long swim.

The call at the warehouse last night had been from someone who'd tracked down FBI Agent Matt Lazlo. Once Sergio discovered the federal agent lived on a boat, all his prayers had been answered.

Americans were not the only ones to train in underwater demolition.

FLIR thermal imaging cameras had identified two people onboard the sailboat. Given the two beverage cups from a

Central DC coffee shop in the front seat of his government issue car, and a hat, very like the one Scarlett Stone had worn in the park last night, sitting on the dash, Sergio was pretty sure she was the smaller of the two heat sources. Or, rather, she had been.

After attaching the limpet mine to the hull of FBI Agent Lazlo's yacht, Sergio had swam out of the harbor and around the headland to where he'd left his vehicle. He'd felt the boom when he'd set off the bomb, but he'd been far enough away not to be bothered by the impact, largely absorbed by the sea wall. Lazlo was regrettable collateral damage, but who knew what the Stone woman had told the FBI Special Agent.

Leaving him alive was too big a risk.

Sergio slicked the cold Atlantic out of his hair as the sirens grew louder and more insistent. The breeze was frigid and he shivered. He stowed the drysuit in the trunk along with the rest of his gear. Job done. Now he had to get back to work. Sergio Raminski had duties that couldn't be put aside. And later he had to check on the prisoner. Make sure she was still alive and no one had touched her. Hopefully he could arrange her release just as soon as he informed Dorokhov about Scarlett Stone's death.

He didn't allow himself to feel remorse for killing the woman. She'd been an active part in the game. A willing participant. Angelina LeMay however was a woman who'd been in the wrong place with the wrong friend. She was an innocent and he'd never enjoyed seeing innocents suffer. Maybe that was why he was doing what he was doing. Maybe that was why he was risking his own life by crossing not just the Russian Ambassador, but the entire Russian Federation.

Matt force-marched Scarlett along the road. He needed to get her out of sight ASAP and talk to Frazer. Having his boat blown to smithereens pissed him off, but he channeled that anger into the more important issue of getting this woman somewhere safe. At least he'd finally convinced her not to hand-deliver herself to Dorokhov, but that could change if she found out the truth about Angel LeMay.

The HRT team was still on standby awaiting a ransom demand. Something told Matt the ransom would be the young woman tucked warmly into his side—or at least news of her death.

They dodged around a factory and some residential housing, listening to the sound of sirens piercing the air as they slogged through a field of frosted grass that crunched underfoot. He considered heading to the TacOps site, not far away, but Scarlett didn't have security clearance. Although he didn't think she had an agenda beyond redeeming her father, he wasn't about to break protocol or risk exposing his colleagues. There was too much at stake.

He hoped to hell none of his neighbors had been hurt in the explosion. It was winter, and no one except him used their boats for full-time accommodation on that side of the pier. Still, boats either side of his would have been damaged and maybe sunk. Fucking Russians.

Scarlett tripped and he anchored his arm more securely around her shoulders. He liked the feel of her pressed up against him, even though it was a one-off situation. A cover. Might as well enjoy it. The rest of the morning sucked but at least they were still alive.

Being in the teams had taught him to appreciate the good things in life and not get stuck on the bad. Shit happened. Every. Single. Day.

It took fifteen minutes to reach his intended destination and by the time they got there, Scarlett was breathing heavily, almost running to keep up with his much longer stride. He didn't have time to be courteous and slow down for her. Her life depended on them both getting out of sight as fast as possible.

He guided Scarlett to the rear door of the nursing home where his mother now lived. He propped her up next to a bush near a fire exit. "I'm going to go in the front door. I'll check in. Give me five minutes and I'll let you in through this fire door."

She grabbed his arm, eyes a little desperate. "Won't it be alarmed?" Her hair was a mess and she wasn't wearing any make-up. Those brown eyes of hers were so dark they were almost black, and she had freckles that were only visible up close. *Freckles.* Freckles were a killer, as were soft shell-pink lips.

"I've got it covered."

She nodded. He stared at her.

On the surface, she was pretty, but nothing spectacular. Girl-next-door beauty that he saw every day in the course of his work. So, what was it about this woman that had called to him from the very start? He'd thought it was the heels or the dress, but even now, mussed up and in jeans, he wanted to pull her close and place his lips upon hers.

What had Frazer said about Scarlett? *Don't get attached?* The guy knew what he was talking about. Annoyed with his reaction, he took a step back and she dropped her hand. The expression on her face became more uncertain the longer he continued to stare. He shook his head to clear it. Not the time to be thinking about women. He had a job to do.

"Wait here," he ordered. He walked around the front of the nursing home—Glen Lawn—and into reception, past a fake Christmas tree covered with more tinsel than Hollywood. There was no camera surveillance out front. Just a buzzer and an alarm system.

"Hello there, Matt. You're here early." The friendly voice belonged to Rhonda, an RN who generally took the nightshift.

"Hey, Rhonda." He leaned over the counter and gave her a smile. She was good people. "I wanted to check in on Mom before work." Realistically he had no idea when this goatfuck would be resolved. Not that Scarlett was his responsibility. He *could* just hand her off. But the assholes had upped the stakes by blowing up his boat, trying to kill an FBI agent who also happened to be a decorated former Navy SEAL. That should get the authorities hollering. "I have something I want to bring in through the side door—will you disarm the alarm for me?" They did this all the time for heavy objects as that fire door was closer to the rooms.

"No worries." She flicked a switch. "No change, I'm afraid. Your mom had a peaceful night."

After more than seven hundred days of the same, he hadn't expected anything else. "Thanks. I won't be long." Matt nodded and walked away.

"Merry Christmas, Matt."

He paused. Even with all the shiny decorations, he'd forgotten it was Christmas Eve. He'd never been a big fan of the holidays, too many reminders of his father, or lack of one. "Merry Christmas, Rhonda."

He pushed through the double doors into one of the main corridors, down the end, turned right, then opened the side door and motioned Scarlett inside. She was the perfect picture of woebegone and he felt a twinge of compassion that battled with the knowledge she'd brought it all on herself. She started this, but the Russians sure as hell wanted to finish it.

He didn't like bullies, didn't like men going after innocent women and children—although calling Scarlett innocent was a stretch. Naïve, definitely. Innocent? He flashed back to that image of her retrieving that damn screwdriver and felt himself getting hard. He set his teeth and ignored the problem.

"Why are we here?" she asked quietly.

It was barely six AM and the halls were empty.

He put his finger to his lips and took her hand. He told himself it was expediency, nothing to do with savoring the feel of her slim fingers against his. He tugged her along and she half-ran to keep up. The best way of keeping Scarlett Stone out of trouble, he decided, would be by keeping her off balance. Giving her too much time to think would be a mistake.

They went up one floor in the elevator and took a left. Strode down the corridor until he reached a plain, brown door with the number thirty-two on it. He knocked gently and when there was no reply, he let them quietly inside. His mother was alone and lay asleep on a twin bed with an ornate wooden headboard. He'd decorated the room two years ago with the same floral paper she had in her home—a house he'd rented to a young family because selling it felt wrong. Various tubes were attached to his mom, and a heartbeat monitor, but apart from that, it looked like a normal old folks' room.

She'd sacrificed everything for him when he was growing up, and he intended to make her as comfortable as possible for as long as she needed. His mom had already been abandoned by one asshole named Lazlo and he wasn't about to let it happen again.

She lay on her back, although the nursing staff turned her regularly to prevent bedsores. Her hair was bright white, almost colorless. She was only in her late sixties, and so peaceful looking it was hard to believe she'd probably never wake up. He went over and kissed her cheek. It felt paper-thin. "Hey, Mom. Just came to say 'Hi.'" He kissed her again and moved away, trying not to think about the futility of what was happening here.

Losing friends in combat *hurt*, but they'd chosen to fight and to sacrifice themselves for their country and their brothers. He respected that sacrifice. His mother hadn't chosen this. But her indomitable spirit refused to let go.

Some days he wished she would and the thought made him feel guilty as hell. But human. All too human.

He wasn't capable of caring for her on a day-to-day basis. Bringing her here, keeping her close was the best he could manage. The added guilt of leaving her with strangers sometimes kept him awake at night, but he knew it was the only way to keep his sanity. And it's what she would have wanted.

He knew it. It hurt anyway.

Scarlett pursed her lips and looked distressed when she stared at the woman in the bed.

He stood in front of her and pressed his hands to her upper arms. "Don't worry, we're not staying long. Take a seat." There was no reason to think the bad guys would follow them here. With the size of that explosion, they'd assume they were food for the fishes.

He took his mother's phone and went into the bathroom. Scarlett followed him and closed the door after them. Damn. He'd wanted to do this without her listening in.

His cell was in his pocket, but he didn't want to use it and give away the fact he was alive to anyone listening in. He pulled it out and checked the number for Frazer.

Before he could dial, Scarlett caught his wrist. "Who are you calling?"

"ASAC Frazer."

Her eyes grew huge. "Call my cell instead."

"You don't trust my boss?"

She shook her head, "It isn't that exactly, but…" He could see the doubt in her eyes. She still believed her father had been set up and someone in the FBI was responsible. "Okay, call Parker instead."

Her eyes begged him to do as she asked.

"Fine." He dialed Parker. It made sense in many ways, but Scarlett didn't need to know that.

"And don't use any names. Who knows what the NSA can flag these days." She looked so serious he refrained from eye rolling.

Parker answered on the third ring.

"It's me."

"What's up?" Parker didn't ask why he was calling from an unknown number.

"Someone just blasted my boat to kingdom come."

"Shit. The girl?"

Matt noticed he didn't use her name either. Was he as paranoid as Scarlett? Maybe Matt was the naïve one. He looked at her standing beside him in his mother's bathroom, and wondered how life had gone from normal to so fucking complicated in twelve short hours.

"Whoever planted the bomb probably thinks we're both dead at the bottom of the marina."

"You talk to Frazer yet?"

"You were my first call."

"That must have been her idea."

"How'd you figure that?" Matt asked.

"Because you're a rule follower and would immediately call your boss. She's smarter."

"I respect the chain of command."

"Rule follower. Linear thinker."

Matt resented the fact he was right. "I'm hanging up and calling Frazer any second now."

"Don't. You made a good choice. No one can trace this call or listen in. I also put a lock on anyone trying to track the signal on Scarlett's cell. Russians are definitely looking for her. Might be useful later."

"How did they know she was with me? I wasn't followed."

"Assuming you weren't targeted for your previous actions?"

"The same night as this shit is going down?" Being a former Navy SEAL was not something he advertised for obvious reasons. "How likely is that?"

"Not very," Parker agreed. "I'm presuming the Russians had your identity from the party last night. When they lost Scarlett, they went looking for you instead. Can she hear this?"

"No."

She was trying to eavesdrop, but Matt held himself away from her and Parker spoke softly so his voice didn't carry.

"The LeMay girl is still missing and there's been no ransom demand yet. I suspect they are holding her for barter. I have some programs running on the Russians from the embassy, but they haven't popped anything as to where they might be keeping her. Yet. They will, but they need time, usually a few days."

Scarlett held up a bottle of mouthwash with a questioning look on her face.

She wouldn't use mouthwash without permission, but took it upon herself to bug foreign dignitaries?

He nodded. She unscrewed the cap and the sharp scent of mint flooded the air.

"Frazer wants us to start looking into Richard Stone's case on the off-chance someone made a mistake. We've got to be subtle about it. Unfortunately there's no way Rooney and I can skip Christmas with her family—much as I'd like to—which means I'll be working on this from West Virginia."

Matt felt a prickle of surprise run over his flesh. "He doesn't actually believe there's something in those old files, does he?"

Scarlett's dark gaze swung to his and he saw a spark of hope shoot through her eyes. *Christ.*

"No. But he's wondering why the Russians overreacted the way they did—that's going to go double when he hears your boat was scuttled."

Matt remembered the mass of fiery objects shooting through the air and figured *scuttled* didn't quite cover it.

"We checked those surveillance tapes of Dorokhov's office, but they only kept a few days' worth—at least that's what they told us. Nothing on them points to anything aside from the guy being an asshole."

Matt laughed at the understatement. "Any idea why they were watching him?"

"Nope. I'm not in that need-to-know loop, and neither is Frazer." And if Frazer didn't know, it was going to be hard for any of them to figure out. "Can you stay where you are for a few hours?" Alex Parker asked him.

Matt thought about it. "No." He needed to talk to Rhonda, who went off duty in about fifteen minutes. He had to tell her to forget she saw him today. But there were other people who worked here and knew his face. Wouldn't take long for one of them to call the cops and tell them the FBI agent they were so worried was at the bottom of the ocean was actually hunkered down in his mom's suite. No way was he luring bad guys here. They needed to leave ASAP.

"You have a few choices." Parker thought fast on his feet— like the combat vet he was. "One is tell the world you're alive while we stash Scarlett under guard somewhere. The other is you both go under the radar until we find proof linking the Russians to the attempted murder of a federal agent, which should be enough to at least expel Dorokhov regardless of his diplomatic status...Actually that's pretty much it."

So either he helped Scarlett avoid these assholes, or someone else did. Matt rubbed the back of his neck as he watched her. She was now trying to fix her hair in the mirror above the sink, looking frustrated that one side wanted to stick up.

"What?" she demanded when she caught him staring.

He said nothing.

It was Christmas.

It was a hell of a time to drag other federal agents or US Marshals away from their wives and families on indefinite assignment. After the goatfuck up in Minnesota where two US Marshals had been shot dead by a bunch of terrorists while protecting Vivi Vincent's eight-year-old son, the organization was still reeling from loss. Matt had no plans for the holidays aside from taking a few days off to spend Christmas with his mom, but the gut-wrenching bottom-line was she wouldn't care if he was here or not.

The other thing he'd learned in the teams was the job came first. A personal life happened when the smoke cleared. As much as he wanted his life back, he didn't want to abandon Scarlett when he could protect her just as well as anyone else could. Better than most.

"The bastards blew up my boat," Matt told Parker, which seemed to be answer enough.

"Can you access a computer? I'm going to send you the case files Frazer copied—should keep you occupied for a few hours."

"Yup." Matt kept a laptop in a locked desk here so that he could work and keep his mom company at the same time.

"Good. Don't even turn it on until I get you a new email identity that can't be tracked back. Then I'll forward your email to that account. First, I need to organize some transportation and supplies for you. It'll take time. An hour tops."

For a cyber-security guru, the guy was savvy about what someone needed to disappear. The advantages of working clandestine ops for the CIA? "I appreciate it. Thanks."

"Lazlo," Parker said, his voice serious this time. "They think you're both dead. My advice—keep it that way."

CHAPTER NINE

Andrei Dorokhov's head pounded from the aftereffects of lack of sleep and the alcohol he'd used to drown his fury last night. The dull pain in his brain and gritty feel at the back of his eyes suited his mood. He got off the metro at Farragut North, rode the escalator up to 17th Street. Taking his time, he cut through the park, past the statue of "Damn the torpedoes" Admiral Farragut. The double chalk mark on the bench closest to him told him where to meet. A rush of satisfaction washed through him and he let out a long, slow breath. It had been a long time.

He didn't pause or stare too long at the chalk, just walked on by, head up, black fedora pulled low. The streets of Washington DC had altered little in the time he'd been away, and the codes he'd used to communicate with his assets were etched in his brain.

It was old-fashioned tradecraft, but sometimes the old ways were the most effective against those who relied on electronics and biometrics. Still he didn't take chances. The hat and glasses disguised most of his face. The cane he carried and his slight affected limp deceived the human eye. Dorokhov was confident in his ability to blend into an American landscape. Easy as apple pie.

He'd been a good handler, a top spymaster, but now, rather than enjoying the spoils of his success, he was worried he was going to get exposed. More than a decade after the fact. It was intolerable. All because a stupid little girl hadn't understood that the game was over, and he'd won.

His lip curled.

He came to Lafayette Park and looked at all the Christmas lights decorating the nearby streets.

He usually enjoyed the American holidays. He wasn't a religious man. He liked the glitter, the superficial sense of affinity for one's fellow man regardless of religious or political ideology. Stone's runt had ruined it for him, but she'd paid for her audacity. A nice little Christmas bonus for the disgraced former FBI agent who'd been the bane of his existence until he'd framed the bastard for the very crimes Stone had accused him of committing. It was his crowning moment in the SVR, but unfortunately the spy ring had fallen apart after that, and he'd eased into his diplomatic role, deflecting any attention he might have gained by becoming inactive. There was no benefit in burning his former sources—it gave the opposition too much information on what secrets might have leaked and you never knew when leverage might be useful. Russia played the long game with more patience and stealth than the Americans dreamt of.

Andrei forced himself to relax. The CIA and FBI hadn't spotted anything fourteen years ago, no reason to believe they were any smarter now. And they'd have to tread very carefully before they accused him of anything untoward. He was the Russian Ambassador, not some low level attaché.

He kept walking through the bustling streets, people busy trying to get their work done so they could go home for the holidays. The politicians were done, of course, but their minions kept the hive buzzing with activity. He'd always liked minions.

A pain shot through his forehead, reminding him of his over-fondness for vodka and his current situation. Andrei had insurance—knowledge was power after all—but maybe it wasn't enough. Perhaps a little extra-incentive was wise at this stage. His phone vibrated against his hip. He answered it. "Yes."

"You blew up a fucking FBI Agent? One who just happened to be a decorated Navy SEAL? Are you out of your fucking mind?"

"You told me to take care of my side of the problem. That's what I did." Dorokhov enjoyed the sputter of anger on the other end of the line.

"I told you 'low profile'. Now we have a Crisis Management Unit on scene and NCIS screaming blue fucking murder. Every Navy SEAL in the world just joined the cause. Shit."

He ambled down the western side of the White House. The current US President, Joshua Hague, was an indecisive twit. He enjoyed seeing him squirm as the threats of Islamic extremists hit closer to home. They'd been threatening his homeland for decades. "Let them all get involved. Let NCIS and the FBI fight amongst themselves trying to figure it out. I can arrange some chatter so that they are all nicely pre-occupied with a possible terrorist plot against retired Navy SEALs, rather than looking at me, or you."

He walked around to get a good view of the White House from the National Christmas Tree. It was an elegant building, so small for all the power it contained. A sniper stood and changed position on the roof. Andrei watched for a moment. Security had been beefed up in the aftermath of the recent assassination attempt, and the unexpected death of the Vice President.

Dorokhov wasn't sure who was replacing Ted Burger, but whoever it was had to be better for the Kremlin. Burger had been an intractable curmudgeon who hated Russians on principle. The guy had been smart, and ruthless. He had feelers out among the politicians and had people searching for dirt on those most likely to be chosen to replace the VP. Dirt was worth more than a diamond encrusted Fabergé egg to men like him.

"The FBI know you were after the girl. You're going to be top of the suspect pool."

"I have a solid alibi, as do all my people, not to mention 'diplomatic immunity'."

The man growled. "I should have cut your throat all those years ago—"

"*Da*. You should have." Dorokhov taunted him. *Or not betrayed your country.* "Did you do your part yet?"

"It's arranged."

"The other loose ends?" Dorokhov walked further along the path heading to the Mall.

"I'm taking care of them."

"Then we're done talking."

"Wait." There was a beat of silence. "What about the other woman?"

"What about her?" Dorokhov looked up at the pewter sky. He wanted snow to coat the city in beauty and remind him of home, but it looked like he was going to get nothing but dreary rain.

The long pause on the other end of the line suggested the man was weighing his options. "It might be worth holding onto her for a while…"

Dorokhov smirked. His thoughts exactly. He hung up. Strolled onwards, past the peaceful Vietnam Memorial, which shimmered in the dawn. He'd never been a fan of war; he saw his former role as a way of preventing needless death by balancing the scales of power. Every country did it. He'd just been better than the rest.

He continued onward. The streets were quieter. Workers at the office now. Too early for tourists. Too cold for locals. He strolled toward the Lincoln Memorial, a familiar sense of anticipation uncoiling inside him that made him feel alive again. He'd missed this.

His contact sat on one of the stone benches at the base of the lower steps. Woolen hat. Tall collar. Sunglasses.

Dorokhov sat heavily, about a foot away, breath freezing in a cloud of mist. The bench was unforgiving, reminding him he was too old for this kind of life.

"I want my daughter back."

He smiled. "I don't know what you are talking about."

LeMay's knuckles shone brightly against pale skin. "Do you want me to expose you?"

Andrei's upper lip twitched in a sneer. "And sacrifice yourself? You don't have the balls."

"I want my daughter back," LeMay repeated. "I'm not kidding."

Dorokhov narrowed his gaze, the headache still grinding his temples. "Why was she there? What were you hoping to find?"

"I didn't know she'd gone until the feds turned up. *I* told her to decline the invitation."

"Are you telling me it was a coincidence she just happened to take Stone's daughter there?"

"Angel and Scarlett have been best friends since they were toddlers. I tried to discourage the relationship but…"

"You didn't know Stone's brat planted electronic listening devices in my office?"

LeMay's face went waxy pale. "She did not."

"Oh, but she did."

"That stupid little bitch. Did she discover anything?" LeMay's eyes were now wide with fear.

Self-preservation always trumped real compassion—an asset in an asset. Dorokhov smiled. "No. I'm more careful than that. So you didn't set this up?"

"Why would I?"

"Maybe you were craving a little excitement?"

"I like my life just fine. The past is the past."

"The past is never the past. I still have all the evidence I had before."

LeMay's lip curled. "I'm not working for you ever again."

"Not even to save your daughter?"

The eyes shifted nervously to scan the trees that edged the Mall. "The FBI are in my house and watching my every move."

"Were you followed here?"

"Of course not. I told them I needed some air. They didn't have time to sort out a tail before I left." The heaviness of the bags under LeMay's eyes suggested lack of sleep and parental worry.

"You know how much I dislike being crossed. I dislike being crossed by Richard Stone worst of all."

The laugh was bitter. "I think you got your revenge on the man. *I* didn't cross you. My daughter didn't cross you. Scarlett loves her father; he must have told her he suspected you were the spymaster back then. What does it matter anymore? Stone is dying, did you know that?"

"He needs to die faster. No one makes a fool of me and gets away with it."

"Please let my daughter go," LeMay tried to cajole, but had always been bad at this part of the game. "She's just a young woman who likes to party—she meant no harm."

Dorokhov allowed a small smile to crease his cheek. "I'm sure she's enjoying quite the party right now, wherever she may be."

"If you touch her…" LeMay's voice vibrated with anger.

Dorokhov laughed quietly and stood. "Empty threats, my friend. You'll be grateful to get her back even if she's in pieces." He sauntered away down the Mall. Once his official duties were over for the day, he might just pay a visit to Angel LeMay and see exactly how much she liked to party. He was intrigued, and feeling a little vindictive. He'd earned it.

———

Richard Stone lay on the bed after receiving his latest dose of chemo and wished he was dead. Every cell in his body rebelled from the poison in his system. He didn't know why he bothered. Maybe just to cost the system as much time, trouble, and money as possible—a tiny fleck of revenge in comparison to what it had done to him. Maybe he kept going because death was the ultimate admission of failure. It wasn't because he hoped to be exonerated. Whoever had set him up had taken care of that long ago.

He looked around at concrete walls, at the grim-faced doctor and nurses in charge of his treatment. *This* was his life, this barren existence of mental and physical purgatory. He'd be better off dead. If he wasn't so damned stubborn, he could just refuse treatment and let the cancer invade his body and ravage what little was left. With his luck, it would anyway.

Three other patients were receiving treatment. One was on dialysis. Another, a diabetic, was having blood sugar levels checked. The last was writhing in pain on his bed.

One guy was a terrorist, another a member of a Mexican drug cartel, the other had killed four people while holding up a gas station. These were his peers. No wonder he felt sick. Thank God for isolation, although some days he thought his head would explode from the pure monotony. He wanted to hike a mountain, feel the sun on his skin, and make love to his wife.

Fat chance.

Years ago, he'd offered to conduct psychological studies on his fellow inmates, but the people in charge didn't want him talking to anyone. He knew the cover story was because he might pass on more secrets to the Russians—as if he knew anything the real spy hadn't already divulged to his Russian benefactors. The reality was someone, somewhere, didn't want him figuring out, and revealing, exactly who had set him up. They were scared of him, and that made him ecstatic.

Another bout of nausea rolled through him, and he curled onto his side, panting against the desire to puke. Sweat made what was left of his hair stick to his forehead. He caught a whiff of rank odor and realized he stank of BO. Great. With his luck, he wouldn't get the chance to wash up before Susan visited and this was how she'd see him on Christmas Eve. Stinking and sickly. *Jesus.*

Anger at the unfairness still hummed in his veins, not because *his* life had been ruined, but for Susan. No one should have to endure what she'd endured. It was a long time to hold onto the hate, but he had plenty of reason and little else to occupy his time.

It wasn't healthy—he smiled grimly at that thought—but it beat the other thing in this hellhole that was even worse than anger, apathy. He hadn't figured out which of his colleagues was the real spy, but he'd narrowed it down to six names—all so-called friends.

He swallowed the saliva that pooled in his mouth.

What difference did it make? He couldn't reveal them without putting Susan and Scarlett at risk and no way was he doing that. He was so proud of them, and so sorry for everything he'd put them through. He'd never in a million years imagined he'd end up here.

He'd written his suspicions in a notebook using a code he and Susan had developed when they were first dating. At the time, it had been harmless fun. Now it was life and death. No doubt, the warden would pass that book onto the FBI after his death. With his luck it would fall into the wrong hands and no one would ever discover his suspicions.

No one would care.

He did it anyway.

Nausea boiled in his stomach. He leaned over and vomited into a cardboard tray, heaving until his throat hurt. Great. He rinsed his mouth out with some water, then wiped his hand through his hair, pulling out a few strands as he did so.

Poor Susan, she'd wasted her entire life on him. At least Scarlett was young. Hopefully one day she'd move past all this ugliness and have a good life.

His shackles jangled as he moved his legs. At least he hadn't crapped his pants this time. He was grateful for small mercies.

A big guy with tats on every inch of skin shuffled past, baring his teeth.

Asshole.

While Richard might be "the biggest traitor of the new millennium" according to the judge who'd sentenced him to six life sentences without the chance of parole, he was still a former fed in the eyes of many inmates. He was glad to have a cell to himself. In the general population, he wouldn't last an hour.

Another wave of nausea rolled over him. Sweet Jesus, chemo sucked.

He caught a movement out of the corner of his eye and instinctively jerked his knee around to defend himself. It deflected a shank that had been aimed straight for his gut, and the hard plastic slid deep into his thigh instead, going through muscle like a red-hot knife. Pain shot though him and flamed up his body. The other guy's shackles rattled noisily across the floor. *Fuck!* The guy—a member of a Mexican drug cartel—lunged again, aiming at his face this time. Richard grabbed the guy's wrist and held on tight, trying to cry out, but his voice wouldn't work, and he had no real strength in his arms. Where the hell were the guards?

Chanting started nearby, like some schoolyard brawl.

"Stick the fucker," said the white supremacist asshole in a rare show of interracial harmony. Richard's hand was slipping, and the knife was edging closer to his eye. *Damn.* This was not how he wanted to go out.

His muscles were shaking, but he twisted sideways, some old FBI training coming back to help him. The guy fell across him, pinning him to the bed. The IV stand crashed to the floor as he twisted, and he shoved the Mexican's head in his bedpan. The skinhead started laughing his ass off. Finally, there was a yell, and the alarm was pressed. Sirens wailed. Lights flashed.

Thank God. He'd survived the attack. Then he felt something press against his abdomen a moment before it pierced the skin and slid deep. Pain flooded every synapse, every nerve in a wave of agony. The Mexican leered close to his face. "*Marlon* said to say 'Hi' motherfucker."

Richard started to black out as the guy pulled out the knife and stabbed him again. God! The pain was indescribable. He'd seen a thousand movies where people got stabbed, but he'd never imagined the all-consuming nature of the pain. A guard ran in and pulled the man off him. Too late. The Mexican went quietly, grinning madly, obviously pleased with himself. Richard pressed his arm tight against the wounds. Marlon? What the hell? Wasn't he dying fast enough to suit the bastard? *Fuck.*

Medical staff rushed around him. Other inmates were being locked down. It was getting hard to breathe. "Please," he told a guard he'd known for years. "Tell Susan to be careful. It's dangerous." His vision pixelated to gray monochrome. Dammit, he needed to warn her. "Marlon…"

CHAPTER TEN

Scarlett paced the motel suite, which had a small sitting room, kitchenette, and large bedroom. Plenty of space to move around in, but she didn't know how long she could stand being cooped up. Energy swirled inside her. What if she couldn't prove her father was innocent? What if Dorokhov kept coming after her? She was scared for her own safety, but she was also angry with herself. She'd dragged first Angel, and now Matt, into this mess.

A thought hit her. "You can't pretend to be dead. What if your friends see it on the news? You can't do that to them." She didn't want other people hurt because of her actions.

"Most of them are OCONUS and won't hear about this for a few days, by which time hopefully it'll be over. Anyway, they're big boys, they know how this shit works. They can handle it. My mother isn't going to worry. Frazer will tell Jed Brennan, who works with me." He shrugged. "That's the best I can do. The others will have to suck it up for now."

My mother isn't going to worry. He'd slipped it in so casually.

"What about you?" he asked.

"Me?" she snorted. "No one has any reason to believe I was on your boat except maybe Angel. Could ASAC Frazer let her know I'm okay?" He grunted, which she assumed was acquiescence. She rubbed her arms, upset at the thought of being estranged from her best friend even though it was her own fault. "My boss is in Scotland and most of the grad students already left for the holidays. No one from work is going to miss me for at least a week, probably two. I do need to contact my mother at some point today." She saw refusal in his expression and held up her hand. "She expects to hear from me and will freak if she doesn't. We have a secret code for letting the other person know we're okay. You can make the call, or even Frazer—which would make sense because he'd call her if he really thought I'd died on your boat, right?"

"Yeah, he would." He ran his hands through his short hair. "Fine, okay, we can probably figure out something to tell your mother, but the bottom line is, she needs to convince the world she's worried about you, otherwise the Russians won't buy the ruse that you're dead."

Her mother understood the stakes better than most. She paced from the door to the table and back.

"You're driving me nuts." Matt sat hunched over a laptop at the tiny dining table. He pointed to a chair. "Sit."

"I'm sorry. I'm not good at doing nothing." She stopped moving but knew it wouldn't last long. If her brain wasn't busy then her body was. "Can I check my email?"

"Sure," he drawled. "Because dead people download their messages."

Heat rose in her cheeks. *Dammit.*

Earlier he'd acted as if he was attracted. Now he acted like she was an annoying kid—and she got it, she totally understood she'd caused him a lot of trouble, got his boat blown up and almost got him killed. But he'd made choices too, like drugging her and preventing her from going to Dorokhov last night. Those decisions had compounded the situation, even if they'd saved her life. This nightmare wasn't all her doing, or at least his involvement in it wasn't.

But maybe that wasn't fair. He was trying to help. Chivalry wasn't dead.

"What are you doing?" she asked.

"Frazer sent me some files to read."

"My father's case?"

He leveled a hard stare in her direction. She found herself missing the twinkle that had been in his eyes when they'd first met.

Regret that she couldn't go back and change what she'd done simmered in her mind. Then she remembered her father's warm eyes and the deep abiding love he had for his family and his country and she shook it off. Regrets were a waste of time. She and Matt had never had the chance of anything more than a few hours of mindless passion, and that was only assuming she'd carried on lying to him about her identity.

Mindless passion seemed like a hell of an alternative to where she found herself right now.

A shiver brushed over her skin.

It wasn't just his good looks that attracted her. Whatever was going on behind those eyes intrigued her. She wanted to get to know the real Matt Lazlo. The man beneath the uniform, behind the badge. The tension in the room ramped up. Her skin sizzled with an electric charge. Her nipples hardened and her pulse sped up. She pressed her thighs together, trying to dispel the arousal, but it only made things worse. Bad enough to be stuck here with a man who believed her father was guilty; she didn't need to be lusting after him, too.

She needed a distraction and fast. "Can I read the files?" It might be her only chance to look at the evidence the FBI had gathered.

Matt stared at her long and hard, obviously weighing the pros and cons. Finally, he shrugged and nodded and dragged a second chair beside his.

"How's your shoulder?" she asked as she took a seat. His thigh was so close to hers they almost touched. His arms bunched with muscle as he tugged up the sleeve and she saw a two-inch graze that could have been so much worse.

She caught his gaze. "I am sorry you got hurt."

"Just a scratch." He rolled the sleeve back down.

She swallowed, painfully aware of him beside her. *Concentrate.* He'd arrested her, remember? Handcuffed her and dragged her into FBI HQ.

For your own good. To protect you.

Her fingers tapped on the tabletop. He stared pointedly in their direction and nodded toward the file on the screen. "You want to look at this or not?"

Scarlett started reading and almost managed to forget Matt Lazlo sitting so close she could feel his heat and smell the clean scent of soap he'd used in the shower.

The first set of papers detailed a list of dead drop locations and ciphers supposedly found in her father's home desk. They were definitely Russian ciphers and undoubtedly from after the break-up of the Soviet Union. The second was a list of information purportedly handed over to the Russians, including the names of agents abroad. Then evidence to verify her father's ability to access the information with his security clearance. Her throat closed reading the names of the six dead agents. Two had died in prison—horrifically beaten and tortured though the authorities denied responsibility. Three had suffered mysterious "accidents" and one had eaten a suicide pill—one he hadn't been provided by the US.

It was a terrible toll but one she didn't believe her father had caused, not even for a second. He was another victim.

Next was the initial interview. She read the transcript. Endless repetitive questions about his involvement. Every single time he denied being the traitor, and urged the interviewer to keep searching for the real spy. He'd been set up—he must have said it a hundred times.

Then she came to the polygraph results. The Examiner concluded "Deception Indicated."

"That's a scientific pronouncement?" she scoffed.

"The polygraph is just a tool, Scarlett. That's why this information is with the case file and not stored in evidence. It's inadmissible in court because it isn't an exact science."

"So what's the point?" she muttered angrily.

"It's leverage," he said patiently. "He failed and then he confessed. Get over it."

Fine. She might not be an expert on human nature, but she understood pride and self-preservation. She knew when to regroup and back off.

Next came the confession. That was hard to read. Her father admitted to selling secrets to the Russians over a period of five years, for more than three hundred thousand dollars in cash.

"They never found a penny." Nausea churned in her stomach, making her glad she hadn't eaten anything today.

"Maybe he spent it?"

"On what? The house was mortgaged to the hilt and he drove a Pontiac and mom had a Chevy van."

"Or he hid it. Maybe your mother knows where it is?" He was trying to solve a puzzle, not be insulting. She was trying to rescue her father and clear his name. But from a scientific point of view, objectivity was king.

"Then why didn't she break it out of hiding when the bank nearly repossessed our house in 2008?" Scarlett questioned.

Those hazel eyes of his were a warm mossy green today. They held compassion as well as pity. She loathed pity. She looked away.

The next interview was completely different. After an initial admission of guilt, her father listed dates and times of when and where he'd made the drops.

"This doesn't make any sense." She pointed to the screen. "November twenty-ninth is my birthday. At seven PM, he wasn't at some cemetery in Maryland selling out his country. He was lighting twelve candles on my birthday cake."

"It was a long time ago."

She gave him a withering look. "Kids don't forget that stuff."

Heat jumped the short space between them and she was hyperaware of every breath he took, every slight movement of his body. His pupils flared.

"Maybe he got the date wrong?" Matt suggested, ignoring the weird thing that kept arcing between them.

"He was a devoted father with one kid. It wasn't exactly rocket science to keep track of birthdays." A flicker in his eyes told her more about his own father than he'd ever admit. Damn. "Shouldn't someone in counterintelligence have checked these dates? I assume that was their job."

Matt leaned closer to the screen and frowned. "They should have. The case didn't go to trial though, so maybe the follow-ups didn't go in the case file, but hit some spook's desk instead." He scratched the dark blond stubble on his jaw. His irises had gold flecks and dark rims that emphasized their unusual color.

Irritated, she looked away. She didn't need the angst of being forced to hang out with a guy who knew she was attracted to him but who didn't feel the same way. In her experience lust, or whatever you wanted to call it, was not worth the sticky aftermath. "So, even though he'd have known that by writing that exact date he gave himself a foolproof alibi, he's still guilty? Why is it okay for the rest of the FBI to not do their jobs properly? Why is it okay for them to let details slide when his entire life depended on them doing it right?"

"He *confessed*." His mouth tightened with impatience, but he frowned. "Why foolproof alibis?"

He was interested and she needed to keep him interested.

"Because the LeMays were with us. They were close friends of the family for many years before..." Her throat felt as if she had a rock stuck in it but she wasn't pussyfooting around this anymore. "...Before he was arrested for treason."

Matt tilted his head to one side, eyes narrowed, but he kept his thoughts to himself. Fine. Whatever. She wished she could talk to Angel. Dammit. Scarlett wouldn't blame her friend if she cut her off completely after this.

"Do you want to watch the news and see where they're at in the search?" Scarlett asked, wanting some background noise to distract her from the guy next to her.

"No point. Frazer or Parker will contact us if there's a real break in the case. The rest is misinformation and speculation."

She crossed her arms as a chill spread over her. "Do you trust them?"

"Frazer? I've worked with him for the last three years. He can be a cold bastard at times, but he gets results and he cares about doing the right thing." He rolled his shoulders as if he'd sat in the same position for too long. "Parker is new to me. Cyber-security expert and former CIA by way of the Army. *Trust* might not be the right word for it, not yet, but if I'm going with my gut? Yeah, I trust him. Plus if anyone can link the Russians to that sniper or to my former boat, it's Parker. And Frazer has the political clout to make it work for us as opposed to it being buried deep."

Frazer's name seemed familiar somehow. "Were they involved in that terrorist attack recently? Are you a friend of the guy who got shot?"

Matt shifted in his seat.

She held up her hand in defeat. "Sorry. You don't have to answer. I forgot who I was talking to for a moment." They weren't equals. She was interested because the president had been attacked. But he was talking to the daughter of a convicted spy about something that was probably personal, classified, and none of her damn business. The fact he refused to say anything made him a professional whom she respected, but it reminded her of their differences and that stung. She gave a little self-deprecating smile. "I guess, on paper, this would be the perfect opportunity for me to try and seduce some cooperation out of you." Inexplicably tears gathered in her eyes and she had to blink rapidly to hide them. She tried to stand and move away, but he caught her arm.

"What do you want from me, Scarlett?"

She sucked in a jagged breath. "Nothing. I don't want anything from you." She tried to shrug him off, but he didn't let her. A ball of emotion scraped the lining of her throat.

What did she want? She wanted him to trust her. She wanted to be treated like an equal. Not a traitor. She wanted other things that weren't important right now. "I want to find out who set up my father. I want to find the real traitor and I want my country to apologize to former FBI Agent Richard Stone before he dies." Her voice quivered but didn't break.

"So let's look at the files. See what we can find." He said it reasonably, unemotionally, because it wasn't his father rotting in prison. And he didn't believe her anyway.

She sat back down. She was being stupid. "Of course." Time was running out and the Russians had backed her into a corner.

She glanced at the other dates for her father's supposed acts of treason. Birthdays, her parents' wedding anniversary. It couldn't be a coincidence. It was a message. His colleagues either hadn't checked, or hadn't cared. "He deliberately used dates when he had an alibi and no one ever questioned any of them?"

Matt peered closer, then pulled up a series of scanned images of what looked like scientific traces.

"Are they the polygraph charts?"

Matt nodded. "Frazer somehow managed to get his hands on the classified audio files as well. Want to listen to them?" He watched her closely.

She straightened in her seat. "Of course."

Matt clicked a button. An unknown male voice listed the date, time, and case number, then asked her father to confirm his identity.

"FBI Agent Richard Stone. This is bullshit, Ken. You know it."

She felt like she'd been flattened by a truck. The Examiner didn't reply to her father's angry comment. To hear his voice so strong and indignant sent a wave of pure grief right through her. Matt didn't notice. He was trying to follow the questioning and match up the scanned images of the polygraphs.

Oh, Dad.

She pushed the sorrow away. There was no time for this. She couldn't afford to wallow in grief, not when there was a faint hope she could still clear his name. But the cancer was taking him from her even more permanently than the so-called justice system. It wouldn't be long before none of this made any difference. She didn't want him to die in disgrace. She didn't want him to die, period.

"Are the lights on in the room?" the Examiner asked.

"Yeah." Her father answered. "It's lit up like Gestapo HQ."

There was a long pause, as if the Examiner was giving her dad a silent reprimand. "Is today Wednesday?"

"Yeah, Ken, today is Wednesday, unless you're in Australia in which case it's already Thursday. These questions need to be more cut and dried, you know? Otherwise you could end up making a big mistake."

Scarlett wanted to smile, but she knew his bravado hadn't lasted. At some point, not long after he failed this polygraph, he'd crumpled and capitulated.

Matt carried on working through the audio and the images, comparing them in excruciating detail and rewinding certain sections and replaying them. Timing segments, making notes on a pad of paper.

He repeated the process over and over. Scarlett went to make them both a coffee. She hadn't gotten a Ph.D. at twenty-two by knowing how to relax or how to sleep or how to not ask questions. When she returned, Matt was leaning back in his chair and tapping his pen on the table. She could tell from his expression he'd noticed something squirrelly.

"What is it?" She tried to suppress her excitement.

His expression shut down. As a SEAL and federal agent, it was probably a necessary requirement to hold back secrets, but as a partner in an investigation, it was frustrating as hell.

He's not your partner.

"I did a psych degree prior to becoming a frogman."

"Impressive."

His eyes narrowed. "We can't all be child prodigies."

"Hey, that's *your* prejudice showing through, not mine. I thought it *was* impressive. A guy who looks like you could have done many things with his life that didn't involve getting an education." She winced. Jesus. He reduced her to a social idiot. "NFL player, cop, mayor of a small Texas town, male model, super hero, professional belly dancer." If she just kept babbling maybe he'd miss the fact she'd just told him she thought he was good looking. Like she needed more nails for her own coffin.

He released a heavy sigh. "The point being…we did polygraphs on one another and then played truth or dare," his sudden grin was wicked, "so I have some experience with this stuff. These traces don't seem to jive with the interview or the answers your father gave."

Truth or dare with a polygraph machine? Maybe she wasn't the only nerd in the room.

"So what are you saying? This isn't dad's polygraph chart? Why would someone substitute it?" Scarlett contained her excitement. There were probably all sorts of reasonable explanations, though she didn't believe any of them.

"It's likely he took more than one exam and this audio tape is for a different polygraph trace." He was frowning at the images. "Or they mixed up the traces accidentally." He pointed to the screen. "Does that number there look different from the rest?"

She peered closer, aware of Matt's face so close to hers that if she turned her head just slightly her lips would brush his cheek. "It's a little darker than the other numbers, and looks a little offset."

"Almost as if someone used Letraset on it afterwards."

"Letra-what?"

He grimaced. "Never mind. You just reminded me how young you are."

She turned her head and held his gaze. "I'm not that young, Matt, and you're not that old."

He held her stare, the gold flecks in his eyes starting to glow.

She forced herself to turn away. This situation wasn't about her obvious attraction to Matt; it was about her father. "I thought the FBI had proper procedures for this sort of thing."

She pushed down her sense of elation. She knew better than to get her hopes up. But someone was actually questioning the evidence rather than just gung-ho following the hysteria of mass hate.

"They do, but after a case is closed it's possible someone took out the evidence and somehow mixed it up. Or maybe someone spilled something on the paper copy and wanted to hide the fact they'd screwed up." He checked the file again. "Pre 9/11 the systems weren't fully computerized. The FBI was probably the most technologically poor law enforcement agency in the world at that time, thanks to a director who didn't believe in technology."

Her father had often bemoaned the computer systems at work where he hadn't even been able to send attachments with his email.

"Maybe when this was digitized, someone mixed things up and tried to cover their tracks rather than risk getting fired."

Scarlett rolled her eyes. It seemed everyone got a free pass on their mistakes except her dad.

Matt went over to the couch and picked up one of the burner cells Parker had provided and called the guy. "Can you give me a location on a guy named Ken Maidstone, who worked as a Polygraph Examiner for the Bureau back in two-thousand?" He wrote something down on his little pad of paper. She checked over his shoulder. The address was about an hour's drive away from where they were holed up. "Any updates?" He was quiet as he listened but it didn't look like good news. "He lives close enough I'm going to pay this guy a visit. Charts in the case file don't match the audio recording of the session. I want to ask him a few questions. See if he remembers the case."

As if he'd forget one of the most notorious spy scandals in history?

He hung up. Scarlett shrugged into her sweater, then grabbed her jacket.

"You're not coming," Matt said firmly, checking his weapon, not looking at her.

"Yes, I am."

"No, you're not."

"My head will explode if I stay here." She crossed her arms over her chest. The idea of him leaving her behind hurt, and that was too stupid for words.

He stood motionless, for a big guy he had stealth and stillness down to a fine art. "Look"—the patronizing tone made her want to smack him, which beat the whole lust thing hands down—"I don't think this guy is going to talk to the daughter of a man he helped put away for espionage."

"I'll stay in the car."

He looked unconvinced.

"I *promise* I'll stay in the car."

He narrowed his eyes, but his jaw relaxed a fraction.

"Come on, Special Agent Lazlo. I'll be good. I always keep my promises." She wasn't above begging. "It doesn't make sense to leave me here with the Russians after me. Anything could happen." Now she was playing on his sense of chivalry. It worked.

"Fine, Dr. Stone. But if you disobey my instructions in any way, I'm going to spank your ass so hard you won't be able to sit for a week."

Her spine stiffened. "I didn't know you were into abusive relationships—"

"Hey, some people enjoy it." He opened his mouth, then pressed his lips together as if clamping down on the next words, eyes going molten before he masked it.

A wave of sexual awareness rushed through her and made her mouth parch. It wasn't as if she'd never had sex. She'd had sex—passionless, boring *are-we-done-yet?* sex.

He was older than she was and had seen things in the military and as an FBI agent she couldn't begin to comprehend. She got that. And he was trying to warn her that despite the spark that shimmered between them, they were incompatible.

Duh.

What he didn't understand was, incompatible was her norm. She didn't fit with anyone. Anywhere. Being a misfit, a reject, was standard operating procedure in her world. If not because of her father, then because of her place in the education system, her age. She didn't fit in. Period. She was used to it.

It was the heat that passed between them, the weird electric sizzle that didn't seem to care he'd arrested her last night, that was extraordinary. So a few sexual innuendos were not off-putting. They were thrilling, because no one had ever gone there with her before and certainly not a guy she was attracted to as much as she was attracted to Matt Lazlo.

Telling him that would humiliate her and scare the crap out of him, so she kept her mouth shut. Emotional masochism was not her thing. So even though the man tempted her on a physical level, she wasn't going to go there. He was putting up the same barriers as she was and that was a good thing. She was too smart to fall for him. And, apparently, he was way too professional to fall for her.

He grabbed the laptop and cash and cells Parker had organized for them. "Fine. Bring everything. We may as well get a motel closer to where Maidstone lives. Should help throw anyone on our tail off the scent."

She jammed on her sneakers. She had nothing with her except the clothes she was wearing. Just before he opened the door, she touched his arm. "Thank you. Thank you for trying to help my dad."

Eyes as cold as sea glass pinned her in place. "I'm not doing this to help your father, Scarlett. I'm trying to figure out why the Russians are so pissed they don't give a shit if they take out others with you. I'm trying to keep you alive to see Christmas Day because that's my job. I still believe your father is a traitor to the United States and the antithesis of everything I believe in and fought for."

The words hit with a meaty punch to the stomach. Thankfully, she was well practiced at hiding pain beneath a calm exterior and a nod of understanding. Didn't mean it didn't hurt.

She dropped her hand. "Of course. Let's go."

CHAPTER ELEVEN

Matt glanced at Scarlett. She sat in the passenger seat of the SUV Parker had arranged for them, an indifferent expression on her face. Matt wasn't fooled. He'd hurt her feelings. Couldn't be helped. He wasn't about to pretend he was doing this for a man who'd admitted his crimes. Matt was detail-oriented, tying up loose ends was one of the reasons he was so good at his job. Trying to find out why the Russians were so damn pissed with Scarlett for trying to bug Dorokhov would be the key to ending this thing. A certain amount of anger and posturing was expected. Snipers and bombs were taking things to the next level, which meant someone had secrets to hide or a giant ego—or both.

He sipped a can of Red Bull—another habit he'd picked up in the teams and never quite quit—and checked the route finder as they headed north.

Ken Maidstone lived in a small town just north of Leesburg in northern Virginia, situated at the base of the Blue Ridge Mountains. It was a historic area set in wine country, with the Potomac winding its way lazily along its eastern flank.

According to the information Alex Parker had dug up, Maidstone's wife had died of lung cancer about five years ago, and he'd retired from the Bureau one year ago. Now the guy did some freelance consulting.

Being Christmas Eve, traffic was nose-to-tail, fist on the horn. Matt had never gotten the polar opposites between theory and practice of the goodwill toward all men. He hadn't been one of those kids surrounded by a million relatives and a huge sit-down turkey dinner. When he'd been in country, it had been just him and his mother.

He suspected he had that in common with Scarlett.

He didn't want to miss this Christmas with his mom. Guilt ate at him, but part of him knew the most important part of her was already gone. It didn't mean he could just abandon her though.

He glanced again at Scarlett. Maybe he *should* transfer her to protective custody with the US Marshal Service? He was veering over the line toward personal and that would bring nothing but trouble. The idea of getting to know her better, of pursuing some sort of relationship once they'd cleared up the mess she currently found herself in, was tempting. He avoided making those kinds of mistakes whenever possible, but the idea of a relationship with Scarlett had slipped past his guard from the very beginning.

Relationship?

He didn't even know her. She looked innocent, but she was trouble with a capital T.

She was also courageous, smart, and loyal. Even as he considered the option of handing her off to someone else, he dismissed it. He was a part of this mess now—they'd already proven his death meant less than nothing to them, so fuck them.

It was good to know where he stood so he could return the favor if it came down to the wire.

And the idea they would hurt a woman…He didn't understand men like that. Who knew what the hell they were doing to Angel LeMay? And when Scarlett found out he'd lied about her best friend, she was going to go through the roof. Frazer hadn't gotten back to him on whether or not there was any progress there. The idea Dorokhov felt powerful enough to take the daughter of a United States Congressman without retaliation seemed nuts, and yet even though they were looking, there was no proof the ambassador had been involved.

What was really going on? What had Scarlett stirred up with the stunt she pulled last night?

He bet Richard Stone wasn't half the man she thought he was. He doubted the guy deserved anyone as devoted or loyal as this young woman who was sacrificing her own life in a quest to prove his innocence.

"Why did your father confess?" He wanted to push her, make her view this from his perspective. Wanted to open her eyes so it didn't hurt quite so much when she was finally forced to confront the truth.

She turned to face him. Young, sweet, pretty. Hair tousled, dark eyes wide, skin pale. "What do you mean?"

"Your dad. One minute he denies everything, then he just admits it. Why?"

"I thought about it,"—he bet she had—"when they told him he failed the polygraph he knew the chances were he was going to prison. I think someone must have threatened me and my mother if he didn't go quietly. He knew he couldn't protect us from inside jail and I assume he didn't know who he could trust. Also thinking about that confession he wrote…if anyone *had* checked the details even a little they'd know all the information he gave was false—"

"What is a spy except a professional liar?"

Her mouth pinched in anger. Her brows rose and her tone turned sarcastic. "Silly me. I just assumed they taught basic law enforcement procedures at the FBI and verified information."

Some asshole in a yellow sports car zipped by him and got blasted by horns of oncoming traffic. Insanity. The weather was as grim and oppressive as he felt. Christmas felt about a billion light-years away. "Did your father have any pressure points? Any deep, dark secrets?"

She shook her head and bit her lip. Damn, he wished she'd stop doing that because even though he was trying to drive a wedge between them, her white teeth on those lips made him hard as a horny seventeen-year-old.

"Could he have been having an affair?" he asked.

"No."

"Gay?"

"No."

"Pedophile?"

"*No.*"

"Bestiality?"

She shot him a look filled with venom, but her voice was cool and placid as a northern lake. "He liked dogs and children the same way any good, healthy man does."

"Were your mom and dad into partner swapping or kinky swinger parties?"

Her eyes became huge. "Obsessed with sex much? Where do you even get these ideas?"

"From the case-files of other spy cases in the eighties and nineties," Matt said evenly. "CIA mole Karl Koecher and his wife attended sex orgies to try and gather information.

Hanssen set up a close-circuit TV camera so his buddy could watch him having sex with his wife—the wife didn't know."

"Ewww on both those counts." She scrunched up her shoulders. "I'm beginning to think most federal employees are closet perverts."

Matt had been trying to dig deeper into the type of person her father was, but her disgust was so genuine he grinned. "Most of us are deprived rather than depraved."

"Deprived?" Her eyes ran over his torso and down his legs. "I doubt it." Embarrassment burned her cheeks, and she looked away, but there was also a shimmer of interest, of heat. Shit. He kept his eyes on the car ahead of them and refused to think about the fact she was attracted to him. Frazer's words came back to him in a rush. *Women like that...they can bring you to your knees.*

He was beginning to think the guy knew what he was talking about, because the idea of being on his knees in front of Scarlett didn't seem like such a bad thing. Shit.

"I know what you're doing, you know," she said.

Really? Because he had no fucking clue.

"You're demonstrating how worldly and experienced most people are compared to me."

Maybe at some point that might have been his intention, but it had backfired on him big time. Now he was just thinking about sex. She'd told him she hadn't dated in school. Was she a virgin? The heat, the *interest* he saw in her eyes might be simple curiosity rather than lust. He was an asshole for pushing it. The fact he had pushed it told him he was playing with fire. He wanted her, and flirting with her was not a good way to keep her at arm's length. Time to back off. Keep it professional.

"Not a lot surprises me anymore, from sexual preferences to *Modus Operandi* for murder." He caught her eye. "If I made you uncomfortable, I'm sorry. It wasn't intentional."

"You don't make me uncomfortable." The tinge of pink in her cheeks looked good on her, but she managed to hold his gaze. "Talking about my parents' sex life does. My dad and mom were devoted to each other and not in some weird, creepy way. He worked hard, and she was a kindergarten teacher until she had to stay home with me after his arrest. It's not impossible he was doing something on the side with someone, but it didn't fit the perception of my childhood. I never picked up any vibes that they were anything except madly in love with one another. They still are."

Her words made him question himself. Was he letting his own bias influence him? Not everyone's father was an asshole. Apparently, even convicted spies were better fathers than his had been. "Could he have had a gambling problem?"

She shook her head. "He had no interest in slots or poker that I know of. I used to make him play Old Maid, but he hated it. I know everyone wants to believe he's guilty, but I don't see it. My mom visits him as often as possible; she's with him now. She still wears her wedding band and kept his name. Financially we struggled but I managed to get scholarships through college—"

"*That's* why you worked so hard."

The line of her throat rippled as she swallowed and looked away. "Maybe."

No *maybe* about it. Her choices suddenly made a lot more sense.

He was aware how fine-boned she was, next to his six-two, two hundred pound frame. He still didn't understand why she attracted him so damn much. He hadn't been interested in a woman for a while—even the blonde from the Christmas party had gone home alone despite an invitation for a play-date. He'd told himself he was too busy with work and his mom to get involved, but as soon as a woman turned up that his body paid attention to he was on a fricking road-trip.

It's work.

Sure.

"Look." Scarlett geared up to give him a lecture, and he quashed a grin. "Back in the year two-thousand, no one considered the Russians a threat. Their economy had tanked and they were supposedly our 'friends'. But Dad didn't trust them and was certain former KGB elements were trying to penetrate all aspects of American society from the ground up."

"Why was he so sure?"

"He knew some of the players involved from his earlier years in the Bureau and didn't think they'd changed their ways." Her voice was gruff, as if holding back emotion. Or secrets. He maneuvered around a minivan and got honked at for his audacity even though he never even broke the speed limit. *Merry fricking Christmas.*

"He said they were crooks at best, spies at worst, and most were probably both. No one at the Bureau wanted to listen, so they shifted him over to a counterfeit case where thousands of designer handbags and soccer shirts were being sold across the country. Trouble was when he fingered an organized crime figure as the major culprit, it was another Russian. He lost credibility. The powers-that-be thought he had a beef with the Russians. When they later turned around and arrested him for spying, they said he'd used his previous accusations as a smokescreen for his real allegiance."

"Maybe he did."

Her face was perfectly expressionless, but he knew what she was thinking. She was thinking he was a moron. "Maybe he did. Or maybe he was set up to take the fall for the real Russian spy, which effectively punished one of their biggest critics, removed his voice from the arena, while protecting their real asset. Pretty neat solution." She turned to stare woodenly out the window.

If it were true, it would be a hell of a coup. He didn't believe it. The FBI was better than that.

They'd driven through historic Leesburg and now they were in Thornton.

On the edge of the commuter belt, it was surprisingly small and unspoiled. A short main street with coffee shop, antique shop and hardware store all next to each other. The street was decorated for the festive season. A thirty-foot pine stood in the town square draped in multi-colored lights. Santas waved overhead from their plastic sleighs. Kids skipped beside their parents, bundled up within an inch of heat exhaustion. Middle class America was alive and well here. He'd grown up in a town like this. Missed it some days. Barely thought about it most of the time. He'd been a fatherless brat and yet he'd had a fantastic childhood. It made him miss his mother—not the woman in the bedroom at the nursing home, but the woman who'd dragged him up hills and through woods just to appreciate the beauty of the countryside.

Beauty in nature had always been her solace and she'd passed that appreciation on to him.

The sky was leaden and seemed to be waiting to cut loose with either rain or snow. Damn. He hated getting cold and wet.

Ask any frogman who'd endured BUD/s and they'd tell you the same thing. None of that cold shower shit, thank you very much.

He turned up a side street into a residential zone, drove along slowly, not wanting to bring any attention to them, up a hill, then right again into some new houses. Every house was slightly different, but they all somehow managed to look the same.

"Number seventy-three." Scarlett pointed. "Up on the left."

Matt drove past and around the block.

"You missed it."

"A little discretion, Dr. Stone, goes a long way—a bit like checking to see if the hallway you access to break into the Russian Ambassador's office has a surveillance camera."

She blew out a breath and crossed her arms over her chest. "I'd like to see you build a processor using nano-elec-tro-mechanical relays."

"What? No flux capacitor?"

"Trust me, if I could do time travel I wouldn't be sitting here with you."

"You stick to your expertise. I'll stick to mine." Which should be looking at linkage between serial killer victims and creating profiles. He had sixteen active cases on his desk in various stages of analysis. More than forty victims waiting for justice. Unfortunately, there was only so much he could do when he was supposed to be dead.

He parked. "Stay here." He held her gaze with an unspo-ken "or else" as she huddled down into her seat. Her cheeks tinged pink. Maybe she was remembering what he'd said to her earlier about spanking her if she didn't do as she was told? The empty threat had backfired on him big time.

He got out of the car, put on some aviator sunglasses, and stuffed his hands in his pockets. One way or another, Scarlett Stone was going to be the death of him.

————

It was lunchtime, Christmas Eve, and he hadn't slept in thirty-six hours. Lincoln Frazer wasn't used to being kept waiting. Rather than being in the office, tracking down serial killers the way he was supposed to, he was inside one of the most secure prisons in the world, hoping to talk to the most notorious spy in FBI history. ADX housed foreign and domestic terrorists, cartel leaders, white supremacists, serial killers—some of whom he'd had a hand in sending here—as well as several spies. Frazer was only interested in Stone who, on paper, had seemed like such a damn good agent before his arrest. Maybe that's why the rest of the FBI were still pissed. Richard Stone's record had been exemplary, which didn't fit the profile of the usual resentful egotistical underachievers who gravitated toward selling out their countries for cash.

Less than twenty-four hours ago he'd been in a private meeting with the President of the United States discussing issues of national security, and vainly hoping for a quiet Christmas. The president had assigned him and his team another task that would have to wait until this mess Scarlett Stone had instigated was diffused. So far, Miss LeMay was nowhere to be found. No ransom demand had been made. Her parents were on the edge of going to the press and plunging the US into a diplomatic crisis with Russia, that, combined with the tensions simmering in the old Soviet Block countries and the Middle East, might be the impetus for all-out world war.

So far the FBI had urged patience to the LeMays and managed to keep a lid on the kidnapping story. He didn't know how much longer that would last.

Had Richard Stone sent his daughter to spy on Dorokhov? If so, why? He needed to find out so he could limit the damage. He'd spoken to Parker when he'd gotten off the flight and heard about Lazlo's narrow escape. Being willing to take out one of his agents in pursuit of this woman pissed him off. Diplomatic immunity or not, Frazer intended to find a way to make Dorokhov back off before any real damage was done. Hopefully Richard Stone held the key because he had better things to do than wear out the carpet of another federal facility.

He checked his watch. He'd been in the visitor area outside the warden's office for eighty-six minutes. The secretary sent him another pained smile, but his usual charm wasn't working and the woman remained tight-lipped. Must be losing his touch.

A harried man with stooped, narrow shoulders strode in, followed by a correctional officer who looked like Muhammad Ali in his prime. The man in the cheap suit stopped short when he saw Frazer. His hand went to his forehead and a look of obvious irritation crossed his features. Bureau of Prisons didn't always play nice with other feebs, especially feebs who had used all their contacts to strong-arm their way inside a supermax prison on Christmas Eve.

Happy Holidays.

Obviously, the guy had forgotten Frazer had an appointment, which was better news than deliberately being kept waiting.

Frazer held out his hand. "ASAC Lincoln Frazer. Thank you for seeing me at such short notice, Warden Baumann." He hadn't told the man who he wanted to talk to because he hadn't wanted to tip his hand. "I realize Christmas Eve is not the best time to request an interview with one of your inmates, but I can assure you this won't take long. It's imperative I speak with the prisoner ASAP."

Once again the charm wasn't working as the man carried on walking into his office and dropped hard into his chair. The CO followed and Frazer went after them.

"Is there a problem?" he asked.

"No," the warden answered quickly. Too quickly. "Who is it you want to talk to?"

"Richard Stone."

The warden lost what little color he had. "Stone?"

"Yes, sir. Is that a problem?"

"Yes." The man opened a bottom drawer and pulled out a bottle of scotch. Three shot glasses followed, but Frazer declined the one offered to him. The warden poured two small measures and handed one to the CO.

The two men chinked glasses and tossed back the spirit. The warden wiped his mouth and both men put their glasses back on the table with a thunk. There were no "cheers".

Frazer raised a brow but said nothing. It had obviously been a tough day.

"I'm afraid you can't see Richard Stone, ASAC Frazer."

"What about tomorrow?" he persisted. He didn't want to call in more favors but he would. This was too important to be shut down by petty bureaucracy or federal infighting.

"Christmas Day?" The warden gave a small humorless laugh that turned into a groan. "This is really important to you."

He maintained eye contact. "Yes, sir."

The warden dragged a hand through his hair and inadvertently disturbed his comb-over. "That's unfortunate, and I'm afraid it isn't going to make much difference."

Frazer opened his mouth to argue but Warden Baumann carried on talking. "Richard Stone was attacked this morning during his chemo treatment. He's been transported to a medical facility at Colorado Springs Air Force Base and is not expected to survive."

Frazer felt as if someone had smacked him on the back of the head with a two-by-four. Someone had gotten to Stone. This was not good. This was really not good. Why? Why after all these years? Was it revenge for what his daughter had done, or the ultimate way of silencing the man, once and for all? Why would the Russians kill one of their own agents? Did the Russians have that sort of reach? Frazer didn't know, but sure as hell hoped not.

"So," the man eyed him tiredly, "I'm afraid you can't talk to him."

"Can I see his cell?" The guy had obviously had a shitty day, but Frazer's wasn't over. "And is it possible to share any information on the person who attacked him?"

The warden rubbed reddened eyes. "Juan Marquez, he's a member of a Mexican drug cartel. Marquez is diabetic and visits the infirmary almost daily to get his blood sugar checked. He stabbed Stone three times, twice in the stomach. Marquez is serving consecutive life sentences and the chance of him ever getting out is slim to none. Why do you want to see Stone's cell?"

Frazer decided to go with some measure of truth, a classic element of any good lie. "We are concerned with recent activities of a former Russian contact of Stone's. That's all I'm at liberty to say."

Baumann shook his head. "The guy spends ninety-five percent of his time alone in a concrete box. All his mail is screened and copied, and he has no access to the internet, but fine, go check out his cell. Officer Knell can escort you."

"Is Stone's wife with him?" Frazer was going to have to talk to Lazlo about how to break the news to Scarlett. Maybe she'd be better off not knowing until they knew whether or not her father was going to make it.

The warden picked up the phone. "She's being escorted to the hospital as we speak. Stone is under armed guard regardless of his condition. Now I have to try to track down the daughter while my wife berates me for not being home and spending enough time with our grandchildren." Baumann's pinched features showed his frustration.

Frazer didn't tell him he knew where Scarlett was, even though it would save the guy time and effort. It was imperative she remain hidden and the moment she heard about her father she'd be on a flight to Colorado. He couldn't risk it. She couldn't risk it. If the bad guys found out she was alive, the game would change back to hunt mode and Frazer wanted to buy her some breathing space.

He thanked the warden and followed Officer Knell through security, where he handed over his weapons and badge. "Do you know the prisoner?" he asked as they walked along gray institutional corridors, going through locked door after locked door.

"Pretty well. We both arrived about the same time. He never gives me any trouble. Compared to most of the guys in here, he's a fricking saint."

The impression of thick walls and the suffocating sense of confinement pressed down on Frazer's head and chest. This was his greatest nightmare. This institutionalized destruction of freedom. And that was the point for those who'd earned it.

What if the guy is innocent?

A trickle of unease ran down his spine. This whole situation felt wrong. He could see no reason for Richard Stone to send his daughter on a wild goose chase after all these years of holding his silence.

So Scarlett acted alone. Probably. Trying to prove her dad was innocent.

So *why* attack Richard?

What if Richard Stone *had* been framed and the real spy heard about what Scarlett had tried to do…? What if they feared she'd discovered something? They'd be more dangerous than ever.

Stone had never once claimed innocence, not after his confession. Part of it had been the assurance his wife would receive his pension, but Frazer couldn't help thinking that the only really compelling reason for a man to keep his mouth shut was to protect his wife and child. Would Stone have endured this hellhole simply to keep them safe?

The answer was yes. If he'd believed the threat was real.

That was sacrifice. That was a man who understood devotion.

Why hadn't he asked for them to be placed in protective custody?

Because he didn't know who to trust.

The thought sent a bolt of unease racing through his body. His instincts were screaming that something was off about this whole situation. The more he dug the more it stank. There was an increasing possibility that the FBI had let Stone down. His colleagues had let him down. And, in all likelihood, someone inside the FBI was still dirty.

He held the knowledge tight inside.

Knell led him to a door and unlocked it. Inside were more steel bars, which Knell opened, then stood back watching him. "Be my guest." He indicated Frazer go inside with the thrust of his chin.

Frazer entered the concrete rectangle with its concrete bed, concrete desk, concrete stool and four-inch wide narrow slit of a window that faced the courtyard. It was like the Flintstones' without Wilma or Dino to make things better.

Frazer repressed a shudder at the idea of being trapped inside a place like this for any length of time. Then he remembered a dark pit in a lonely West Virginian wood where many women had died and realized this, at least, was a lot more humane.

Books lined the shelves. Some writing paper and pencils were arranged neatly on the desk. A box of letters that looked to have been written by his wife and daughter sat there. He read a couple, but they were filled with the day-to-day happenings of normal life, heartbreaking in their mundane detail—painting the hall, fixing the dishwasher, planting tulip bulbs. However unexciting to the rest of the world, it must have been a lifeline of sanity for the condemned man.

He eyed the cell again with its small TV and heavy locked door. There were books on the shelves. Everything from Shakespeare to Ludlum, Lee Child to poetry. He pulled out a thriller and flicked through the pages.

A call on the radio had Knell stepping out into the hallway. He put his head back inside. "I'll be back in a few minutes."

Frazer nodded, grateful to be alone. He put the novel down and noticed a small notebook tucked against the shelf, behind the other books. He pulled it out, looked inside, saw scribbles that he couldn't decipher and felt his heart pound. He palmed it quickly and slipped it into his pants' pocket. Maybe it contained something useful. Maybe it was demented ramblings, but he didn't have time to figure it out right now and it might be a clue.

He swept his hand under the pillow, found a picture of Stone with his arms around his wife and a young Scarlett. A handsome man, beautiful wife, happy family.

Why would he throw that all away?

Frazer stared at that photo for a long time. He turned it over and saw the date written in blue ink. December 12, 2000—the day Stone had been arrested for passing secrets to Russia. Frazer frowned and turned it back over. The picture had obviously been taken along the Washington Mall in the summer, but was dated in December. Why? He slipped it into his pocket just as Knell came back in the room.

"Find anything useful?" Knell asked.

"Just the firm desire never to break the law." Except he had broken the law once. The lines between right and wrong had blurred drastically that day.

The man shrugged. "It's not so bad when you get to go home at the end of your shift."

Frazer nodded and concentrated on the here and now. "Can I take the letters?" He pointed at the neat stack.

Knell frowned. "No, but I can arrange to get you copies."

"Okay." He walked past Knell into the corridor. Being outside the cell didn't lessen the feeling of oppression. "Did Stone have any issues with the other prisoners?"

Knell gave him a *you-must-be-joking* look. "He didn't mix with other prisoners. Not only was he in here for espionage, he was a former federal agent. They'd have gutted him in an instant."

"So the only time he mixed with other prisoners is at the infirmary?" Where they'd gutted him anyway.

Knell nodded and unlocked the first of the series of doors that led to freedom.

Someone had known that the only chance of getting to Stone was during his chemo sessions, and the best chance to do it was by using another inmate who was also a regular in the clinic.

"Any chance of talking to this Marquez guy?" Frazer asked.

"He's an animal. He isn't going to tell you anything you can trust." A note of belligerence crept into Knell's tone. "Marquez has nothing to lose by killing another prisoner. He's not getting out. Saw his opportunity and took it. It can be as simple as that when this place is your entire existence."

Frazer didn't push it. He wanted Knell on his side in case he needed to come back.

After they passed through the next iron gate, the correctional officer put a hand on his arm and leaned close, keeping his voice low. "We're in a blind spot for both cameras and sound right here. Look, the boss didn't want me to tell anyone this, but Richard Stone told me to tell his wife that it was dangerous and to be careful. Before he went unconscious it sounded like he said the name *Marlon*." Knell held his gaze. "I don't know what any of it means, but when I passed the message onto the wife, she looked like she was going to pass out. She kept trying to call the daughter, but the daughter didn't pick up."

Frazer nodded. Silently thanking the man for his confidence. This was a game changer. He needed to contact Parker and Lazlo with this new information and figure out their next move.

"I don't appreciate people bringing their wars inside my prison. Makes for a dangerous time and we have enough danger in here already." The guard started walking again, as if nothing had changed, but they both knew it had. Getting to Stone in here was hard, but not impossible. Someone could have bribed Marquez or threatened his family—Frazer fingered the photograph in his pocket. The tendrils of a possible conspiracy theory seemed to be waving at him with increasing vigor. Frazer had brought down others who tried to manipulate justice for their own ends and wasn't afraid to do it again. People who used their position to inflict hurt on innocents didn't deserve to stay in power. He just hoped Richard and Scarlett Stone survived long enough for the FBI to get to the bottom of this conundrum and find out the truth.

CHAPTER TWELVE

Matt strode down the sidewalk of the quiet residential block. This time of year had an advantage in that there were lots of people visiting friends or relatives they hardly saw the rest of the year. People arrived on the doorstep unannounced. Strange cars parked on the street for an afternoon without comment.

He walked up the driveway of number seventy-three, which had a red SUV parked on the drive. The house and car were nice, nothing flashy. A retired professional could afford this sort of thing on a regular salary if he'd been careful with his money.

He rang the bell and waited. No one answered. After thirty seconds, he knocked loudly on the door. Still no one answered. A door banged nearby. Voices rang through the dank air as someone laughed, then a car engine started and they drove away.

Deciding to take a look around back, he ventured past the attached garage and let himself through the small garden gate at the side of the property. Down a path lined with empty pots and a garden hose, skirting the side of the deck. He walked up the steps and made sure his hands were clearly visible. Best not to sneak up on a former fed looking like a potential threat.

He peered through the kitchen window but saw no one so he went over to the sliding doors and looked into the living room. His blood chilled. The place was torn apart. Christmas tree overturned, decorations scattered. Trinkets and picture frames smashed and lying on the floor. Worse—what he assumed were Ken Maidstone's feet lay in view.

One foot twitched.

Shit. The guy was still alive. Matt drew his SIG from the holster at his waist and tried the kitchen door. It swung open. Senses on high alert he strode inside, down the hall and crouched beside Maidstone, who lay across the threshold between the living room and the hall. He put two fingers to the man's carotid and felt a subtle throb against his fingers. Still alive. Judging from the blood that pooled around his body, he wouldn't last much longer without serious medical assistance.

He grabbed the phone off the side table and dialed 911. "Need an ambulance ASAP. GSW to the chest." He hung up on the operator. Was the perp still inside the house? He didn't have time to search. Maidstone would bleed out.

He lay his gun beside him but kept his senses wide open for any hint of another person nearby. He ripped the man's shirt open and saw a small caliber bullet hole in his chest. He eased the guy up and discovered a much messier exit wound. It looked like it had taken out one of his lungs and the guy struggled to breathe. Maidstone's eyes followed him. Wide with fear and pain. Matt grabbed a small cushion off the couch, pressed it tight against the man's back, applying pressure to try to stop the bleeding.

There was a lot of blood. A series of images flashed rapid-fire through his brain. Blood. Guts. Severed limbs. He shook his head to clear the memories. He saw blood all too often in his work, but never when the victim was still alive. "Hold on, Ken. Hold on, buddy."

The guy's breathing was hoarse and shallow, lungs too weak to drag in a decent breath. Matt had basic medical training but zero supplies and the only real thing that was going to save this man was a trauma surgeon, a blood transfusion, and some serious good luck.

The sound of a siren grew louder. Matt holstered his weapon. Someone started banging on the front door. He leapt up and unlocked it, but it wasn't the EMTs. Scarlett looked at the blood on his hands and then her eyes went to the man on the floor.

"Did he attack you?" she asked as he went back to the injured man.

Maidstone groaned.

"He was like this when I found him." Matt frowned at Scarlett's question. Did she really think he'd shot the guy? "Mr. Maidstone. I'm FBI Agent Lazlo and this here is Scarlett Stone—Richard Stone's daughter. You've been shot." *Duh.* "Hang on, we've got emergency services on the way."

The man turned toward Scarlett, lips parted as if he wanted to say something.

Scarlett clasped Maidstone's hand. "Hold on, Mr. Maidstone. Please hold on. Who did this to you?" She knelt beside him, not flinching as blood soaked into the knees of her jeans.

A ragged sound emerged from Maidstone's lips. Matt and Scarlett both leaned closer to hear what he said.

"Ma…"

"Ma?" Matt asked urgently.

The man tried again. "Marlon."

"Is that who did this to you?" Scarlett demanded. She was on the edge of tears.

The man lost consciousness and she looked at Matt, eyes wide with fear. Scarlett didn't get the significance of the name, but he did.

Marlon was the code name used by the Russians for the same spy Richard Stone had confessed to being. The name had never been made public, and wasn't in the case files he'd let Scarlett read. Why would Stone want this man dead after all these years?

Answer: *He wouldn't.*

Shit. Matt got a very bad feeling about this. They needed to get out of here. Cops and emergency services would do what they could to save Maidstone, but if they found him and Scarlett here, they'd be suspects. They'd be separated, and the fact they'd both survived the bombing would become public knowledge. Scarlett would be vulnerable not only to the Russians but also to this new threat. Because if Marlon wasn't Richard Stone, he—or she—had everything to lose if they were identified.

Matt grabbed Scarlett's hand and pulled her after him.

"We can't just leave him!"

"We have to." He forced her into a run. When he got to the car he opened the car door and pushed her inside. The shooter might be watching them right now. He got in and reversed into a neighbor's driveway before turning around and driving in the opposite direction. Thankfully, the guy didn't live in a cul-de-sac. Matt drove quickly, knowing they had seconds to get out of there before they were detained— and they should be detained. They had information.

They had disturbed a crime scene, but they hadn't shot the guy and didn't know who had.

Damn. His prints were on the phone. He contemplated turning around but the flash of red lights in the rear-view made him abandon the idea. With that one act, he might have just deep-sixed his career.

He called Frazer who didn't answer, so he called Parker next, slowing as he hit the main road and headed out of town. "Maidstone has been shot. Medics just arrived on scene. Place looks like it was burglarized, but lots of things of value still lying around." He'd noticed an iPad, big-ass TV. Wallet on the table.

"Is he alive?" asked Parker.

"Just. Get this, he said 'Marlon' shot him." The silence on the other end was intense. "I called the cops and got out of there. My prints are on the phone and my voice will be on the 911 tape, though I didn't identify myself." *Fuck.* He looked at Scarlett, who sat shaking beside him. They were both covered in blood, but his jeans were more or less clean and it didn't show on his black t-shirt. "We need a place to lay low and figure out our next move." He needed to think.

Matt heard a mumbled conversation, then Parker was back on the phone. "Nothing about this feels right. I'll call Frazer again—he's been out of touch for the last few hours. We need to arrange protection for Maidstone in case the guy survives, which I can do." He reeled off an address for them to head to. Matt repeated it to Scarlett, who plugged it into the GPS system.

Matt kept alert for cops, thinking aloud. "Why shoot this guy now? Did someone know we were going to see him?"

"They couldn't listen in to our phone conversations or intercept our email—I made sure of that. But Frazer got permission to access the case file last night. Someone knows we're looking at the evidence." Someone *inside* the FBI was the unspoken subtext. "It appears someone is trying to clean up any loose ends."

"This goes well beyond Scarlett breaking into Dorokhov's office last night."

"She stirred up a hornets' nest. She thought Dorokhov might have something to do with her father's arrest. If her father wasn't *Marlon*, maybe the real spy panicked."

Which likely made Maidstone an accomplice who needed silencing. "*Could* Dorokhov have set up Richard Stone?" asked Matt. Russians had money and therefore power, but could they have orchestrated setting up an FBI agent?

"Not without help from the inside."

His gut churned at the idea of being fooled.

The idea that the Russians had gotten the better of his agency, had lied and manipulated the confession and conviction of an innocent man was...inconceivable. Except why else would someone be cleaning house—two attempts on Scarlett's life, blowing up the residence of an FBI agent, the shooting of the man who'd stated Richard Stone had failed the polygraph. Too many things happening too close together to believe they were all unrelated.

Stone had been caught at a dead drop with Top Secret information. He claimed it was already there when he arrived and he'd been following a tip off. What if he was telling the truth? What if Scarlett had been right about her father all along?

Matt couldn't believe he was starting to entertain the possibility that Scarlett's father might actually be innocent. Fuck. If that were true, Richard Stone was a patriot who'd been betrayed, locked up, and forgotten, and everything that had happened to him and his family was a win for the Russians and an insult to the American way. And Scarlett was the only one searching for the justice that had so far eluded her family.

He caught her eye.

"Is this my fault? Did I get that man shot?" Her eyes were huge and he was immediately reminded of when he'd first met her eighteen short hours earlier.

Matt shook his head. "No, but I think you scared someone into taking action."

"So I was right?"

Matt didn't want Scarlett getting her hopes up. It was hard to believe the system he'd dedicated himself to for so long was this flawed. "It might just have been a burglary gone wrong. Even if Maidstone was shot because the polygraph evidence was tampered with, it *still* doesn't mean your dad is innocent." But he didn't sound convincing; he sounded like he was grasping at straws.

She pressed her already bloodless lips together and nodded. Her skin looked icy white as shock started to set in. "I get that. I even get the fact you need to believe in the justice system you represent. But be careful, Matt. My father believed in it just as fiercely as you do. And look what happened to him."

———

Scarlett's hands trembled in her lap. Seeing a man bleeding from a bullet wound brought home the magnitude of the risk she'd taken, and the fact she wasn't the only one in the line of fire made it worse. She'd been wrong to stir things up. She should have accepted everything that had happened.

But her father was innocent.

How did she let the destruction of her family slide? How did she live in a society where she knew the justice system was a sham?

Matt drove slowly and steadily out of town. His hands were smeared in blood but his breathing was normal, his eyes extra-vigilant in the rear-view. Calm in a crisis. Trained for situations like this. Unlike her.

Her teeth clacked together noisily. "S-sorry. I can't s-stop shivering."

The blood that had soaked into her jeans was drying, making the material stiffen. The sticky sensation made her skin itch. Her stomach flipped and she couldn't stand it any longer. She unclipped her seatbelt. Undoing her button and zipper, she lifted her hips so she could slide out of her jeans.

"What are you doing?" Matt's eyes went to her legs.

"I can't stand it. It's making me feel sick." She pushed them off, sneakers and all, then kicked them into the footwell. She plucked tissues out of a box in the console, spat on one and scrubbed at the rusty-red blotches that marred her knees. "I can't deal with the idea of his blood on my body. It sounds awful and selfish, but I can't."

Matt blew out a controlled breath. "Fine. I get it." He cranked up the heat. "But don't take off anything else without warning me first. I'll crash the damn car." He muttered the last under his breath.

She dragged her shirt as far down as possible and it covered her upper thighs. Refastened her seatbelt. "Will we be suspects?"

"If anyone saw us running out of there covered in blood and tagged our plates then we will definitely be suspects. Me being with the feds will only get us so far."

As she knew too well.

"We need to find somewhere to regroup. I feel like a headless chicken running around with no real idea what the hell is going on."

She drew her knees to her chest and hugged her legs. "You think Maidstone is dirty?"

Matt turned those clear hazel eyes on her. The gold in them glinted. "Honestly? It's a heck of a coincidence for him to get shot if he isn't involved in this in some way."

"Do you know who Marlon is?"

He hesitated, clearly debating whether or not to tell her the truth. She'd thought they were beyond that. Dammit.

He nodded curtly. "Marlon is the codename the Russians used for their spy. The spy your father was convicted of being."

"You don't think my father orchestrated that, do you?"

His fingers tightened on the wheel. "I don't see why your father would have arranged a hit unless he's after revenge before he dies. It still doesn't make sense."

"The way Maidstone said the name, it was as if Marlon himself had shot him."

Matt nodded. "That's how it sounded to me too."

"Which would mean my father isn't 'Marlon' and is therefore innocent." Scarlett spelled it out. No more room for evasion.

"Unless there were two spies and they only caught one." Matt suggested.

Crap. If she couldn't convince this man, she'd never convince anyone. "Why won't you even consider he might have been set up?"

His jaw flexed as he considered his words. "Because it's easier to deal with the thought of one man being dirty, than the idea that the FBI, as an institution, fucked up, imprisoned the wrong guy and destroyed his family."

He believed her. He finally believed her. She didn't think he even fully realized it yet.

They sat in silence as the wheels put more and more distance between them and Thornton. Finally Scarlett whispered, "How will he ever get justice if no-one fights for him?"

Matt was silent for another moment before he said tightly. "You're fighting for him, Scarlett."

"What if I'm not enough?" That was her greatest fear. That she wouldn't be able to prove him innocent in time to set him free. That she wouldn't be able to fight through the red tape and bureaucracy, even if she did find the evidence.

Matt took her hand, squeezed her fingers. "If your dad is the guy you think he is, he'll understand you tried. If he isn't, then he was never worth the effort anyway."

There was a bitterness in his words that Scarlett realized wasn't aimed at her father, it was aimed at his. "Not all dads are like your father, Matt."

He jerked his head in a nod, obviously not wanting to talk about it. He cleared his throat. "We need to clean up and grab some food." They were approaching a gas station. Matt reached back and groped for the laptop case and put it on her lap. He pulled up beside the restroom. "Stay in the car. I'll be right back."

———

A hand stopped Frazer's forward progress toward the operating room where doctors were struggling to save Richard Stone's life. He opened his jacket to reveal his badge to the

US Marshal who blocked his way. "The warden said he was going to call to allow me access to Stone as soon as he was out of surgery."

The man looked him up and down. "Warden isn't in charge here. I am."

"Wrong." A nurse who barely reached Frazer's chest interrupted. "*I* am. Out of my way, both of you." She glared at them until the US Marshal dropped his hand.

Frazer didn't have time for a pissing contest. He glanced left and saw a woman, probably in her mid-to-late fifties, pacing in a nearby waiting room. He turned on his heel and knocked on the door, opened it. "Mrs. Stone?"

She looked up at him. Her red hair had faded a little with time, but her deep brown eyes combined with a bone structure that would keep her beautiful until she was a hundred. Her daughter had inherited the eyes and face. No wonder Lazlo was hooked.

Her expression turned wary when she saw his badge. Lips pursed over barely concealed loathing. "What do you want?"

"My name is ASAC Lincoln Frazer."

She appeared even less impressed.

He looked over his shoulder. The marshal was standing guard over the entrance. Combined with military security, it should be enough to keep Stone safe for now. "I came to the prison today to speak to your husband about your daughter."

Susan Stone's head snapped up. "Scarlett? Where is she? What have you done to her?" She pulled out her cell and shook it at him. "I've been trying to reach her to tell her about her dad, but she's not answering." She marched toward him. She was way beyond being intimidated by a gold badge or federal title. "Is she safe?"

"Mrs. Stone." He lowered his voice so it wouldn't carry through the glass. "Your daughter is safe, I assure you,"—a spark of relief flickered through her eyes—"but something happened last night that I need to talk to you about."

"What? What happened?"

He looked over his shoulder and saw the marshal eyeing him through the window with a sideways glare. He turned back. "I need your promise that what I'm about to tell you stays between us."

"And Richard," she insisted. "I don't keep secrets from my husband." She stopped talking and swallowed audibly. Assuming the man lived.

"How's he doing?" he asked gently. Ideally, he'd hypnotize the woman to try and calm her down, but somehow treading on her civil rights seemed wrong. She'd already been through so much.

"Not good. The knife nicked his liver." She covered her face and her shoulders shook, though no sound came out.

Frazer used the opportunity to get closer and lay a supportive arm on her shoulder.

She pulled away. Eyes wide and furious. "Don't touch me."

He backed off. "Look, I don't have much time to do everything I need to do and I need your help."

"Why would I help you?" She began pacing with her arms crossed, so wound up he didn't know if she'd be capable of helping anyone.

"Because Scarlett tried to plant an electronic listening device in the office of the Russian Ambassador last night and now someone is trying to kill her."

"What?" Susan Stone stopped pacing and sank to a chair. "No. Oh, no. Why?" She shook her head in denial, then glared at the cell phone in her hand and then at the sign on the wall that said cell phones couldn't be used. She gave a watery laugh. "It seems I'm the only member of this family who knows how to follow the rules. I can't even bring myself to call her from here. I have to go out to the coffee shop every single time."

"Please give me a few moments to explain." Frazer sat beside her. Close. Closer than strangers usually did. He needed to establish a sense of trust, fast, and he didn't want anyone overhearing what he had to say. "She's fine, but please don't let anyone know that—no one at all. There are hopefully only seven people in the world who know she's alive and you are one of them. My team members are the others. Keep trying to reach her on her cell. Keep being upset and loud and irritable when she doesn't answer." She glared at him. "But please know she's okay for the time being."

Susan searched his face, looking for something worth trusting. Finally she nodded. "I guess I don't have much choice but to believe you." Her face hardened. "And she can't know about her father if she's in danger. She'll come here if she does, and then they'll know how to find her. Whoever 'they' are?" she said bitterly, clearly not expecting an answer.

"Right now the people trying to kill her think she's dead. I want it to stay that way. The agents guarding her will keep her safe, but I can't guarantee they won't tell her about her father if they think she has a right to know." They were already lying about Angel LeMay. He pulled the photograph out of his pocket. "Do you remember this photograph? I found it in Richard's cell."

She took it with a smile on her face and nodded. Then she turned it over and frowned at the date. "That wasn't written on it before, and it isn't Richard's handwriting." She ran her finger over the faded ink then turned it back over. "It used to sit on Richard's desk. It went missing out of the frame on the day Richard was arrested. I assumed…" She frowned. "I don't know what I assumed. That the FBI had taken it? There were so many people in and out of the house that day. A group of kids were over, playing outside after school. I remember having to call their parents to come and pick them up, even as the FBI executed their search warrant." Her laugh sounded strangled. "I had another copy of the photograph made from the negative—digital cameras were new back then and we didn't have one. This was in Richard's cell?" she asked.

Frazer nodded. He'd send the photograph to the handwriting specialists in Questioned Documents and see if they came up with anything. Unlikely but always possible.

"I think someone took something personal from him, something from inside your house, to prove they could get to you any time they wanted. He kept it under his pillow to remind himself why he was there."

He looked up. Found Susan Stone watching him carefully, but she didn't jump all over him with thanks. Too many years of no one believing their story had done serious damage to the Stones' faith in the system.

"I need your help with something else."

"What could I possibly help the FBI with?"

He didn't blame her for her skepticism. He checked the surroundings. No one could see as he carefully drew Richard Stone's notebook out of his suit pocket. "I took this from your husband's cell today."

She took it from his fingers and flipped open the first page. Her eyes widened at the unintelligible scrawl and understanding dawned. "Why would I help you?"

He held her gaze. She was a smart woman. More intelligent than the reports indicated—*don't bother with the wife, she's a crackpot*—or maybe there was a reason for that, or maybe he was reading too much into every little detail now. "I think your husband may have been set up. I believe whoever did it is, or was, another FBI agent. I think they arranged to have him killed today because they are scared that even after all these years their secrets might come out."

Her eyes filled with tears, but she didn't let them fall. "Am I supposed to be grateful that someone is finally doing the job Richard was so good at?"

"No, ma'am." The silence was heavy and condemning. "I don't expect gratitude. But I do believe this book might hold vital clues, and I don't have time to go through official Bureau channels, especially when I don't know who I can trust. So I need your help because I believe you know the key to this code and I *know* you want your husband to get out of prison."

"If he survives," she said.

Frazer was well aware of his failings. He blew out an angry breath. Not anger at her or her husband, but at the bastard who'd set this up so convincingly. "Will you help me? If you won't, I need to know now so I can try another avenue."

It took a few seconds for her to lose her stiffness. She sank back in her seat and put her hands over her face. "Yes," she said tiredly. "But we need the copy of *To Kill A Mockingbird* from my house."

He raised his brows. "That's the key?"

She nodded.

"I'll organize it." Then he frowned. "I didn't see the book in your husband's cell."

She started pacing again. "He memorized the code. He and Scarlett have those annoyingly perfect memories. I need the book."

It would take hours to get the book out here. Who did he trust? Rooney and Parker were stuck in West Virginia going through the evidence in the case files to see if they missed anything, trying to find a link between the LeMays and Dorokhov, trying to link the Russians to the kidnapping, shooting or bomb by monitoring the police and federal investigations. Shit. Too much for them to handle alone. They didn't have enough people on this, but he couldn't risk asking for more because then whoever was the real villain would figure out they were onto him. And the last place Lazlo should take Scarlett was the Stone family home—he had to assume it was being watched. Under normal circumstances he'd turn to Jed Brennan, but the agent was still recovering from a gunshot wound and even the dinner last night had tired him out. The guy wasn't fit for cloak and dagger maneuvers, not yet anyway.

He paused. There was one guy, but he didn't like owing the spook any favors. Right now he didn't have a choice. Hopefully Patrick Killion was near DC.

"Would a photocopy do?" he asked.

"Yes."

"I'm going to need permission for someone to break into your house."

"There's a key in the peg basket in the garden shed."

His friend from the CIA wouldn't need a key. "You don't think that's a little lax with security?"

She shrugged. "Scarlett might be super smart with a great memory for facts, but it doesn't mean she doesn't forget her keys on a regular basis. I got into the habit when she went to college, forgot about the spare key until just now. Tell whoever it is that the book is in my bedside table. There's a photocopier and fax machine in Richard's office."

Fourteen years in prison and the guy still had an office at home. Frazer pulled out his cell phone, but Susan Stone pointed to the sign forbidding its use.

"Fine." He had one of Parker's gizmos with him so he should be safe from electronic eavesdroppers when they were outside. "But I want you to come with me. In fact, we stick together everywhere except the restroom until I can arrange a bodyguard for you. You're in danger. I need to keep you safe."

"Unbelievable—or maybe I finally went crazy and I'm imagining all this, huh?" One side of her mouth curled up in a sad smile. "If my husband ever recovers I think he might like you, ASAC Frazer."

"Let's hope we get the opportunity to find out."

CHAPTER THIRTEEN

Matt washed up in the restroom, grateful he was wearing a black shirt and the blood didn't show. He scrubbed his hands and forearms with soap, watched the dirty, brown water circle the drain. The memory of blood smeared on Scarlett's skin was not something he wanted to dwell on. There was a very real possibility it could be her blood if he didn't figure out exactly what was happening.

He didn't know who in his organization he could trust. He needed to talk to Frazer ASAP, but the guy's cell went straight to voicemail.

He dried his hands and shoved the crumpled paper towels in the trash. Inside the store, he loaded up with sandwiches, bottled water, chips, wipes, Band-Aids, dental floss. Browsed the t-shirts and found matching his-and-her tourist numbers, a couple of quilted lumberjack shirts, a pair of thick hand-knit socks that might keep Scarlett's feet warm.

If he could quit picturing her bare legs he might be able to get the image of her naked and under him out of his head, but so far no dice. He found a travel blanket. That would help—as long as she was the only one under it. He glanced at the TV in the corner and saw the news was on. The camera panned to a shot of Quantico Harbor and in the corner of the screen was a picture of him in his dress blues. Matt wore a cap in the photo and right now he was wearing shades so he didn't think the girl on the register was going to ID him—not that she'd looked up from her cell phone.

"Can I get a coffee and hot chocolate too, please?" Something to warm both him and Scarlett that didn't involve friction.

He paid with cash, grateful again to Alex Parker for bailing him out in his hour of need. He went back to the car and climbed in.

Scarlett took the drinks and smiled gratefully as she placed them in the cup holders. "Roofie-free, I presume?"

He sent her a doleful look.

She grinned. Her hair was a mess, but it didn't seem to make any difference to the way his blood heated whenever he saw her—like his body was wired up for her, and her alone. Why did he have to be interested in *this* woman? She was ten years too young and more complicated than the IRS. He leaned over and placed the bags on the back seat. Noticed a squad car pull in beside them in his peripheral vision.

Matt didn't know if the cops had linked this car to the shooting incident. Rather than hurry away like a guilty suspect, he took Scarlett's face gently in both his hands and kissed her.

The sensation hit like a thousand volts and blew every fuse in his body. He'd been wanting to do that since they'd met, but she tasted like nothing he'd ever experienced.

Heat flooded him. Her sweetness overwhelmed him. She didn't pull away. Instead she blew his mind by opening her mouth and sweeping her tongue hungrily across his. If he hadn't been sitting down he'd have fallen over. He slid his hand into her soft hair and angled the kiss deeper. Dammit he wanted her, and she wanted him, if her parted lips and rapid breathing were anything to go by. The urge to drag her against him was huge. He ignored it.

He pulled back. Her pupils were wide and dilated, giving her the darkest eyes he'd ever seen. The expression in them was a mixture of arousal and wariness.

Dammit. He didn't want to be the asshole responsible for hurting her this time around.

Her jaw tightened and she got a determined look on her face that replaced the uncertainty, and the desire. It told him she was ready for whatever happened next in the fight to clear her father's name.

And maybe that was what it was about her that got to him, her unswerving, unwavering loyalty. Nothing had shaken her belief in her father. Not a confession, not a conviction. It was a little humbling when he was the one who was supposed to fight for justice.

The cops had moved inside the store so he ignored the fact his heart was trying to punch its way through his rib-cage, and drove calmly away. He didn't know if Scarlett had seen the police and damned if he was explaining his reasons for kissing her when all he could think about was the way she'd responded, and the knowledge that if they ever got the chance he'd like to take it a hell of a lot further than a kiss.

Frazer had warned him, but he'd thought he could handle it.

She drew her knees up to her chest, and he couldn't help looking at her bare legs.

Christ. Sweat broke out on his brow. He cleared his throat. "It's hot in here." He adjusted the heater.

She drew in an audible breath. "It is now."

He huffed out a rueful laugh. Some of the tension that had gripped him let go. They had other things to deal with. His libido would have to wait.

"What's the plan?" she asked.

He saw the sign for a picnic area up ahead. "I'm starving. Let's eat."

She rolled her eyes but looked relieved. "You're such a *guy*, Lazlo."

"Hey, I *am* a guy." If she needed proof all she had to do was kiss him again.

He drove another mile or so out of town, pulled up in a small gravel area off the main highway. Judging from the trickle of people and pooches heading down a nearby pathway, it appeared to be a popular dog walking spot.

He grabbed the shopping bags from the back seat and handed her the wipes.

From the smile on her face you'd think he'd showered her in diamonds.

"Thank you." She ripped them open and set her foot on the dash as she cleaned every inch of skin.

Fuck. Shit. Perfect.

He was definitely a guy, and so hard it was a wonder he didn't pass out from lack of blood to the brain. Now he understood why women weren't in the SEAL teams. All it would take was one look at those legs and all the guys would be standing around drooling like idiots.

Which was a dumb ass reason to penalize women, he realized.

Women were on the firing line of every conflict in history so maybe they should all have combat training. Then, when war broke out, or the psychos got busy with their knives, they'd have a better chance of survival.

His gut churned just thinking about it. Bad enough his best friends being in the firing line. The thought of Scarlett being hurt…the idea made his trigger finger itch.

When she was finished wiping her legs and then very carefully cleaning her hands, he passed her the travel blanket, which she spread over her knees.

Hallelujah.

"Thanks." She stroked the soft wool and he did his best to get his mind on the problem at hand. Not think about those hands on him. Obviously he needed some down time. Or sex. Lots of sex.

Or a cold shower.

He swallowed and looked away.

This wasn't like him. He didn't go gah-gah over women. Sure, in the old days when he'd gotten back after spending months in stinking hellholes with nothing but hairy guys and the constant threat of death for company. Then he'd obsessed about getting laid. But lately?

He figured he'd matured. Judging the gutter depths to which his brain had sunk, not so much.

She handed him the pack of wet wipes and he used them on the steering wheel and gear stick. Then again on his hands and face before he reached back for the sandwiches. He was starving. "Ham or turkey?"

"Festive sandwiches. Awesome." But her tone lacked enthusiasm.

"Yeah." He grew somber. Damn. "Sorry, this is a pretty crappy Christmas, huh."

"It's my own fault." Her lips drooped sadly. "At least I have company." Then she looked away, but not before he saw the shimmer of tears in her eyes.

Ah, shit.

He unhooked his seatbelt, pushed his chair back as far as it would go, undid her belt, and pulled her across his lap. Her shoulders started to shake as she tried to fight him, but he wasn't letting her go. Huge great keening cries came out even though she tried to keep it all inside. He thought of what she'd been through over the years, and all the stress of the last twenty-four hours, culminating in finding Maidstone bleeding out in his living room and the idea that someone had finally started to believe her story.

He hoped the guy made it. There was a good chance Maidstone would tell them everything they needed to know, now that he was on Marlon's shitlist. He rubbed his hand up and down Scarlett's back, feeling the hard ridges of her spine, knowing she needed to de-stress and let it all out.

"I'm so sorry for getting you caught up in this." She hiccupped. Her hands gripped his t-shirt so tight she was going to rip out the few chest hairs he possessed. He didn't care. "I'm sorry you aren't with your mom for Christmas the way you should be."

Another bout of tears had him holding her tighter. The weight of her in his arms was insubstantial, fragile and delicate, but he knew it to be deceptive. She was as strong as a spider's web and had entangled him in her life just as effectively. And she was super smart, which he found to be a total turn on. Obviously his inner high school geek was in heaven.

Her legs were cold. He grabbed the blanket and spread it over her, resting his chin on top of her hair as he rocked her. It took a few minutes for his heat to warm her through and she burrowed closer. Shock, probably. The desire he felt for her wasn't going anywhere, but right now he was content to hold her until the tears subsided.

"I always hated Christmas Eve." He felt her focus on his words and not on her own misery, so he carried on. "I tend to give the impression that my dad was never a part of my life, except he showed once on Christmas Eve."

"What did you do?" Her fingers had eased their iron-man grip on his shirt. He was going to have marks.

"It was like discovering Santa was real because he'd made my greatest wish come true."

"Santa isn't real?" She sniffed.

He huffed out a laugh. "My mom let him spend the day with us; probably the night, too." Matt would put his fist through the guy's face for that alone—keeping his mother dangling on a string. "But he was gone before I woke up the next day." Leaving that desperate little boy devastated on what was supposed to be the best day of the year. "We never heard from him again, but every Christmas I'd be wishing as hard as I could that he'd come back…"

"He never did?" Scarlett's voice was small.

"Not then. Thank God." But the kid he'd been hadn't known that until later. "He got in touch once when I was in the Navy. I told him if I ever heard from him again I'd send one of my buddies to kill him." Her hair tickled his jaw, but he didn't move. "I was *probably* joking. Anyway, he never tried again." His arms tightened around her. She felt good. She felt right. "I told myself I didn't want him hurting my mom's feelings anymore. I've never been a fan of men using women or deceiving them for sex."

There was silence for a moment. Then a pensive, "Maybe he thought he loved her when he first met her? Maybe it was an honest mistake."

"Maybe." Matt allowed himself a slight lessening of tension. "But he married her, he ditched her, and he hurt her. Once I was old enough to figure that out, I never wanted to see him again."

"How old were you?" she asked.

"Eight."

Her fingers rubbed his chest. He covered them with his own.

She'd been twelve when she'd lost her father. Richard Stone had been taken away by the justice system, a system Matt believed in and fought for, every day. The idea it might be corrupt was not reassuring. He didn't want to get to the end of his career and discover he'd been played for a fool by something else he'd believed in.

A rumble filled the car's interior.

Scarlett's shoulders started shaking again, with laughter this time. "Sorry." She pressed her hand to her stomach. "I'm starving."

He lifted her back onto her own seat. He was damned pleased with himself for not turning the moment into another excuse to kiss her.

Gold star for Lazlo.

He had a handle on this. He wouldn't mess it up with all the complications that came with sex.

Then she smiled at him and her eyes sparkled with happiness. His heart skittered like a teenage girl's. If he'd been anywhere except in a semi-public place he would have kissed her, and a whole lot more if she'd let him. Damn. He was doomed.

She took the ham sandwich and he took the turkey. Seemed appropriate under the circumstances. He checked his cell. No signal. Dammit. He needed to speak to Frazer.

CHAPTER FOURTEEN

They drove for another hour, down quiet country roads and through small towns all dressed up for the holiday. She didn't allow herself to dwell on the kiss—she'd seen the cops pull up beside them and knew he'd done it as some sort of camouflage mechanism even though the kiss itself had almost melted her bones.

Later, when he'd held her in his arms and she'd cried like a baby—that had affected her more. She could count on the fingers of one hand the number of times she'd been in a man's arms since her father had gone to prison.

Matt's embrace hadn't felt like any of those other embraces. It had felt super-sized and bulletproof. Strong enough to protect her from Dorokhov. Smart enough to help save her father. Gentle enough to deceive her foolish heart.

She'd never met anyone like Matt Lazlo before. He was not your average man, and her response to him was anything but ordinary. There were plenty of jerks in the world, but it seemed wrong to compare Matt to them.

He was a former SEAL *and* an FBI agent.

Despite what her father had gone through, those things meant something to her. She respected him. Respected what he stood for. Somehow in the short time they'd known one another, they'd become allies. And something else, too, something she didn't dare put a name to.

They passed a sign. Greenville. For some reason the name of the town seemed vaguely familiar, though she didn't think she'd ever been out this way before. "Why've I heard of this place?"

"It was on the news last month." He cleared his throat. "Serial...killer..." *Cough.*

The memory connected. "Agent Rooney is Senator Tremont's daughter? The one whose sister was abducted all those years ago?" A shudder moved through her. "We're not staying at the same house, right?"

Matt sent her a sideways glance. "Guy's dead, Scarlett. No one there is going to harm you."

Oh, my God. She tried not to breathe too deeply. Tried not to panic. She couldn't even watch horror movies and he wanted her to sleep in that house? On Christmas Eve? No one in their right mind would want to stay there.

Suck it up, Scar. This is all your own doing anyway.

They drove a few more miles out of town, then turned down a leafy driveway. "Eastborne" was written on a small discreet sign. She sank further into her seat.

The house when it came into view took her breath. An old, red-brick mansion, creeping vines growing over the entire west wing of the house. White trimmed windows. White portico. It was gorgeous, but a little girl had been stolen from this beautiful house eighteen years ago and you could almost see the sadness etched into the stone. "It looks like it has a thousand bedrooms." A thought hit her. "Is the senator here, too?" The woman had just announced her retirement.

Matt nodded.

Was she putting the senator in danger? Or would the fact they were staying with a senator keep them safe? Maybe it didn't matter as long as Dorokhov believed she was at the bottom of the seabed.

"Special Agent Rooney helped catch the guy who killed her sister, right?" A light went on in one of the downstairs rooms. A shiver of fear crawled over her shoulders and raised gooseflesh in its wake.

"Yeah. And Frazer shot the guy. He's dead. He isn't coming back, Scarlett."

But the ghosts of his victims seem to hover in a dark cloud over the place. She needed a distraction. "Is this what your grandparents' place looked like in England?"

He shrugged. "They had some big old country estate in Gloucester, but not enough space for their youngest daughter and her infant son apparently. I haven't looked into it. Mom didn't talk about them. They didn't want her, so I didn't want them. Probably a little immature in terms of attitude, but it works for me."

She smiled. "I can live with immature. I just don't like nasty."

"I don't like nasty either." His hands tightened on the steering wheel. He was probably remembering the important work he did, work she was taking him away from.

"Have you caught many serial killers?" The idea of a human predator was chilling; someone who enjoyed killing for killing's sake. Who would do that?

"It isn't like the way they show it on TV. I rarely get to arrest anyone." His quick grin suggested he did it sometimes though, and enjoyed it. She almost made a joke about him arresting her, but didn't want to destroy the easy truce between them. "My profiles have helped narrow the suspect pool and aided convictions, but the most important thing in catching serial killers is good police work and solid investigations."

He was being modest. Obviously he was good at his job. Good at tracking down killers. He was tough and smart—she could see him going head-to-head with monsters. She didn't like that idea at all. "What qualifications do you need to be a profiler?"

"Behavioral Analyst," he corrected, then shot her a glance. Maybe he realized she needed to be distracted from the huge hulking shadow of horror that the mansion represented. Stupid to be nervous of a building when she was being hunted by someone as ruthless as Andrei Dorokhov and some shadowy spy.

"You need a four year degree and three-to-ten years of experience in the FBI dealing with violent crime. But it's very competitive, so even if you cross all those boxes you'd need to find a way to stand out of the crowd."

"Like maybe being a Navy SEAL?"

"It didn't hurt." He slid her another grin.

A little pop of lust reminded her of the feel of his lips on hers. She'd much rather think about lusting after Matt than about serial killers. The timeline put him probably in his mid-thirties.

"The most important quality is the ability to avoid getting sucked into the darkness of the crime scenes, and being able to see clues amongst the gore—my time in the military got me used to gore." Silence simmered for a moment. "You also need a really good memory."

"I have a good memory." Scarlett sometimes wished she didn't, because maybe then past slights wouldn't hurt so much.

"But I couldn't cope with the subject matter." She swallowed to ease a suddenly dry mouth. "It's too…"

"Yeah." Matt nodded slowly. "It is."

They were almost at the house. A huge, elegant holly wreath decorated the front door. Somehow the reminder of Christmas didn't make it feel any more festive. She squared her shoulders. She could do this. It was just a house, not the *Lubyanka*.

Alex Parker stepped out the front door and indicated they drive around the side of the house. He was in jeans and a gray long-sleeved t-shirt. They pulled into a five car garage beside a Bentley, an SUV, an Audi, and a Mercedes.

Crikey.

Matt got out and slammed the door. She scrambled to follow, dragging her blanket around her waist like an extra-long kilt. Parker raised a brow at her attire, then nodded his head to indicate they follow him. Even without its disturbing history, the house was so out of her social circle the whole experience felt surreal. She felt like she was in a movie. Groomed grounds, dormant and cold, surrounded by a dense, dark forest. She shuddered as she remembered what had happened in those woods.

They went inside, through the mudroom into a big, brightly lit kitchen to find Mallory Rooney pouring champagne into glasses of orange juice. Scarlett hovered uncertainly near the center island. The last time she'd seen Rooney was when Scarlett was being questioned at FBI HQ after she'd broken into the Russian Ambassador's office.

What did she think about Richard Stone's daughter turning up at her family home? Especially during the first Christmas they'd had since they'd solved her sister's abduction case.

"Matt, Dr. Stone." Rooney nodded determinedly. "I'm going to take these through to my parents in the drawing room and I'll be right back." She headed off with the tray.

Parker pointed to the stove. "There's soup and bread if you're hungry. The housekeeper went off to a carol service but she'll be back later. I told Mal's parents this was a time sensitive matter and the less they knew the better. Trust me. They won't interfere."

"A federal judge and a retired senator minding their own business? What did you put in the soup?" asked Matt.

Alex grinned. "I have a few aces up my sleeve."

"Thank you." Scarlett smiled. Then it faltered. "But considering what happened to Maidstone, perhaps we shouldn't stay here."

Matt put his hands on her shoulders and she relaxed a fraction.

Alex's eyes flickered over the connection. He turned away and pulled bowls out of the cupboard, serving up food even though Scarlett wasn't sure she could eat.

"Right now the Russians and feds believe you're dead and no one's looking for you, yet. That will change as soon as the cops run that print from Maidstone's house. I have an alert placed inside the system so we'll know when we need to start worrying. It won't be long."

"I-I don't want to put you out," she stammered.

"She's freaked about what happened here." Matt ratted her out.

"I had the security completely overhauled." Parker held her gaze and obviously recognized her unease for what it really was—cowardice. "You can relax for a few hours. It's safe. I wouldn't let Mallory stay here if there was any danger."

The FBI agent came back into the room with raised brows. "Wouldn't *let* me?"

Parker mouthed a curse.

"Busted," Matt said in an amused undertone.

Parker grimaced. "How about 'Would do everything in my power to help keep you safe?'"

"Better." Rooney leaned up and kissed him on the cheek. "But you need to work on remembering that while I might be pregnant, I'm also a federal agent who can take care of myself. I have a job to do and I don't need you to protect me."

Parker managed to choke down whatever he wanted to say, with effort.

Rooney handed Scarlett a pair of yoga pants.

She took them, surprised and grateful. "Thank you. Congratulations on your pregnancy, by the way. I had no idea."

Rooney smiled. "It's not for general consumption as I'm not that far along. But it might help you understand why Alex is so over-protective. The pants are capris on me, so shouldn't totally drown you."

She went into the mudroom and slipped the pants on beneath the blanket. When she was done she folded the blanket neatly and placed it on a stool beside the backdoor so they didn't forget it on the way out.

By the time she got back, Matt had grabbed a bowl of soup and started eating. Apparently nothing put the man off his food.

"Is Maidstone still alive?" he asked between bites.

Parker nodded. "In ICU, but he doesn't look good. Frazer managed to finagle some security for the guy."

"How do you know the guards are trustworthy?" Scarlett asked, then grimaced. These people all worked for the FBI too.

Alex Parker grinned. "He was able to hire some people from my firm at a very good rate. Trust me, they'll keep Maidstone safe."

"But *why* should I trust you?" she asked in all seriousness. "No one has ever listened to me before. How do I know you're not just placating me until I'm arrested or Dorokhov turns up to claim his prize?" She shifted from one foot to the other, half-tempted to run and not knowing where she'd go. Was she being a fool? Was she being lulled into a false sense of security? Matt trusted these guys, but she didn't know them at all. She didn't really know Matt either, for that matter—he'd arrested her once already, she had no doubt he'd do so again if ordered.

But she did trust him, as naïve and dumb as that seemed.

Alex's gray eyes were suddenly piercingly direct and she felt as if she was seeing another side of the seemingly easygoing guy. "You shouldn't trust us. Not without more information. But know this—if I was going to betray you to the Russians or to some other unknown entity, I wouldn't do it here. I wouldn't put Mallory in danger—gun and all." He acknowledged his fiancée's stare with a humorless smile. "But look at it this way, if you're mistaken about your dad being innocent, then all we're doing is giving you protection while Dorokhov cools his jets—no harm, no foul. On the other hand, if you're right about your father, then the FBI and CIA fucked up, and there's a good chance a Russian agent is still active within the US system." His lips curled slightly. "One of my specialties is cyber-security, which means he's probably circumventing everything I do from the inside. That makes me look bad."

"*Now* you care about appearances?" Rooney snorted as she chewed a piece of fresh bread.

"Well, my future wife seems to like her job, and I want to know she's working for the good guys." Parker shot Rooney a grin that turned him from nice looking into devastatingly handsome. The glow on the other woman's face said she knew exactly how gorgeous her man was.

"So assuming I'm right," *because she was*, "you guys create profiles. What type of characteristics are we looking for in a spy?" Scarlett asked.

Matt and Rooney looked at each other. Matt gave Rooney a nod.

"Most exhibit antisocial behavior—think classic sociopath who only care about their own needs with no sense of right or wrong." Rooney looked enthusiastic about her subject. "Many show traits of narcissism and grandiosity with a huge sense of entitlement, decided lack of empathy. When they don't get what they think they deserve they blame other people and can be petty, vindictive, and vengeful."

Matt took over. "Impulsive, immature. Emotionally unstable assholes unable to form a commitment. They can't stick to one career choice, often have affairs and can be reckless to the point of lunacy because they think they're better than everyone else."

"None of that sounds like my dad." Scarlett interrupted. "He was career law enforcement, did a stint in Vietnam and was given a medal for bravery. He and my mom were high school sweethearts."

"Profiles can be wrong." There was sympathy in Rooney's eyes. "But, you're right. Richard Stone doesn't fit the typical profile of a spy."

"And I'd agree on the psychological traits of spies with one caveat," Matt added. "If someone was being blackmailed because of some indiscretion then they might spy for Russia for different reasons."

Rooney nodded in agreement. "Motive is everything. Can we actually assume Dorokhov *was* a spymaster?"

"I checked out some more of his background but frankly the information is spotty," Parker admitted. "Dorokhov has been what the Russians professionally term as 'framed' and is now squeaky clean. Even his KGB roots have been sanitized. According to documents, he's a career diplomat with modest Russian origins. In reality he's been holding hands with leaders in the Kremlin for the last twenty years—he and the president both served in Germany at the same time and have apparently been friends ever since."

Powerful friends indeed. Powerful enough for the man to be confident in acting alone? Scarlett hoped so. The idea Dorokhov had the approval of his government in killing her sent a shiver of unease along every nerve in her body.

"Have you heard anything new on the other investigations?" Matt asked between bites. He noticed she wasn't eating and pushed a bowl and a hunk of bread in her direction. "Eat."

She didn't think she could, but when the soup hit her tongue she discovered she was ravenous.

"Bomb blast on your boat is a federal investigation involving too many agencies to name. All members of Special Forces community have been told to ramp up personal security."

"I shouldn't be wasting time or resources like this." Matt's jaw firmed.

"You gave us an advantage that we needed to run with," said Rooney. The female agent turned her clear gaze on Scarlett. "Have you given any thought to just disappearing?"

She felt her eyes bug. "I-I can't. I have a job, a scientific reputation—"

"Which will mean zip if you wind up dead," said Matt.

She folded her arms. "So if you had to give up being a federal agent…you'd just be okay with it?"

He raised his brow. "I'd have considered the risks before I took the law into my own hands."

Rooney had effectively reminded him that this whole situation was Scarlett's fault. *Great.*

"You know why I did it. No one would listen to me. My plan was to call Dorokhov and then see what he said when he put the phone down afterward. That was it. No State secrets. No great invasion of privacy." All three operators exchanged glances. "I had to see if I could find any information that would prove Dad innocent before…" she trailed off, not wanting to think about the other battle her father faced—a more personal one as cells metastasized throughout his body. She closed her mouth. Nothing she said could change what she'd done. "I made a mistake. I'm sorry."

"If it's any consolation, I'd have done the same thing. Except I wouldn't have gotten caught," said Parker.

Scarlett rolled her eyes. "I'll bear that in mind next time."

He grinned at her. "Your transmitter looked interesting. How does it work?"

"It powers itself by parasitically picking up any available electromagnetic waves—not a unique feature, obviously. Output frequency mimics the nearest source within the room—generally a cell or laptop. Hops on a cellphone or Wi-Fi network to transmit data when anyone within range is online or makes a phone call." She crossed her arms. "But rather than silicon I built the chips using Gallium Arsonide."

Parker's eyes narrowed thoughtfully. "Which has switching logic hundreds of times faster."

"Exactly." Scarlett nodded. "The speed at which the chip operates makes it virtually invisible to electronic detection—"

"I hate to break up your geek-fest, but Scarlett can show you her circuit diagrams some other time," said Matt coolly. "The fact that Maidstone isn't dead is going to create a major headache for the person who tried to kill him."

"We can use that," Rooney murmured.

"What do you mean?" asked Matt.

"I doubt the killer thought Maidstone would be found alive, let alone that you and Scarlett would be the ones to find him. When they find out, they're going to wonder if Maidstone told you anything."

"We might be able to smoke him out with false information." Matt's gaze turned inward.

"So we need a plan ready to go for when they ID the print."

"You could dangle me as bait." Scarlett tucked her hair behind her ear. She'd kill for a hairbrush.

Matt shook his head. "No way."

Rooney tilted her head to one side. "I'd vote for that plan, but the trouble is we don't know if the spy or the Russians would fall for it. If it's the Russians, we're back to massive international incident and no clue to 'Marlon's' true identity."

"So how do we find out who the real spy is?" Scarlett asked.

"We're searching Maidstone's bank accounts for any indication he took payouts." Parker pulled two beers from the fridge and handed one to Matt. He held one up for her but she shook her head.

"Someone hid that list of ciphers in my father's desk. Someone, probably the same person, had to persuade Maidstone to switch the traces of the polygraph test and falsify the results."

"Who was assigned the case? Who searched the house after his arrest? Shouldn't they be our major suspect pool?" asked Rooney.

"Ridley Branson was on the team—I remember him being in our house and looking scarily fierce," said Scarlett.

All of the expressions in the room grew hard at the mention of the top counterespionage officer in the FBI. If he were corrupt, what would that do for morale?

"I'll get the names of people who conducted the search ASAP, but we can't limit the suspect pool." Parker stared at her until she wanted to look away. "Some of the information passed on was high level clearance but not all of it was specific to counterintelligence. And the real spy could have broken into your residence and planted evidence just before they set your dad up to take the fall. It's not that difficult. Frankly it could have been anyone from FBI HQ or the surrounding field offices. Not forgetting the Agency."

"CIA?" Scarlett whispered.

Parker took a drink out of his beer bottle, wiped his mouth before answering. "Aldrich Ames was CIA. The Agency works closely with the FBI on espionage cases. Someone there would know the status of the investigation and all the likely suspects."

It was overwhelming.

"So we can't rule out anyone at this point," Matt agreed. "The only clue we have that never made the previous investigation is Stone's suspicion of Dorokhov. His name was never in the files—why not?"

"Someone kept him out of the official investigation," Rooney interjected.

"Which again points to someone close to the case." Matt frowned. "Dorokhov has to be involved, because as soon as Scarlett tried to bug his office there were multiple attempts on her life, and more telling, the hit on Maidstone."

"Was he ever suspected as a spy handler?" Rooney asked.

Parker shrugged. "Not on any available electronic document I can find. But the guy rose too far too fast to be anything except a senior member of the SVR. His reputation is squeaky clean on paper—the Russians excel at rewriting history to suit their purposes."

Dorokhov had kidnapped her friend. "Did he hurt Angel, do you know? Did you talk to her?"

No one said anything for a long moment. Rooney stepped in. "No. But I'm sure it wasn't a pleasant experience."

A wave of hot then cold rolled up her spine and down her arms. "When can I talk to her?"

"As soon as the danger's over," Matt said firmly.

Whatever had happened to Angel was entirely Scarlett's fault, and the knowledge seemed to reverberate around the room. No one would meet her gaze. She'd never forgive herself for getting her friend mixed up in this.

"So our best clue to Marlon's identity is on life support?" Scarlett said, feeling miserable.

"There are lots of clues, we just have to find them." Parker opened his laptop and started tapping away. "I've set up some computer programs looking at signals from cell phones associated with government agencies and GPS units for Bureau cars that might have pinged towers in Maidstone's neighborhood today. If something pops we might get a head-start on figuring it out. Nothing yet."

"Given the now mandatory polygraphs and background checks, this person has been beating the system for years." Rooney watched the screen over Parker's shoulder.

"Easier to do when you have one of the top polygraph technicians in your pocket." Matt sounded pissed.

Scarlett couldn't keep quiet any longer. She thrust her bowl away from her as she processed the conversation they were having. "So are you guys actually saying you believe my dad might have been set up?" All three of them looked at her, but her gaze stayed on Matt. "You really believe me?"

His eyes went from cool hazel to warm green.

"I believe you, Scarlett," he said softly.

"Really, really?"

His lips twitched and she remembered the moment she'd first seen him. Humor sparkled in his eyes, but his mouth tried to pretend it wasn't there. He nodded.

She threw her arms around his neck and hung on so tight he probably couldn't breathe. She didn't care that the others were watching. She didn't let go. "Thank you. Thank you, thank you, thank you."

He wrapped his arms tight around her waist and hauled her closer. She inhaled his warmth and strength. He spoke to the others over her head. "But proving it without getting killed is going to be a bitch."

———

As Matt's arms closed around Scarlett for the third time that day he knew he was screwed. He had a mother who depended on him for everything and a career that mattered. But somehow Scarlett had snuck under his guard and gotten him *involved*. Not just because he was on the case, but because he cared what happened to her. He cared that they found out the truth about her father, and not just because it was his job. He cared. Full stop. Period.

Shit.

When she found out he'd lied to her face repeatedly about Angel LeMay being found safe she was going to freak. It wouldn't be a loud freak. It would be a silent withdrawal and he wasn't sure he'd be able to regain her trust. He'd been following orders—*yeah, that's not gonna fly after you kissed her*. If someone within his organization was undermining national security, he was damn sure he was going to do his best to stop them—even if it involved deception. Unfortunately Scarlett wouldn't see it that way.

She pulled out of his arms, which was just as well. He'd already gotten way too involved and now Rooney and Parker knew it too.

"You guys should catch some sleep," Parker said.

Rooney nudged him with her elbow. "Unfortunately, *we* need to spend some time with my parents, whether we like it or not." She twisted her lips. "Dad's selling the place in the New Year and it's supposed to be our last 'family' time together. A final goodbye to my sister."

"I'm sorry for your loss, and for invading your home like this." Scarlett sounded small and sad and alone. Damn.

Rooney's smile had a razor's edge to it. "Oh, don't worry. I said my goodbye to my sister when we found her." A hint of vulnerability swept over her features and then was gone. Parker wrapped his arm around her shoulders.

"Anyway, we have twenty-plus bedrooms. It's not like we don't have the space. But I need to give them a few hours. And so does Alex."

The guy pulled a face. "Here I thought I had the perfect excuse to avoid the whole Christmas thing."

"In which case you don't know my parents very well."

"I need to grab a shower, then we'll start going through names," Matt offered. "Let's see who's still alive. Narrow down the list while your programs crunch data."

Parker nodded and they followed him through a servant's staircase and along the west wing. He turned on the lights as they went and Matt felt Scarlett relax beside him as beautifully decorated hallways failed to reveal any blood spatters or curdling visions of horror.

Parker opened a door and indicated they go ahead. "It's a two-bedroom suit with its own bathroom. Windows are secure and there are locks on the external door." He held Scarlett's gaze when he said the last, clearly trying to reassure her. She bit her lip and nodded. She looked like a stiff breeze would snatch her up and sweep her away. Time to get her to rest.

A laptop sat on a desk.

"The house Wi-Fi password is written on the pad of paper over there. So are Frazer's FBI passwords so nothing looks too suspect coming from this location."

"How did you get Frazer's passwords?" asked Matt.

Parker shrugged. "It's what I do. I'm seeing how long it takes for him to figure it out."

"He's going to kill you."

"I'm giving him a demonstration in cyber-security."

"You hack mine?" Matt asked him.

"I didn't get your password, but I got into the system through a backdoor and read your private email," he admitted.

Matt shook his head. "Why do we even bother?"

"I contacted the company and pointed out the potential for breaches. I even sent them a patch they can use to plug the hole if they want."

"You could have charged them big money for that," said Matt.

"I have money." His smile was sharp. "Next time they have a problem I'll be the first person they call."

Matt wasn't fooled. "Bet you a twenty you can't guess my password before we crack this thing."

"I'll take that bet, but I should point out I don't 'guess'. Don't be tempted to check your email or social media accounts right now." This to Scarlett. "The window to solve this thing is closing."

Scarlett let out a startled laugh. "But I wanted to update my Facebook status to 'Still avoiding the Russians who are trying to kill me.' Hashtag, 'feelinghunted', hashtag 'MerryChristmas.'"

"Except you don't have Facebook."

Scarlett's brows rose in obvious surprise.

"Could be worse," Parker said quietly.

"Seriously?"

"You get to hang with a gorgeous guy," Parker's lips quirked, "and Special Agent Lazlo."

"Funny." Matt held the door for the guy and jerked his head, but at least Scarlett was smiling again. Alex Parker's eyes were serious as they connected with his on the way out.

He got it. They needed to talk. Alone. He also needed to have a discussion with Frazer, but not in front of Scarlett.

He gave the man an almost imperceptible nod. He'd persuade Scarlett to get some sleep, and then find him.

———

Raminski didn't know why they still had the girl, but he knew better than to ask questions. He'd left his boss enjoying the embassy Christmas party, which should easily last another couple of hours. He entered the room and scanned the figure sitting cross-legged on the mattress. Dried blood smeared her face. Her cheek was red and swollen. But she was still fully clothed and didn't cower away in fear. Hopefully that meant no one had raped her when he'd been gone. He'd purposely only left one guard on duty, not wanting to give a duet the opportunity to tag team should they be so inclined.

She still wore the blindfold, but he wore a nylon mask just in case she did something stupid like try to see his face. She was certainly determined enough. It was better for everyone if she couldn't identify him.

"I have a present for you. Open your mouth," he whispered in a low, gravelly voice. She had to be hungry by now.

Her lips twisted with disgust. He gently took a handful of hair and tugged her head back. "I'm not here to hurt you, Angel."

He almost smiled at the stubborn tilt to her jaw. He put his thumb on her chin and exerted just a little more pressure to get her to open her mouth for him. "There."

He popped a grape inside and watched her demeanor change from disgusted to surprised. He fed her another, and she swallowed it greedily.

"Why are you doing this to me?" Her husky voice scratched over his body like sharp, painted nails. She opened her mouth eagerly now, like a little bird. His grip on her hair changed until he was cupping the back of her head, soothing the sting with his long fingers against her scalp. The pain from the beating Mikhail had inflicted was evident in the stiff way she moved. In her sharp gasp as she grabbed one of her ribs.

He put another grape in her mouth, but this time his fingers lingered. He traced her bottom lip, then bit another grape in half and rubbed the broken, bleeding fruit over her lips like gloss. She licked the juice off. He could see her breathing was a little uneven, didn't deceive himself that it was anything but fear.

"My parents will be worried about me."

"Yes," he conceded.

"It's nearly Christmas."

"Yes," he said again.

"How long will I be here?"

He hooked a strand of blonde hair behind her ear. She didn't pull away.

"You said I could go home if I told you the truth. Are you asking for a ransom? Daddy will pay."

He said nothing, just fed her another grape. She chewed and swallowed and he found himself entranced by her lips, which were full and a natural, deep red.

"My father *will* pay, you don't need to threaten or hurt me." Fear trembled in her voice, almost overtaking the calm. Maybe she sensed his attention had wandered to her body.

He tutted. "I only made promises about what happened if you lied to me."

"Your promises sounded like threats to me."

"Then you weren't listening."

"Then why aren't I home yet?" she snapped. Her voice broke, but she recovered quickly. "Are you going to kill me?"

He kept silent. He'd done many dubious things for his country. Killing her was still a possibility in this duplicitous game of cat and mouse.

"If you do…will you promise me something?"

"You want more promises?"

She ignored his teasing tone. "Don't let it hurt. I'm not good with pain."

He flinched. Fed her another grape. He didn't know whom he was tormenting more. Him or her.

"I won't hurt you," he promised.

"I guess I'll just have to take your word for that. Won't I?" She smiled. With her blindfold and bound hands she looked like some erotic lover but that was his fantasies taking over. Fantasies where she hadn't been drugged and snatched from her own home, beaten, and kept captive.

He was a fool for treating her any better than a stray dog. Getting attached could ruin everything. She'd reeled him in like a salmon on a line—and he hadn't even put up a fight. The phone in his pocket vibrated. He stood and moved away from her.

The text message had him staring at the screen wondering what the hell he was going to do now.

Raminski did not like this. He did not like this at all. Dorokhov had ordered him to bring Angel to him. Maybe she was being released, but his gut was telling him no.

He knew what the man would do to her. But there was nothing he could do to stop it that wouldn't get them both killed. He picked up the black sack and put it over her head. "It would be best if you didn't struggle."

She began kicking and fought despite her bound arms. He managed to bind her flailing legs, but only after she'd kicked him in the jaw. The stars were his reward for being a heartless coward.

Finally when she was immobile, dripping in sweat, he lifted her in his arms. "Do everything you are told and you might survive this day."

She started crying. Great gulping sobs. He couldn't stand it. He put her down for a moment. Even though his boss was going to be pissed, he pulled a syringe out of his pocket and jammed it into her butt. He waited thirty seconds for her to crumple and then he picked her up again.

Scarlett Stone was dead. Why did Dorokhov want this one? The answer was pressed against his body with soft curves and slim limbs. He said a little prayer and walked her out to his car. He willed her to survive whatever came next.

CHAPTER FIFTEEN

She'd made him swear he wouldn't leave her alone.

The sound of the shower coming on and the idea of Scarlett being naked in the next room made Matt burn. The idea of making love to her had tempted him since the moment they met. The fact they'd only known each other a ridiculously short amount of time seemed irrelevant. Life and death stakes had circumvented the usual dating game rules. Maybe it had ramped up the attraction, but he was feeling pretty damn invested now.

Yeah, he had a job to do, but it was impossible when all he could think about was the woman wet and naked in the next room.

Maybe he was the one who needed a quick catnap—except sleep wasn't what he was craving if he got horizontal in the next ten minutes.

Life was short. Nothing was guaranteed.

He thought about his mother, lying comatose in a hospital bed. She always told him to go for what he wanted. People died. He'd lost some of his best friends to war. Jed Brennan had been shot and had almost died just a couple of weeks ago.

Jed had crossed the line with Vivi Vincent and was still a damn good FBI agent.

There wasn't even a real moral dilemma. Scarlett wasn't wanted by the law, she wasn't a witness, she wasn't her father, and even if that was a real issue, the case against Richard Stone was looking increasingly suspect.

So what was the problem?

He knew exactly what the problem was. If he made love to Scarlett Stone he would get hooked. He was already half-way there and they'd only shared a kiss. Sex would bring him to his knees, just like Frazer had warned.

What the hell was so wrong about being on his knees in front of a hot, wet, naked woman?

Nothing that he could think of.

Wasn't it Christmas? Wasn't this the time of miracles? Because he was pretty sure sleeping with Scarlett hit miracle territory.

He started walking to the bathroom, moving too fast for second thoughts. He stripped off his t-shirt and dropped it on the floor. Kicked off his shoes, and opened the shower door.

Scarlett let out a scream so he put his hand over her mouth before Rooney and Parker broke down the door to see what the hell was going on. Not that they hadn't guessed he was in over his head.

He kept his eyes on hers, which were wide and terrified until she realized it was him and not some serial killer intent on making her his next victim. Her hair looked almost black, plastered against her skull. He needed to ask her if this was okay, but the words wouldn't come. Just because she was attracted didn't mean she wanted sex. He knew she wasn't that experienced, didn't want to scare the crap out of her or assume she'd want to do all the things he wanted to—

She put the tip of her tongue against the palm of his hand and answered his silent question.

He jolted. "Are you sure?" He took his hand away and ran a thumb over her bottom lip. "Really sure?"

"Yes." She didn't try to cover herself and he let himself look. Small breasts, narrow hips, long legs he was already torturously familiar with. Everything about her was small but perfectly formed. Slight. Delicate. Slim. Strong.

Something twisted inside him. Maybe it was the level of faith she had in him. Maybe it was something else.

"Ever made out in the shower?" His hand dropped to the button on his jeans and her eyes followed the movement with an uncertain look that made him pause.

She shook her head.

"Want to try it?"

A grin lit up her features.

He shucked his jeans and stepped into the shower.

Hot spray ran over her shoulders and rivulets of water ran between them. He wanted to follow the water with his tongue. Wanted to touch, taste. He wrapped his arms around her and kissed her, trying to ease into this. But his body didn't want to take it slow. It wanted to plunder and take. *Slow it down asshole.* He shook from the effort of doing just that.

Scarlett wasn't hesitant or shy—a surprise, but a good one. She felt warm and smooth in his arms and very, very female. She opened her mouth and kissed him back, wrapping her arms around his neck and pressing her breasts to his chest. He gripped her hips and pulled her more firmly against him, his arousal impossible to miss.

He kissed her again, heat wrapping around them both, building inside him even though he tried to control it. To take things easy. He didn't want to go too fast for her. Didn't want to be another asshole who disappointed her.

He eased back an inch and watched as the water dripped off the tips of her tight, pink nipples. He lowered his mouth to catch a drop, licked his way back up to her mouth.

"You taste good." He was hungry for her. Ravenous. She didn't smell like lemons anymore. It was strawberries now.

"You're good at tasting." Her lips nibbled up his neck to nuzzle below his ear. "You smell amazing."

He slanted his lips over hers and took the kiss deeper. Her tongue followed his, turning the kiss from playful to volcanic in a heartbeat. Their hands explored each other, stroked and smoothed, traced contours that he'd only guessed at beneath her clothes. He reached for the soap and ran it over her collarbone, down to her navel, back up over her breasts, the dusky pink of her nipples vivid against the paleness of her skin.

"You're beautiful," he murmured.

Her eyes told him she only half-believed him so he figured he'd show her. He cupped her breast, rolled her nipple between thumb and forefinger. Her lips parted on a gasp as he did the same to her other breast. Her eyes grew slumberous, breath shallow and fast.

He turned her in his arms, his other hand gliding lower as he tasted the pulse that pounded at the side of her throat. He rubbed the soap in slow circles as he moved lower, reaching between the apex of her thighs and urging her legs apart. She opened, tentatively at first, and he was reminded this was new to her. Take it easy. Take it slow. Pressed against her lower back, he was so hard he was hurting. But it wouldn't kill him to wait.

It wouldn't kill him to stop.

She could have no doubt as to how completely turned on he was, and he didn't want her freaking out and regretting anything that happened between them. He wanted this to be something they did again and again when the danger was over.

Which would probably freak her out if she knew. Too new, too intense, too uncertain.

He slid the soap between her legs, over her slick folds, pressed harder on her clit before returning to her breast. He nibbled the skin of her ear, her neck, felt heat pour off her in waves.

As he repeated the movement she groaned, and her head dropped back against his shoulder. She opened her legs wider, making his head spin just from the feel of her satiny, smooth skin.

He dropped the soap, but he didn't need it anymore. He moved one hand back over her nipples. Her hips bucked against him as he sank two fingers deep inside her, she went on tiptoes and braced her hands against the wall.

"Oh, God, that feels good."

No kidding. He turned her around and dropped to his knees, exactly where he'd been dreaming of being since Frazer had put the image in his head. Probably not the effect his boss had been going for.

He put his mouth on her, and her knees buckled. He held her up with one hand wrapped around each thigh as he made love to her with his lips, tongue and teeth. Her body tensed, her muscles quivered, just moments before she cried out. He waited for her to recover before kissing his way back up her body.

She ran her hands over his shoulder and then down his front until she found him hard against her stomach. She wrapped her fingers around his rigid flesh and moved her hands over him until he thought his own knees might buckle.

"Tell me what to do," she demanded, kissing the side of his mouth.

"You're doing just fine on your own."

"I want you inside me."

As much as he wanted to take her in the shower, as much as it pained him physically not to slide deep inside, he couldn't.

"Matt...oh, dammit." She leaned her forehead against his chest as if she was going to burst into tears.

What the hell? Was she having regrets? Had she changed her mind?

"We don't have a condom."

He picked her up in his arms and turned off the faucets. Stepped out of the shower with a cloud of steam billowing in his wake. "I have condoms in my wallet."

"More than one?" She flicked water out of her face. "I don't know whether to be horrified or grateful."

"Are you asking if I'm a man slut?"

Her cheeks flushed pink. He was trying not to let his amusement show because laughing at a naked woman never went over very well. He carried her into the bedroom and dropped her to her feet.

"It's none of my business." She looked away.

"You're naked and I'm naked. It's definitely your business." She started to shiver so he snagged a towel from the rail just inside the bathroom door and wrapped it around her shoulders, dragging her closer, inch by perfect inch. "When I was in the military I got hit on, a lot. Sometimes I took advantage of the opportunity, sometimes I didn't. But a friend of mine ended up married to a woman he barely knew when she got pregnant after what should have been a one-night-stand. It was a shitty situation, especially for the kid." Matt was not going to repeat his friend's or his father's mistakes. If it ever happened, he was gonna be the best god-damned, hands-on dad he could be, and the best goddamn husband any woman could ask for. The fact that those kinds of thoughts were in his head before he and Scarlett made love wasn't lost on him. He wasn't about to declare undying love, but he'd known from the moment he saw her she was a woman he *could* love, given time.

He caught her hand. This conversation was about so much more than safe sex, but maybe it needed to be said. Maybe if anyone deserved brutal honesty it was Scarlett. "When I was younger I was with a lot of women, but I haven't been with anyone in quite a while—over a year now." The atmosphere pressed heavily around them. "I haven't wanted anyone in a long time."

Her eyes flashed and her gaze heated. He gave her time to digest what he'd said to her. Time to change her mind.

He turned away, found his pants, tossed his wallet on the bedside table.

When he turned back a shadow passed through her eyes. "I've never been very good at sex."

The fact she wanted to pretend whatever was going on here was just sex amused him. He tipped her chin. "You're beautiful, Scarlett. And you're hot. The fact that other guys don't know how to make love to a woman is not your fault."

She laughed, just the way he wanted her to. "The feminist in me wants to object to that statement, but I'm too curious about whether or not you're right to bother." Her eyes flashed to his and her lips formed a small smile. "But I don't want my insecurities to ruin this." He could see the nerves in her eyes, in the tense way her fists clenched.

"Scarlett, what I'm telling you here is you can't ruin it. It's already spectacular." He nipped her bottom lip, then again harder, forcing her to think about the physical sensations, not old hang ups. "How about I worry about the details and you concentrate on feeling good?"

His hands curved down her hips and rested there. His lips made love to hers, long, sweet kisses that drew her out of herself, drew her back into the moment. She put her hands on his shoulders and stood on tiptoes to reach him, taking the kiss deeper, heating his blood as her hunger grew. His hands slid over her bottom, her skin unbearably soft. Did she know how good she felt?

He lifted her off her feet and laid her on the bed, taking his time even though his heart felt like it might explode from the way it hammered his ribs. This wasn't about him getting off. This was about him not fucking up. He followed her down, them both lying on their sides, facing one another. He traced a finger over the delicate line of her collarbone and swept it slowly down her arm, down her hip. He was trying so hard not to rush this.

Her body was perfect. Small pert breasts, a gently curved stomach, narrow, finely arched feet. The sight of the dark curls between her legs made him so hard it hurt, so he moved his gaze upward.

If anything she was too skinny, which seemed to go with her hyperactive mind and the highly stressed events of the last days. He wanted to savor the discovery of each part of her, but he was almost scared to touch her and risk screwing it up.

Her hands ran over his chest, across his shoulders, and down his arms until her fingers entangled with his. He brought her fingers to his lips and kissed them. "Are you sure about this?"

"Have you changed your mind?" There was a sadness in her eyes, almost a resignation. Some asshole had pulled a real number on her.

"I want you so much I'm scared I'm going to embarrass myself as soon as I get inside you."

Her gaze heated. She pushed against his shoulder, so he was flat on his back. Now she was the one doing the exploring. Hot hands ran over every inch of his body. She kissed his chest, then moved lower, down to his navel, and his erection throbbed painfully. She touched him, and he jerked in her hand.

Unable to stand it, he dragged her up the bed and captured her lips with his. He touched her again, but there was no playing anymore. His hands got greedy, desperate. Sank between those dark curls to make sure she was ready for him. Blood heated until it seared his veins. He grabbed the condom and rolled it over himself. She opened her legs for him, and he swore his head exploded. He eased between her thighs, cradled against her heat, unable to shake the feeling that nothing had ever felt this good before. He eased slowly inside her. Her fingers tightened on his back, nails biting into his skin. Sweat broke out on his forehead and he paused for a moment.

She swept her hands into his hair and whispered. "I'm okay."

He held her gaze as he sank deeper. She groaned, not looking away. The sound traveled through his bones in an erotic caress. He moved deeper, pushing her thighs wider apart until he was all the way inside. It felt so good that he couldn't speak any more. Couldn't think.

He moved instead. Small, controlled thrusts. Wanting to make this better than good for her but trying not to freak her out by doing everything he wanted to do to her in one night.

We might only have one night...we might only have an hour.

The thought made him push a little bit deeper, a little bit harder. She tilted her pelvis and wrapped her legs around his hips and, dear God, he couldn't go easy, and he couldn't go gentle. He thrust into her, only grateful she seemed to be enjoying his lack of technique and finesse.

She closed her eyes and tipped her head back, crying out with pleasure. Her inner muscles squeezed him and the climax that tore through his body turned his brain into a white-hot flash of pleasure. Breathing hard, he rested his weight on his elbows and waited until his mind came back down to earth.

When he opened his eyes, he found her looking up at him with a very female smile on her lips.

"Thank you."

He almost snorted. "For what?"

"My first decent sexual encounter."

He pushed her hair back from her face. "You know that's what it's supposed to be like, right?"

"That's why I'm thanking you." One side of her lips quirked up.

"Hey, it was a joint effort. And it's only gonna get better next time 'round."

Her pupils dilated at the implication they'd be doing this again. If he had his way they'd be doing it. A. Lot.

He kissed her one last time, rolled over onto his back. He didn't want to leave her, but he knew he had to. "Get some sleep. I'll work on that list and wake you in a couple of hours."

He climbed out of bed and headed to the bathroom. Got rid of the condom. He grabbed his clothing in the darkness and left the room, quietly closing the door behind him. From her steady soft breathing, Scarlett was already fast asleep.

In a moment of post-coital clarity, Matt realized he'd messed up. Things had just gotten complicated, not because they'd had sex, although his FBI colleagues would not approve. But because he hadn't told her the truth about Angel. Judging from how deep her loyalties ran, Matt had the feeling it wasn't the sort of deception Scarlett would forgive easily. He'd screwed up. Big time.

He could fix it. As long as they all survived this SNAFU, he could fix it. But it was a big *if* considering the LeMay girl had been missing for a full twenty-four hours with no word from the kidnappers. And they had to find a spy who'd managed to remain hidden for more than fifteen years. *That* was an entire FBI career. Matt didn't want to think how many lives and operations had been jeopardized because of this person. He didn't want to think about being ordered around by someone who might have a knife ready for his back. What he wanted was to nail the guy's ass to the wall and then throw darts at him. What he wanted was for Scarlett to be safe so they could all go back to their lives—lives that might someday become intertwined. Suddenly he felt like that little boy on Christmas Eve, praying his father would come home. It seemed, even after all these years, all the disappointments life hurled at him, he still believed in miracles. God help him.

A knock on the door had him reaching for the weapon in his belt.

Parker called out, "Only me." He came into the room, eyes taking in every detail. "Scarlett asleep?"

Matt nodded and wondered if the guy could tell he'd had mind-blowing sex just from looking at his face. Probably.

"Bad news. Richard Stone was attacked in prison this morning during his latest round of chemo."

Shit.

"Maidstone died on the table. Cops IDed the print on the phone. Locals issued a BOLO. You're now a person of interest in a murder investigation."

————

Andrei Dorokhov strode along the top floor of his residence and entered the last room on the right. His wife was wrapping Christmas gifts with her assistant and wouldn't miss him for an hour or so. The anger that had been growing over the last twenty-four hours was poised to burst out of his skin.

Raminski stood beside the bed. An unconscious female was passed out on top of the covers.

"I wanted her awake," Dorokhov snapped.

"She struggled." Raminski shrugged. "I didn't want her kicking out the taillights while sitting in traffic. I may have misjudged the dose. Apologies, Your Excellency."

Although his expression was contrite, there was something in the man's tone that suggested he disapproved.

Dorokhov narrowed his eyes. There was more than enough anger to go around. "Strip her." His smile was evil.

Between the LeMays and the Stones they'd managed to stir up more shit than a Moscow sewer. A little payback was a good reminder of why they shouldn't cross him. He was particularly skilled at revenge.

He undid his tie and poured him and his assistant a large whiskey. When Raminski finished removing the woman's clothes he stood back for a moment, lips pinched tight. Ugly bruises mottled her skin like spray paint. Mishka had always been enthusiastic in his work.

Raminski had left the girl's panties in place. Andrei hooked a finger through the silk and dragged them down her legs. He looked at his protégé and smiled knowingly. "There. All done."

He handed the man his drink. He wasn't feeling the slightest interest in what he needed to do. "Would you like to go first? I saw the way you looked at her at the Christmas reception, my friend."

"She's a beautiful woman, Your Eminence, and I bow to your wishes in all things. But…" The man's jaw clenched and his eyes glittered. "I prefer my women willing."

"This isn't about sex, Sergio. Surely you understand that?" Dorokhov laughed, but not with amusement. "It's about power and control and punishment."

Raminski's lips tightened.

Dorokhov raised his brows. "You don't agree?"

"If you have to rape a defenseless woman to prove your 'power' then…" Raminski stood with his head bowed. "I'm sorry. Not everything has to be about fear."

Did the young man really believe that? He'd had high hopes for Raminski, but apparently he was soft.

Dorokhov poured himself another drink. Tossed it back. The angry fire seeped out of him and he felt tired. Very tired. "Get out."

Raminski hesitated long enough to look at the woman on the bed.

"Out!" Dorokhov locked the door behind the man and poured himself another drink. Truth was he didn't have the inclination to fuck this woman. Not when he had a wife who was willing and able to make love to him like she actually meant it. That was a miracle. Not one he intended to squander.

But he couldn't afford to make it look as if he'd gone soft either. He didn't lie to himself. He'd wanted Raminski to rape her so he didn't have to. Watching the deed would have been revenge enough on those who'd messed with him, and would have forged a bond between the two men that would have lasted for years.

Dorokhov sat on the bed, wishing he was more limber, less old and fat and lazy. Even the sight of the woman's naked body did nothing for him. She was too young. Too *unconscious*. There was no fight in her. No fun. The bed squeaked as he moved. It gave him an idea. The only person who knew what happened in this room was going to be him. He started bouncing gently in case Raminski was listening. Gave a few grunts and moans in between shots of whiskey.

The girl's head flopped listlessly to the side, her tits wobbled, the delicate nipples like elegant raspberries perched on top.

She was beautifully made, but it would be like screwing a doll. He bounced harder, wishing he wanted her. Had Raminski knocked her out because he'd known it would take away his fun? Had he done it to protect the girl and make it so she didn't remember anything?

There was little solace in having gaping holes in your memory. The reminder had him taking out his cell phone and photographing her from all angles.

He crawled back on the bed and straddled her body, crushing her hips with his weight. Still she lay there as if dead. He snagged the bottle off the side table and tipped his head back and swallowed thirstily. Then he poured the rest of the liquid over the girl's body and slung the empty bottle at the wall with a fierce cry.

The glass shattered and the silence that followed was heavy and cloying. He climbed off the bed, springs groaning with his weight. He pushed her knees wider apart and rubbed some of the liquor between her legs so she glistened all over. It looked and smelled as if he'd fucked her with a bottle in hand.

He swiped his hands on the sheets, then took more photographs. He gathered his tie in one hand, unlocked the door and found a glowering Raminski standing there talking rapidly on his cell.

"You're sure?" Raminski said as his eyes went over Andrei's shoulders to see Angel LeMay displayed to the world. The spark of anger was quickly masked. He closed the phone with a snap. "The FBI agent and the girl. They're both alive. Do you want me to go after them?"

Anger fused his teeth together. He managed to grind out. "I'll call in a professional this time." He tossed a look over his shoulder. "Take her back to the warehouse. I'm not finished with the little bitch yet. And Raminski…" He let his voice get low and threatening, "Refuse an order again, and I'll send you home in a body bag, *vy ponimayete meniya?*"

CHAPTER SIXTEEN

"Scarlett, wake up."

The bed tipped to the side, and she woke with a start. Matt sat looking at her, concern darkening his eyes. Was he regretting what they'd done, or had something else happened?

"What is it?" Her voice came out all scratchy. She glanced at the clock. It wasn't even midnight. "Didn't I just go to sleep?"

"Yeah, sorry."

She'd drifted off feeling sated and satisfied. Now the weight of their situation settled on her chest, crushing her lungs, and any peace she'd felt earlier fled. The reminder there were bad people out there actively trying to kill anyone who got in their way had her suddenly wide awake. She couldn't believe she'd let herself fall into the fantasyland that they were safe. "What is it?"

"You need to get dressed." From the expression on Matt's face, something awful had happened.

She threw off the covers, not caring she was naked. She pulled on the yoga pants Mallory Rooney had lent her and wished she could pick up some of her things. She hadn't realized how comforting it was to slip into her own well-worn jeans until now. She pulled on her bra, t-shirt, and sweater.

Matt went into the other room. It probably would be best if she didn't act like a love-sick ninny in front of his colleagues. Not that she was—love sick, that was. She couldn't allow herself to fall for him, not until this whole mess was sorted out and her dad was exonerated. Sex was allowable—good exercise, a great stress reliever—but letting it turn into anything else right now would be a huge mistake.

Not like me to make a massive error in judgment.

She shook her head at herself. Who was she kidding? She'd fallen in love with the guy the moment she'd seen him. Who did that? What sort of moron took that sort of emotional flying leap just from looking at someone?

There was a science to attraction—humans found symmetrical features more attractive than asymmetrical features. And she could vouch for every last inch of Matt's face and body being outstanding in the symmetry department—she got hot just thinking about him naked. Maybe humans had an imprinted blueprint for their perfect match that they didn't even know existed until it whacked them over the head with lust.

But there was so much more to Matt than looks. Everything he'd done since she'd met him had been heroic and worthy. She ground her teeth. Obviously the rose-colored glasses obscured the arrest and handcuffs. She did not want to make a fool of herself again.

Trying not to think about whatever crisis had hit, she used the bathroom and quickly brushed her teeth. The only thing Rooney hadn't provided her with was a hairbrush so she ran her fingers through the gnarly mess, pulling out the major knots and then gave up and went to find Matt.

Both Parker and Rooney were in the small sitting room too. Rooney pacing, Parker leaning against the wall watching.

Scarlett's eyes went to Matt but she couldn't read him. A little unnerving, considering what they'd just done together.

"Frazer went to see your father in prison today." Rooney took point.

Her throat parched. "How is he?"

"Alive." Rooney's amber eyes turned compassionate. "He was stabbed by a fellow inmate during his chemotherapy treatment and is in intensive care after undergoing an emergency operation to save his life. Your mom is with him."

A chill of shock shot straight through her. Her knees gave way, but Matt grabbed her before she fell flat on her face. He tugged her over to the couch and thrust her head between her knees.

"He's out of surgery and in the ICU—stable for the time being." Rooney continued, "We believe this attack is connected to your activities last night—"

Furious, Scarlett pushed Matt's hand away. "If everyone had done their jobs properly fourteen years ago, I wouldn't have needed to try to bug Dorokhov's office."

"I wasn't blaming you, Scarlett. I'm sorry for everything that's happened, but frankly I *am* angry. For you, for your father, and for me. The idea that someone in the FBI got away with feeding the Russians information that killed six US agents and got a good man framed for it makes me livid." Rooney's face was pale. Dark circles shadowed her eyes, but there was no censure there. No judgment. She should be resting. She should be enjoying her Christmas break.

Tears burned, but Scarlett blinked them away. "I'm sorry." She shouldn't have snapped at the few people in the world who were actually trying to help her. "I want to go to him," she said quickly. "I need to see my mother." She tried to climb to her feet but when she swayed Matt dragged her back down.

"Your mom doesn't want you there," Rooney stated baldly.

A feeling of cold calm swept over her. "I have to be there for them. What if he dies without me? What if he thinks I don't care?"

Matt hauled her against his chest and rocked her. He didn't seem to mind about his colleagues, or that she was crying all over his shirt again.

"Putting yourself in danger will not help this situation," said Rooney.

"What if we're on the verge of cracking this thing wide open? Proving him innocent? Wouldn't that be more worth your while compared to a bedside vigil of a man who might never wake up?" said Matt. "Christ, if anyone can vouch for that truth, it's me." The pain in his voice yanked her out of her self-absorption.

Other people went through terrible things. She needed to get a grip. Her stomach churned. "Is she okay? My mom? She'll be worried."

"Frazer apprised her of your situation. She's working with him—"

"My mother is helping the FBI?" Everything in Scarlett's life had gone *Twilight Zone*. Maybe she was dreaming all this?

"He can be very persuasive." Rooney seemed to speak from experience. She held out a piece of paper. "They decoded a list of six names of people your father suspected of being the real spy."

Scarlett took the list from Rooney's hands and dropped back to the couch. Her hands shook so violently Matt took the paper from her, covering both her hands with one of his and giving her fingers a quick squeeze. They'd gone way beyond handcuffs and Miranda rights.

"White, MacGyver, Clarkson, Regan, Weber, and Branson," Matt reeled off the list. "Shit."

"According to the evidence logs neither Weber nor Clarkson were part of the team who searched the Stones' house."

"Richard Stone had a lot of time and a hell of an incentive to do a thorough job figuring out that list," Rooney pointed out. "If he thinks they're suspects they should be suspects."

All Scarlett could really think about was someone had tried to kill her father, a man already dying of cancer.

"Regan. Is that Jon Regan? The unit chief from TacOps?" asked Matt.

Rooney nodded. "Back then he was a junior agent, now they are all high-ranking FBI agents. All six are still active."

"Regan's the one who called me in to see the video of Scarlett pulling the double-*oh* shit at the embassy." Matt's gaze was focused on the list. "Why would the guy do that if he had a big-ass secret like this to hide?"

"Did *everyone* in the entire FBI see that video?" Scarlett felt numb.

Parker cleared his throat. Matt looked away.

"At least you weren't wearing granny panties." Rooney went with humor.

Scarlett didn't laugh.

Parker shrugged. "Regan contacted you before they'd identified Scarlett. Maybe he didn't realize the implications then. Or maybe he was given the information from higher up and not acting on it would make him look suspect. Maybe he wanted to look you in the eye and see if you were onto him."

"I don't buy it. I always liked the guy." Matt brushed his hand through his short hair. "We need to know who set up that initial surveillance and why."

Parker nodded. "Frazer is on it."

Matt started pacing.

Scarlett watched him, wishing she could unfreeze whatever was going on inside her. If her father died, none of this really mattered. She wanted him free. To be released, to find justice. To live.

Matt pointed his finger at her and she jumped. "Your original plan. To bug Dorokhov and then see what he said and who he called? Can we backtrack to see who he did call?"

Parker shook his head. "I tried. Russians encrypt the data out of any of their places of business. Top grade military encryption that would take months to break."

"Can you locate all the places the Russians scramble data?"

Parker's eyes widened then he nodded. "It might take a few hours, but yes. Good idea. I'll get one of my people on it."

Scarlett didn't understand why it mattered.

Rooney interrupted them. "What's the most important thing here?"

"What do you mean?" Scarlett couldn't keep up and she was a super-nerd. No sleep and the terror of someone wanting to kill her whole family had scrambled her circuits.

"I mean, do we want Dorokhov, or do we want the real spy?"

"What do we want?" Scarlett held the other woman's gaze for a long time. "*We* want the real spy. We want the truth."

Matt stopped pacing.

"So Scarlett calls Dorokhov. Tells him Maidstone told her something before he died. Something important. Arranges a meet. Says she'll tell him in exchange for letting her live."

"Maidstone died?" A wave of guilt and pity for the man rushed through Scarlett. Then she remembered what he'd helped do to her family.

"Scarlett is *not* meeting Dorokhov." Matt stuck his jaw out and stared down at Rooney.

"She doesn't have to go, she just has to say she will. Someone with his ego and his sense of superiority means he'll definitely turn up. Also he'll want to know what Maidstone said and who it damages." Rooney shrugged. "Without solid evidence of a crime, we can't touch him anyway and he knows it. But the reason we do this is not for Dorokhov. It's to scare the spy into action. We'll need a surveillance team—and Frazer is going to ask Jon Regan for a personal favor in providing that surveillance team. Our job is watching what our suspects—the men on Richard Stone's list—do, where they go and who they contact after Scarlett makes that call. Thankfully MacGyver is in Alaska and White is overseas on assignment, which leaves four."

"Clarkson, Regan, Weber, and Branson. You already talked this through with the boss?" asked Matt.

Rooney nodded. "He's figuring out the fastest way back from Colorado. US Marshals are guarding both your parents, Scarlett. He wanted to stay but knew we needed him here."

"What about the BOLO on me?" asked Matt.

"Frazer spoke to the local police chief up in Thornton and managed to get it revoked, but keep your head down in case someone doesn't get the memo," said Rooney.

Matt rolled his eyes. "Great. Fuck."

Rooney pursed her lips. "We need you in DC."

Matt's gaze hardened. "So this is it? This is all the manpower we can spare in the hunt for the most dangerous spy in US history? We're not even field agents."

Rooney looked from Scarlett, to him, to Parker and nodded. "Yup. This is who we know for sure we can trust, and Frazer, assuming he arrives on time. Basically the plan is to plant the seed that Scarlett knows who the real spy is and see who takes the bait."

"So Christmas is cancelled?" Parker kept his expression bland, but Scarlett noticed a gleam in his eye.

Rooney narrowed her gaze. "Call one of your choppers, Mr. Parker. Maybe we'll be home in time for turkey."

He didn't reply, but one side of his mouth curled into a small smile.

———

Speeding through the air in the dead of night created an adrenaline rush all of its own. Flying blind was both exhilarating and terrifying. The noise was intense. Vibrations ran through his bones. Memories of old friends and missions he still couldn't talk about filtered through his brain. Flashes of the past colliding with the present and what could be his future, if things worked out the way he wanted them to.

Scarlett sat opposite him in the near darkness, just the faint outline of her silhouette visible.

He'd already fucked up the start of their relationship, although Scarlett had a hand in the fiasco. He should never have made love to her until she'd known the truth about everything that was going on. Parker was right—for all his crazy adventures over the years he was a rule follower. Even now he was under strict orders not to tell Scarlett about Angel being missing and feared dead. He planned to change that as soon as the situation allowed—when he was sure she wouldn't race off to her friend's rescue with zero regard for her own safety.

He'd finally figured something out.

Scarlett felt the same way about Angel as he did about his old teammates. Her fierce sense of loyalty was part of the reason he'd fallen for her. Fallen like a HALO jump without a chute. Whether he survived or not was going to depend on whether or not Scarlett caught him. His odds were fifty-fifty, *if* they found Angel alive and well. They dropped precipitously after that.

The pilot circled around a small landing pad at an airfield twenty miles south of the marine base at Quantico and set the bird down without a bump. Parker jumped out first and handed Rooney down the steps. Matt didn't know how he'd feel if it were his pregnant fiancée on the job—but he knew Parker wouldn't be leaving Rooney's side for this part of the op. They had to stick to being teams of two to watch each other's back anyway. There were too many people they didn't trust. Plus, only he and Rooney were legitimate agents of the law and this thing could explode in their faces if they weren't very careful.

He unclipped his seatbelt, then caught Scarlett's arm before she went out the door. Her hair had been calmed by a black woolen knit-cap Parker had pulled out of his overnight bag. Her pretty eyes couldn't be disguised, though she could probably pass for a teenage boy if you hadn't seen her naked.

Lucky him. He grinned.

"What?" she shouted suspiciously over the beat of the rotors.

He didn't know what he'd planned to do, but in that moment she looked so in need of not just a lover, but a friend, that he pulled her toward him and took her mouth. Maybe it was foolish, maybe he was letting his guard down, but he couldn't help himself.

She pulled back. "What was that for?"

"Merry Christmas, Scarlett."

She swallowed. Emotions raced through her eyes like sparks from fireworks. "Happy Christmas, Matt." She kissed him then. Quickly, fiercely. Then climbed down, and he was beside her in an instant, steering her away from the dangerous tail rotor, urging her into a crouched run toward the car that waited for them.

Frazer had arranged for his Bucar, a big black Lexis, to be dropped off at the airfield. Matt got in the driver's seat, and Parker checked it for explosives.

Tracking devices were moot. The whole point of this exercise was they wanted the bad guy to know where they were—or at least to think they did.

The temperature had dropped, the damp, cold air replaced by a low pressure bringing frost from the north. December had decided to hit the deep freeze again just in time for Christmas. Dew froze on the grass, ice sparkled on the trees—it was pretty, but didn't lighten the tense atmosphere. They drove in silence, the car handling well on the slick roads. Not far from the FBI Academy, Parker handed Scarlett her cell phone. Matt watched her in the rear-view.

Rooney turned on the dome light. Scarlett spread her carefully constructed script over the knees of her borrowed yoga pants.

She dialed the number Parker had assured them was Dorokhov's personal cell phone, put the call on speaker.

"Who is this?" The voice was gruff, angry, heavily accented in Russian.

It was four AM on Christmas morning. Most people over the age of twelve would be annoyed at being woken so early.

"My name is Scarlett Stone. I believe you've been looking for me." The plan was not to let Dorokhov speak. "I talked to someone yesterday who passed on information that you need to know." Her voice shook, but she carried on, determinedly. Matt wanted to wrap his arm around her shoulder but she was in the backseat with Rooney.

"I don't know what you're talking about."

"He said you'd say that."

"What do you want?" The tone was impatient and angry.

She was giving him too much room to maneuver. "I'm offering you this information in good faith as an apology for what I did. I made a mistake. I was stupid and foolish and I'm *sorry* and want to make amends. Meet me at seven AM near the Vietnam Memorial and I'll tell you everything."

"Tell me now, on the phone."

"I can't." Her voice cracked. "Three hours. On one of the benches along the path."

"No."

Shit. Everyone held their breath. The tension in the car ratcheted up five thousand percent. If he threatened Angel's life or hinted he still held the other girl, Scarlett would know the truth and all bets were off.

"On the steps of the Capitol Building, facing the Mall. Somewhere I can see everything going on. Is your FBI boyfriend still with you?"

Scarlett's gaze flicked over him. "Not anymore."

"If I see him there the meet is off and I will report the incident along official channels."

Rooney was telling Scarlett to wind the call up with gestures and signals, but she hung onto the phone like she'd been hypnotized.

"Aren't you afraid of me? Of what I might do?" asked Dorokhov.

Matt froze.

"Honestly? Yes, I'm afraid." *Don't feed the monster, Scarlett.* "I wish you were shamed and ruined the way my father was. I wish you were dead. But I'm not powerful enough to fix this on my own. I need my life back." She hung up the phone and everyone started breathing again.

————

The knowledge that Richard Stone's daughter and FBI Special Agent Matt Lazlo had not only survived the destruction of his boat, but had also tracked down Ken Maidstone and spoken to him before he died made him so terrified he couldn't speak. *Goddamn.* He'd thought Maidstone had been dead before he left. He hadn't stuck around in case one of the neighbors had heard the gunshot, which had sounded far too loud despite using a suppressor.

He and Maidstone had gone through the academy together, and he'd helped Maidstone's wife get out of a DUI once, years ago. He'd persuaded his friend to fudge Stone's polygraph as an interrogation tool. Up until after he'd pulled a gun on his buddy, Maidstone had actually believed Stone was guilty. The evidence had been overwhelming—all planted of course.

When he heard they'd found the former polygraph examiner alive, and then found the missing federal agent's fingerprint on the phone at the crime scene, he'd actually thought his colleagues were on their way to arrest him. Instead, higher ups were trying to figure out whether or not the ex-SEAL had gone rogue.

The good news was that if Lazlo or the Stone girl already knew his identity, they'd have screamed it to the world and he'd be wearing metal cuffs with a matching bracelet.

So they didn't know. Not yet.

He ran his hand around the inside of his shirt collar. The fact he lived alone meant disappearing in the early hours of Christmas morning wouldn't be questioned. His odd work hours had been another offense in a long list of grievances his ex-wife had fed the judge. She'd cleaned him out in a divorce after discovering a stripper from a DC bar had been giving him all the joy she'd been refusing. She'd thrown him out of their nice four-bedroom home and he'd moved into a smaller place.

Considering he'd put up with her nagging and moaning for more than twenty years, he didn't know why the judge hadn't given him a better deal. He was the one who regularly risked his life for his country. She was just a stay-at-home mom who didn't know how to cook and certainly didn't know how to clean. She was a freeloader, but because society punished men like him, she got what she wanted and he got the dregs.

Thankfully she hadn't known about his bank accounts in the Caymans.

He'd been enjoying his newfound freedom as a single man, cruising along toward retirement, which was only three lousy years away. Richard Stone's stupid bitch of a daughter had made him rapidly reassess his plans.

The good news was he'd always been careful. Planting false trails. Muddying the waters. Aside from that money in the Caymans, which was in a shell company, there was no evidence that pointed directly to him. He'd made sure of it.

He didn't consider himself a spy. He'd been blackmailed into it. They both had.

Looking back sixteen years, they should have just taken their punishment. Instead they'd believed the false promise of a one-time deal combined with making some seemingly easy money. It had been ridiculously appealing. Once they'd done it, they were owned by the devil. No backing out without going to jail.

He'd earned a lot of money in a short space of time but he couldn't spend it. There had been too much scrutiny to do anything except wait. Too much pressure in the hunt for the traitor who was selling out the FBI and getting people killed. The cash had sat in his bank account, growing, waiting for him to hang up his badge and take off for the sun-drenched beach.

It had taken him two years to extricate himself from that bastard's grip, but ironically Dorokhov had come up with the idea of how to get the feds off his trail—blame Richard Stone, who was always poking his nose into the case even though he'd been transferred out of the section months earlier. Then he'd arranged blackmail material on Dorokhov himself and turned the tables, forcing the Russian to leave the country.

He'd learned from his mistakes. Never made them again. And worked his ass off for little appreciation. But the Bureau wouldn't see it that way. They wouldn't remember his years of service, they'd just remember his one, terrible mistake.

He wasn't going to jail.

Only two people on the entire planet knew of his relationship with Dorokhov. Both had to die.

Sweat ran over his clammy skin, though the temperature had plummeted. He'd been in the office for hours, monitoring the situation, but he needed a break. The streets were empty. The quiet lull before dawn. He lit a cigarette and inhaled deeply, something else he could enjoy without guilt as a single man. He pulled out his phone and looked at the photograph he'd taken earlier that day, of the old woman sleeping so peacefully in her room in the nursing home. He could easily have killed her. He'd be doing Lazlo a favor. But he'd learned from a master that the most important thing in getting someone to do what you wanted was leverage. The knowledge that he'd gotten unseen inside that room would scare the shit out of the former SEAL, divide his loyalty and hopefully make him back off. Otherwise he'd have to get rid of the guy.

As he stared at the screen poised to send the picture, the burner buzzed to life. He answered but remained silent.

"The Stone girl just called Dorokhov to arrange a meeting in three hours."

"Where?"

"She asked for the Vietnam War Memorial. He told her the steps of the Capitol Building. He didn't tell me why she wanted to meet. Just told me to get the car ready."

Sergio Raminski was a liaison he'd cultivated with false promises of riches when Dorokhov had returned to the States. If Dorokhov found out the young man had betrayed him, Raminski was a dead man. And he knew it.

Thoughts raced through his mind. Why did the Stone girl want to meet Dorokhov? Maidstone must have told her something before he died—but what? If it were just his identity he'd be arrested by now. Unless…she was going to use the knowledge and the threat of exposure to get her friend released.

"Where's the other girl?"

"In the trunk of my car. She's drugged. I want to defect. Now. This morning. Before Dorokhov finds out I've been feeding the Americans information."

He blinked as he realized with sudden clarity how he could make this work, but he had to act fast. "Meet me at Fletcher's Cove. I'll make arrangements." He hung up.

CHAPTER SEVENTEEN

In her work Scarlett was confident and logical. Math and physics did not lie. Properties of chemical elements did not spontaneously change. They were a constant you could build upon. The challenges lay in the ability of humans to unlock their secrets. Strangely, espionage seemed to work in the same way. The truth was what it was. But figuring out that truth, interpreting that information correctly, was the key to unlocking its secrets.

She fingered the homemade transmitter that still sat in her jacket pocket.

Being in league with a cyber-security expert gave them access to information that would make any government conspiracy theorist pee their pants. Parker had given her and Matt a second laptop with a program that tracked all the target's cell phones—as well as their own. Plus, official bureau cars and private vehicles fitted with GPS units that were registered to their list of suspects.

They'd stopped at the "office" on the way through Quantico, and Rooney and Matt had picked up body armor and spare ammo. Now, standing in the visitor parking area, Matt thrust a vest at her, so she got out of the car.

"Under your sweater," he ordered.

She took off her black turtleneck, put the vest on over her t-shirt. He helped with the straps, making sure it fitted snugly. As nice as it was to have his hands on her, the vest was the most uncomfortable thing she'd worn next to Angel's high heels.

The thought of her friend brought a pang. They'd been through so much together. Scarlett hoped Angel hadn't been traumatized by her ordeal. She looked at her phone, which was still in her hand. She wanted to call her, but it was the middle of the night and Angel would hopefully be asleep. No way would Matt let her deviate from the plan.

She struggled back into the sweater feeling as if she'd gained thirty pounds, then pulled on her jacket.

"Take the battery out of the phone for now. Let's not make ourselves easier targets than we already are." Matt watched her carefully. It was a little embarrassing he read her mind so easily. She removed the battery and slipped the cell back in her pocket.

A few more hours wouldn't make any difference in talking to Angel, in fact, given her temper it might be best.

"Oh, shit." Parker peered into the backseat where he'd rested his laptop while he geared up.

That didn't sound good.

"Just got a hit on the money trail from an account in the name of R. Branson to an account in the name of Ken Maidstone."

Scarlett felt as if she'd been punched in the chest. "That smug son of a gun. Sitting in that office and telling *me* to be a good girl. Bastard."

"Another hit. Same account. Five thousand US dollars wired to a bank in Mexico this morning. Merry Christmas,

Mrs. Marquez." He checked the chamber of his weapon and slipped it into a holster at his side. Then he did the same with another weapon that he attached to his lower leg.

"For the hit on Richard Stone?" asked Matt.

Parker shrugged and handed Rooney a spare clip.

"Five thousand dollars?" Scarlett's insides felt scrambled. "That's all it costs to kill someone?" She placed her hand on her stomach to stop the unsettled sensation that made her want to throw up. No time for human frailty. She was playing with the big boys now and they seemed impervious to weakness. They all carried weapons. She'd never even touched a gun, let alone fired one. Her dad had been going to teach her. At the back of her mind she still hoped he would.

Parker shrugged. "People have killed for less, especially when it's a lawman in a federal facility. They'd happily do it for free. Okay. We're ready to go." Rooney and Parker were picking up her bureau vehicle, which she'd left here. "We'll get eyes on Branson as he's our number one suspect and lives in DC itself. You guys ready to follow Regan?"

Matt nodded. Checked his watch. "If the guy's on the level he'll head straight for the Center to gear up as soon as Frazer finishes the call."

Scarlett checked her watch. Frazer was calling the guy in fifteen minutes.

"He'll probably do that regardless." Parker stated. "Keep in touch using the burner cells I gave you earlier and trust no one." He threw Scarlett a sad smile. Then they were gone. It was just her alone with Matt and the idea made her heart give a little leap.

Foolish heart. They were on a mission.

"You okay?" he asked.

"Yes." Her voice was small. They were so close to figuring this out. Please let them figure it out and let her dad survive both his attack and the cancer. She'd closed her eyes and squeezed her hands into fists. She hadn't even realized she was praying until a big, warm hand covered hers. She opened her eyes. "Thank you for being here."

One side of his lips quirked and there was a fierce light in his eyes. "Wouldn't want to be anywhere else." She opened her mouth to argue but he read her mind. "My mom would want me to help you. If she knew." He cleared his throat and looked away.

Scarlett climbed up on tiptoe and kissed his cheek. They were both dealing with tragedies regarding their parents. Both needed a miracle.

"Time to go." Matt put her away from him. He was focused on the mission, and Scarlett didn't want to distract him. They headed toward Woodbridge where Regan lived.

Scarlett kept her eye on the dots on the screen. "Weber's on the move." He worked at the academy. Her heart was pounding, and they hadn't done anything yet. They couldn't follow everyone because of their lack of manpower and need for secrecy. It was more a divide and conquer approach, process of elimination. Still, that worked in science too. "So is Regan."

Matt nodded, jaw tight. Concentration levels high. "Which way's Regan headed?"

She gave him directions and they followed at a safe distance. Ten minutes later, Regan's Cherokee pulled into a low building set well back from the road. Matt drove past and pulled over further along the road.

"That's an FBI facility?" she asked.

"Can't tell you."

She laughed. "Classified, huh? You'll just have to wipe my brain with a MIB flashlight at the end of all this."

"And erase the memory of us having great sex? I don't think so." His eyes burned with intensity.

"It was great sex, wasn't it?" She looked at him and grinned. The idea they might do it again sometime hovered unspoken in the air between them.

"Damn right."

The sharp tap of metal on glass had her sucking back a scream.

A masked man dressed entirely in black stood outside the driver's side window pointing a lethal-looking pistol straight at Matt's chest. They'd made a mistake. A deadly one.

———

As a soldier, Sergio Raminski had killed people. He'd lined Scarlett Stone up in his sights and pulled the trigger, more than willing to end her life. But seeing Angel LeMay spread out like a piece of meat had torn apart his soul. He'd thought he could handle it. Killing someone should be worse than violation. But it wasn't.

He hadn't really expected Dorokhov to rape the girl. But he'd done nothing to stop it.

Because he'd kill you.

Didn't matter. Raminski was going to burn in hell for this. He'd done it. He'd kidnapped a woman who knew nothing about what was going on, who'd only wanted to attend a pretty party and meet an attractive man. They could have made love. Instead, she'd been tied up, beaten, drugged and raped all because her so-called friend had wanted to get the dirt on his boss. Foolish amateur. Ruining carefully laid plans with a single stroke of ignorance.

Scarlett Stone should be dead. She should be hurting.

His FBI contact had approached him on a street only days after he'd arrived in DC. Said he'd seen through the shine of the cleaned-up image the powers-that-be had created for their new ambassador. This stranger had understood the man was merciless and brutal. It was as if he'd read Sergio's mind and knew exactly how desperate he was to escape the dangerous treadmill of Russian politics and diplomacy. He'd fed the guy some basic information. Small stuff. Minor stuff. Schedule details. Personnel details. Nothing that mattered. Then he'd copied some files.

That had crossed the line.

They'd both known it.

He saw the white, stone house on the canal and turned into Fletcher's Cove. It was quiet. Doubly so, in the early hours of Christmas morning.

A nondescript, burgundy sedan was parked there and Raminski pulled up beside it in one of the embassy's official Cadillacs.

The window of the sedan rolled slowly down. "Any trouble?"

"*Nyet.*"

"You have the girl?"

Raminski nodded to the trunk. She was dressed and warm and safer in there than anywhere else.

"Where does he think you are right now?"

"Driving her back to the warehouse." He kept his face expressionless. The fact he'd taken her to Dorokhov in the first place made his gut ache.

"You have GPS on this vehicle?"

"I disabled it." He shrugged. "I want to defect. Now. Tonight." His fingers gripped the wheel. The idea of going back...of putting this woman back in her cell, was abhorrent. He couldn't do it.

"Sure, sure." The man nodded. The mist from his breath floated out of the window. "There is an alternative...you could kill Dorokhov."

"What? What do you mean?"

"I mean take a rifle and blow his brains out. You're a sniper. You know where he's going to be at seven AM. He's too egotistical and arrogant not to show up. There's a direct line of sight from the top of the National Art Gallery, East Building. I can get you on that roof. The FBI will leave you alone and let you escape. You return to your embassy full of woe and no one will suspect you. Give it a few weeks and you can meet some girl. Fall in love. I guarantee I can get you a green card."

Raminski stared at the dark reflections on the canal. It was tempting. He wouldn't need to defect. He wouldn't need to change his identity or never talk to his family members back home again. They'd expect him to spy for them, of course, but he'd make sure he fed them nothing of value or disinformation. He'd make himself so useless they wouldn't care if he spied or not. And the idea of putting a bullet through that fat bastard's head..."Why don't you do it?" he asked suspiciously.

"I'm not that good a shot, and we can't be seen to take direct action unless we want to start a war. We need plausible deniability. You have your rifle?"

Raminski nodded. He'd stashed his long gun in this car after the shooting in the park. Diplomatic plates meant it was virtually impossible for the Americans to search.

"What about the girl?" Raminski nodded toward the trunk.

"We'll transfer her to my car. I'll take her back to her parents as soon as I can."

Sadness and regret enveloped him. "She'll sleep for a few more hours." His throat was suddenly gritty. Alive, Dorokhov would always be a threat to him, and to Angel LeMay. Dead, it would be over. He nodded and stuck out his hand across the narrow gap. "You have a deal."

———

"Fuck." Matt couldn't believe he'd made such a rookie error. Regan—it had to be Regan—had spotted the tail and circled around behind them. He raised both his hands and spread them over the wheel. "Distracted by great sex."

The dark figure rapped the glass again and pointed to Scarlett.

"Put your hands where he can see them."

Slowly she raised her hands and laid them against the dash.

He'd let his guard down. Gotten cocky.

"Are we dead, Matt?"

The fear in her voice drove spikes through his heart.

"Depends," he muttered. "Don't do anything rash. He'll shoot first and ask questions later."

The man eased open the driver's side door and then stood back, out of range. After a few tense seconds the figure swore and raised his stocking mask. "Lazlo?" It was Regan, looking pissed. "Nice to see you aren't dead. But what the hell are doing following me, and," his voice dropped to low vibrating fury as he took in Scarlett, "bringing a suspected criminal with you?"

"I'm not a suspected criminal—"

"I saw the video, princess, which was Merry Christmas to me on account of the heels and the lace panties, but it doesn't change the fact you were snooping illegally on what is technically foreign soil."

"If it's foreign soil why do you care so much?" Scarlett retorted.

"Stop." Matt didn't know whether or not this man was the traitor. His instincts said not, but he wasn't leaving Scarlett's survival up to chance.

Regan had been a newly minted agent fourteen years ago, landing a plumb first assignment. He certainly didn't fit the profile of a classic spy. The guy wasn't narcissistic and he sure as hell wasn't an underachiever. He'd gone from the military to the FBI and, despite his acerbic wit, everybody Matt knew liked him. "Frazer just called you?"

"How the hell do you know that?" Regan's eyes narrowed.

"He told you the target for surveillance is Andrei Dorokhov? And that you need to be in position within the next hour."

Regan's eyes flicked between them. He kept his mouth shut, the way a good agent should when questioned about an open case.

"Show me your phone and I can clear this mess up right now." Matt eased out of the car, and Jon Regan took a step back.

Regan took out his cell but didn't hand it over.

"Fine. Call Frazer and ask him what's going on," Matt urged. Regan looked down, and it was all the distraction Matt needed. He kicked the gun out of the man's hand and had him down on the ground, face pressed into the asphalt. He grabbed both wrists and held them firmly behind his back. "Grab the phone, Scarlett. Check the call history."

Matt started rifling through the man's pockets, searching for another cell phone.

"I don't know what the fuck you think you are doing, Lazlo, but I am going to kick your ass and report you for this. And then I'm going to kick your ass again."

Matt could feel the fury locking the muscles in the other man's body. He *was* going to get his ass kicked, but that was the least of his worries.

There was no second phone. No burner. Good news.

"Nothing on the outgoing call log except for one…" She reeled off a number that Matt knew belonged to TacOps.

"My boys are going to be here any minute, Lazlo. You really going to throw your career away over a piece of ass you won't ever see again from the inside of a jail cell?"

"Is it him?" Scarlett ignored Regan's rant. Good for her.

Regan's attention shifted as he seemed to hear Scarlett's words and register the fact that his taunts had no effect.

"I don't think so but if I'm wrong we're both dead. Get in the car. Driver's side and start her up. If he comes after me I want you out of here. Got it?" She hesitated, so he repeated louder, "Got it?"

She nodded and hurried to the Lexus.

Regan stiffened beneath him as Matt let him go and took a big step back. It was a leap of faith. "Talk to Frazer. Do it fast so you know what we're telling you isn't some crazy bullshit, because trust me, it sounds like it's coming from someone who's been mainlining LSD while smoking a joint."

Regan stood slowly, and went over and picked up the gun Matt had kicked out of his hand. Matt didn't try to stop him. No agent liked losing their weapon so there would be reparation. Regan's eyes told him that.

Matt dialed Frazer and tossed the cell back to Regan who caught it one-handed.

He snapped the phone to his ear. "I got Lazlo and the Stone girl sitting outside my office and unless you give me a reason not to I'm going to smack the crap out of the one and lock up the other." His eyes widened and his head went up. "You're fucking kidding me."

He tossed the phone back. Matt caught it but didn't drop his weapon or lower his aim. He put the cell to his ear. "Boss?"

"This wasn't the plan, Lazlo."

"I fucked up. Is he clean?"

"I think so."

Think was faint praise. Regan was watching him carefully.

"Tell him everything about the case, but nothing about the evidence leads we're following. Frankly anyone who has remained hidden for this long is smart enough to fake all the right responses at all the right times. Let him carry on setting up the surveillance on the meet. I want to see how this plays out," said Frazer. "Watch your back. I'll see you in DC."

Matt stared at the phone and then his head snapped back as Regan hit him square in the nose. Blood gushed. Scarlett squealed. Matt didn't even see the guy move. Fuck.

"That's payback for getting my clothes dirty." Regan shook out his fist, which probably hurt as bad as Matt's face. "The rest will come after we sort out this shitfest you've gotten yourself into."

Matt spat onto the tarmac but said nothing. Regan wanted to go toe-to-toe with him, he was more than willing and able.

"We're wasting time," Scarlett said irritably from the driver's seat.

Jon Regan's smile was sharp. "Just drive the car into the compound, sweetheart." He held up his finger. "One question. Black or red panties today?"

Scarlett gave him the bird. The car door swung closed as she pulled away.

They started walking toward the TacOps building. "Her dad might really be innocent?"

"Definite possibility."

Regan blew out a breath and shook his head, staring down at the ground. "God. I had my doubts back then. But I was just the FNG and Stone confessed. *Shit.*"

"One thing," Matt said quietly. "She doesn't know that the LeMay girl hasn't been found yet."

"Great." Regan's eyes shot to his.

They hit the gates and Scarlett stood beside the Lexus, arms crossed, clearly unsure what she should do next.

"She's a feisty little thing. Let me know when you're done with her, I might give her a—"

Matt smacked him on the side of the head. Regan laughed as he rubbed the sore spot. "Yeah, I figured that was the lay of the land. *Lay* being the operative word."

Matt shook his head. Bringing Scarlett into the lions' den was a big mistake, but he couldn't afford to let her out of his sight, and he now needed to keep a close eye on Regan. Good thing she didn't carry a weapon.

"Stand there while I get the wand," said Regan.

Yeah. *Not.*

Matt followed the guy inside with Scarlett on his heels, grabbing onto the back of his t-shirt as if she was scared he was going to disappear on her. His vest chaffed against his skin. Regan ran the wand over their bodies. Scarlett grinned when he nodded reluctantly for them to enter.

She put her hand in her jacket pocket and pulled out a small, flat gizmo. "You're going to have to update your technology."

"Gimme," Regan demanded. He held it up and examined it in the light. He peered down his nose at her as he ran the wand directly over it and got nothing. "This really works?"

"Transmission radius of three hundred feet. Will jump on any cell signal and piggyback a ride home. It's not activated, which is why you didn't pick it up."

Regan looked impressed. "You know I have to strip-search you now, right?"

Scarlett backed up three steps and hit Matt in full retreat.

Regan's grin flashed. *Oh, he was definitely enjoying his revenge.*

"Trust me," Matt said. "I checked her for bugs."

"*All* over?"

"All over." He put his hand on Scarlett's shoulder and squeezed.

Her cheeks went bright enough to match her name. She straightened away from him, going all prim and proper. "I can wait in the car if that makes you all feel safer."

"No." He and Regan said together, probably for different reasons.

Scarlett held out her hand for the bug. "I'll leave it in my jacket in the car." Regan reluctantly handed it back.

Matt held the door wide while she ran back and put her jacket in the car. The yoga pants molded her skin and left nothing to the imagination.

Regan watched her move. "Nice ass."

"I'm going to kill you."

"Oh, you're going to want to." The man grinned unrepentantly. He passed Matt a paper towel to mop up the blood on his face.

Scarlett came back looking at them both warily. "What?"

"Nothing."

Regan led them through to another room at the back just as two other men walked in the door. "What's up, boss?" Both sets of eyes went to Scarlett and though it took a moment to get past the hat and the vest, all four pupils flared as they recognized her.

She shook her head.

"We need surveillance on the Capitol Building steps, ASAP," Regan told them.

Matt checked his watch. "Meet is set for seven AM."

Everyone started bitching and complaining. "Enough." Regan said. "White van's already loaded. Grab your weapons and vests and let's move it. We'll discuss on the way. Complete radio silence on this one. Let's go."

"We'll follow in Frazer's car. He's meeting us there," Matt told him.

Scarlett started shivering and the look Regan gave her was not unkind. "Park behind the American Indian Museum on Maryland. Keep out of sight of the Capitol Building."

"Roger that." Matt nodded, took Scarlett's hand as they strode out of there. They had to move fast, and he wanted to check the location of all players. See if Rooney had eyes on Branson yet. End this thing.

CHAPTER EIGHTEEN

Raminski lowered his FBI ball cap as he was led to the top of the NAG's East Building by a security guard who talked constantly and kept stopping to catch his breath and hitch up his pants.

Raminski wore shades, a windbreaker with FBI on the back, black shirt, black boots. He kept his mouth firmly shut. The guard led him where he needed to go, exactly as the FBI agent had promised. Up the stairs into a tower that was empty of artwork, then unlocking a secure door onto the roof.

"This is it." The guard turned and looked at him. Excitement lit his eyes then dimmed when Raminski didn't respond. "I, er, guess I better get back to my post," the man said nervously.

Raminski gave him a curt nod and waited for him to leave. Then he walked out onto the modern-looking structure, all sharp lines and acute angles, grateful it was still dark. He stared at the Capitol Building approximately fifteen hundred feet away. The breeze was a light, four knots, coming from the north. He laid out flat on the concrete and lined up the shot. It was a tough one. Not the distance so much as the swaying tree branches that might deflect a bullet. He stood and shifted position. Found a better angle. He checked his watch and prepared to wait.

———

The surveillance van was cold with the engine off. They were parked up snug beside the American Indian Museum with a clear view of the Capitol Building through the windshield. Scarlett shivered despite her layers, watching the laptop screen which sat on her lap. She'd put the battery back in her phone because they wanted Dorokhov to believe she was genuinely going to show up and knew the Russians were tracking the signal.

They'd followed the van as it had sped most of the way here using red lights and sirens, turning them off just as they hit the 14th Street Bridge. In less than five minutes, Jon Regan's team had seamlessly planted listening devices under some of the benches and on lampposts at the bottom of the steps of the Capitol Building. Parabolic microphones were aimed in that direction, as were video cameras.

The scene itself was utterly transfixing. Deep navy sky, cold, white spotlights making the dome of the Capitol Building shine. A Christmas tree glittered on the grass below the steps, all beautifully rendered in the reflecting pool. As iconic images of America went, it was pretty soul inspiring.

There was a homeless guy asleep beneath a bench on the south side, but apart from that the streets were empty. The Mall quiet. In most homes across the country children were getting up, eager to see what Santa had brought them. Scarlett had been eleven the last time she'd done that. She'd been a late developer, happy to cling to the fantasy until her bubble had been shattered with nuclear force, and her father had been taken from her.

It had been the end of childish dreams. The end of stupid make-believe. The beginning of cold, hard reality.

Even now her dad might die. The spy might not be revealed and Matt might be pretending to care about her just because of the case.

Ten to seven.

Jon Regan looked at her. "Ready?"

"She's not actually meeting Dorokhov." Matt stood.

"Then what the hell are we doing here?" Regan sounded pissed and confused.

"Watching. Waiting. It's a ruse."

Regan's eyes narrowed. Mouth tightened.

Scarlett's burner cell buzzed insistently in her pocket. It was set to silent.

It was Rooney on the line. "Branson hasn't moved, but a light just came on in the bedroom window. Car's here. Phone is here." But he might not be. They both knew it. "Clarkson is in his office at the Washington Field Office and Weber is at Quantico."

"Does no one in the FBI have a life outside work?" she asked. Her father had. Until it had been stolen from him.

"Apparently not," said Rooney ruefully. "Parker has gone to see if he can verify Branson is in the building, hopefully without getting shot or arrested." She hung up.

Matt's cell vibrated in his pocket. Scarlett watched him. His eyes went wide as he checked the screen, then he swore and dialed another number on his other phone. Opening the rear door of the surveillance van, he stepped out into the freezing cold air. He paced restlessly, back and forth, out of sight of the Capitol Building. Patience wasn't his strong suit. He was speaking quietly but urgently into his cell. Scarlett followed him outside, desperate for fresh air.

He covered the receiver and spoke to both her and Jon Regan who'd followed them out. "Just got a photograph of my mother sent to my email, telling me to back off."

Oh, God. She'd never imagined they'd go after a comatose woman to get what they wanted. "Is she all right?"

"I'm having them check at the nursing home right now. Then I'll get security on it." His knuckles were white. He put the cell back to his ear and paced. Every muscle tense. She knew he wanted to race over there and protect his mother. She was forcing him to stay here.

For the thousandth time she wished she'd gone about this differently, not involving anyone else. But after all these years, Dorokhov and the spy had both disguised their tracks so well she'd never have uncovered the truth alone. Someone was always going to get hurt, but Scarlett would rather it be her than an innocent bystander.

Her cell rang again. She assumed it was Rooney with another update. When she pulled the vibrating cell out of her pocket, she realized it was her personal phone not the burner. She didn't recognize the number. Matt wasn't paying attention, he was trying to make sure his mother was safe. An image was downloading. For some reason she was expecting the same picture Matt had just received. Instead, a blurred image of a young woman curled up in the trunk of a car appeared. Blonde hair was visible despite the blindfold. She zoomed in on the screen and her heart raced beneath her bulletproof vest. It was Angel. *Jesus.* Scarlett looked at the newspaper that was placed beside Angel's head as some sort of proof of life. She couldn't see the date, but she sure as hell could see the photograph of the blast scene at Quantico Harbor.

She frowned. That wasn't possible. Angel had been released the night of the party, before the explosion…Had she been taken again? *No.* No way would the FBI security detail have allowed a congressman's daughter to be kidnapped twice. She froze and stared at Matt's back. Shock blasted through her body. He'd lied. Of course he'd lied. He'd told her what she wanted to hear to gain her cooperation. *Oh my God.*

She felt cold. Detached. She understood why he'd lied to her. Why they'd all lied to her. She wasn't a team member. She was an outsider. She got it. She was used to it even. But the betrayal felt like a sharp knife in her back.

Matt caught her gaze. She smiled, hiding the bile that had crawled up her throat, waited until he turned to do another lap of pacing. As soon as he did, she slipped quietly around the van, out onto the path that led to the Capitol Building. Then she started to run, because the man who held her best friend captive was coming here in just a few minutes, and if she begged him, on her knees, maybe he'd let Angel go.

———

Goddamn it. Matt couldn't believe he hadn't foreseen this. Threats and manipulation were standard fare in these sorts of cases, and he didn't intimidate easily. But if anything happened to his mother he'd never forgive himself. His heart was pounding. The timing was crazy. Dorokhov was due to arrive any moment. He doubted it was a coincidence.

Finally the nurse on duty got to his mom's room. He could hear her breathing hard, as if she'd been running. "She's here. She's fine. *Hallelujah*." She sent him a photo of his mother sleeping undisturbed in her bed. Thank God.

"I still want you to call the cops. I received an unauthorized photograph of her with a very definite threat to her life—" He turned around. Scarlett wasn't there. He assumed she was in the van "—from that location." He walked over to the van and came face-to-face with Regan, who had an odd expression on his face. He looked past the man. No Scarlett. What the hell? Then he spotted her running up the path to the Capitol Building. Oh, shit. He snapped the phone shut and started to run, found himself slammed to the ground, arms pitched high behind his back.

"Use your head, fool. If Dorokhov spots you, he'll bail and this won't mean shit." Regan was hurting the crap out of his arms, hissing in his ear. Then Matt realized that was because he was still fighting the man and forced himself to relax. "Let her talk to him. We've got eyes and ears on them both. There are five FBI agents within a thousand feet. She's a smart woman. She isn't going to do anything stupid."

Matt gave him an *are-you-fricking-kidding-me?* look.

"Think with your head, Lazlo, *this* is exactly what Frazer wanted to happen and you know it. That crafty sonofabitch is probably the one who called her out there."

"I want to know who made that call." Matt drew in a deep breath. Not that easy when he was flattened by two-hundred and twenty pounds of muscle. "And get the fuck off me."

"Promise you're going to get in the van and behave yourself?"

"Yes, sir." Matt was feeling lethal on the inside, but not at Regan. He needed to talk to Parker, needed to know about the call that had made Scarlett race away. If it was Frazer he was going to punch the guy out for manipulating him, boss or not.

He also needed to check where all the players were. The plan hadn't changed. Scarlett should be relatively safe since Dorokhov had to maintain some sense of decorum given the location. He was on camera from twenty different angles regardless of FBI surveillance, and surely he knew that.

Regan let Matt up. He brushed the icy dew off his pants and Regan indicated Matt go ahead of him into the van. On the surveillance monitors Matt watched Scarlett hurry down the path. He was going to tan her ass when he got hold of her, assuming he didn't choke to death on fear first.

He dialed Parker, simultaneously checking the laptop screen for the locations of their suspects and watching Scarlett.

No one had moved. Why the heck did he feel like all hell was about to break loose? He scanned everything frantically, searching for answers. Then a large, black limousine, bearing the white, blue, and red striped flags of the Russian Federation, cruised up Pennsylvania Avenue.

Parker finally answered the damn phone. "Branson is in his kitchen along with his wife, stuffing the turkey—that's not a euphemism."

"Scarlett just got a call on her cell. Who was it?"

Matt heard Parker tapping few keys. "Came from a burner. An image was sent from DC, and...ah, shit. We're busted. It's a photograph of Angel in the trunk of a car with today's newspaper."

Shit.

"Dorokhov is here," Matt told the other man.

"Branson didn't personally send that image. I was watching him at that exact time. But we were working on the assumption the Russians had Angel LeMay. Do we sit on him or come to you?"

"Even though the evidence points to him, Branson feels wrong."

"Yeah. That's what my instincts are telling me too."

The other phones hadn't moved from their offices. Matt didn't like this. He didn't like it at all. Dammit. "Stay on him. Let's see this through."

Matt hung up, then held his breath as a driver opened the limousine door. The burly figure of Andrei Dorokhov pulled himself out of the back seat. The ambassador looked around in the pre-dawn quiet.

"Remember." Regan smacked him in the chest. "First and foremost he's the representative of Russia on US soil. Do not create a diplomatic incident that loses all of us our jobs and starts World War III. Under-fucking-stood?"

Matt nodded, but every step the sonofabitch took toward Scarlett was one step too close.

———

Scarlett physically shook as she stood at the bottom of the Capitol Building steps and watched Andrei Dorokhov walk toward her. His face was haggard, eyes bloodshot, hair dirty-blond and greasy. Thick stubble covered his cheeks and jaw. He was gruffly handsome and exuded a sense of forcefulness that sent a shiver through her entire body. He had her friend in the trunk of a car—maybe even that car. The idea made her want to throw up. What had he done to her?

He nodded toward a bench. "Come. Sit." He indicated she go first. The only person close-by was the homeless guy who was covered by a thin blanket at the far end of the steps. He had long, filthy dreadlocks, which stuck out the top of the blanket, and he hadn't moved an inch. Maybe he was dead. More likely, he was one of Dorokhov's bodyguards, planted early to protect the man.

Ha! Like *she* was a threat. She sat, keeping most of the bench between them. She cleared her throat. "I wanted to apologize for what I tried to do the other night."

"*Tried* to do?" His voice rumbled, and she smelled alcohol on his breath. He'd definitely been drinking.

Damn—what could she say to that? She could hardly say, *oh, no it was the FBI who actually bugged you, not me.* Despite everything, she was a patriot. She had no more desire to betray her country than her father had. "What I *did*. Unsuccessfully." Very unsuccessfully.

He snorted out a laugh. "You Americans." He shook his head. "Is there a reason I shouldn't press charges? Espionage is not something we treat lightly." His gaze was shrewd, assessing as it traveled over her.

She pinched her lips together, then blurted, "I want my friend released. Unharmed."

His eyes narrowed. He looked like a snake about to strike, and Scarlett was careful not to make any sudden moves.

She rushed on. "Before Mr. Maidstone died he told me there were photographs."

Dorokhov's chin came up, eyes full of crimson fury.

She'd been bluffing, but obviously she'd hit the jackpot. Her heart banged in her chest. Her fingers clenched each other for comfort.

"I want those photographs." He stood, and she tried not to cower before him.

Scarlett was terrified, but she couldn't afford to let it show. "I want my friend back. Release her, and I'll tell you where the photographs are."

His hand shot out, and he grabbed her round the throat. "Tell me now."

She was aware of several things happening at once. Pain streaked from her ears to her lungs, down her throat, as his iron grip tightened. The sound of running feet behind her, the vision of two men getting out of the Russian's limousine and running toward them, hands reaching into their jackets.

Then Dorokhov seemed to come back into himself, and he loosened his grip, turning it into a caress, though her neck was sore as hell. "Get me the photos, and I'll find you the girl." He stepped back with his hands raised as if in surrender, and everyone stopped moving. And then, as the first glimmer of dawn shimmered on the eastern edge of the horizon, Dorokhov's head exploded.

———

A fierce sense of satisfaction rushed through Raminski as the bullet hit its target dead center. He would have gone for the girl too, except there wasn't time. He had to get out fast. He ran down the stairs and through the Mezzanine gallery. Out the same way he'd come in.

The sight of the guard's body beside the security desk had him skidding to a halt across the floor. *What…?*

The first bullet hit him in the upper leg and shattered bone like a rocket. He went down hard, the rifle sliding across the floor.

Blood pumped frantically from the wound. He dragged himself toward the rifle knowing he wasn't going to get there before the next bullet hit. It was the other leg this time, the pain just as excruciating. He rolled onto his back, panting, so he could see the face of his murderer.

The American. The FBI agent.

His hands tried to stop the bleeding. "Why?" he asked. "Haven't I done everything you asked?"

———

"You did, Sergio. I'm sorry." He pulled the trigger again—headshot this time.

The FBI agent put the handgun that had killed the guard beside the dead Russian and placed the guard's gun back in the dead man's palm. He wore latex gloves beneath a thin, woolen pair. He moved carefully, making sure he didn't track blood with him. The feds would arrive shortly and see that the night guard had discovered the sniper who'd killed Ambassador Dorokhov trying to escape and died in a shootout.

Terribly sad. Very brave. The guy deserved a medal.

Raminski would take the fall as a disgruntled employee—maybe rumors would circulate that the Russians themselves had offed Dorokhov but wanted to make it look like the Americans did it, only to be foiled by Barney Fife.

The threat of war would be averted, and he'd use the ensuing storm to disappear from view. One last loose end to tie up, and he'd already baited that trap.

It might not be the perfect crime, but it was pretty damn good. He slid out into the shadows and the coming dawn.

———

As soon as Dorokhov grabbed Scarlett, Matt started running. He didn't care about the mission or the spy or anything, just getting Scarlett away from that fat, ugly sonofabitch so he couldn't hurt her—and possibly beating the crap out of the asshole for laying hands on her—diplomatic immunity be damned.

He was done following orders.

He leaped over hedges and hurdled small walls, realizing he should never have listened to Regan or Frazer. This was a stupid plan, and they were no closer to figuring out who the traitor was than they had been yesterday morning. Scarlett's original idea had been more sensible—and that had fucking sucked too.

His feet pounded the ground, and he was aware of Jon Regan in close pursuit. Then he saw Dorokhov's bodyguards get out of the car, and the homeless guy roll out of the bench where he slept and jump to his feet, weapon in hand, and Matt pushed harder. No way was he about to let the Russians grab Scarlett. No goddamned way.

His arms pumped, lungs burned, but he was still fifty feet away when a rifle shot rang out. He ran harder. Blood sprayed in a wide arc and Dorokhov toppled over.

"Get down!" he shouted, the words echoing off the hallowed stone above him. The homeless guy grabbed Scarlett and pushed her to the ground, behind a low stone wall. Matt finally recognized his boss. He dove for cover next to them, breathing hard. Jon Regan plowed in beside them. They all lay there panting, catching their breath. Dorokhov's body twitched on the sidewalk, gruesome. Frazer was on his cell, calling in emergency response teams from the local cops—hopefully getting backup that would find the shooter and not arrest them on the spot.

Frazer ran in a crouch toward the Russians—FBI creds on display, pointing toward the north side of the Mall where the shot had come from, and indicating they keep low.

The Russian bodyguards looked toward their fallen comrade who was obviously beyond anyone's help and climbed back in the vehicle, which was probably the safest place they could be right now.

"You okay?" Matt asked Scarlett. He turned her toward him. She nodded but seemed unable to speak. There was blood on her cheek. He wiped it away with his thumb, but her eyes were wide and pupils dilated. In the totally freaked-out-zone. The fingermarks on her neck made him glad the asshole was dead, but not like that, not in front of Scarlett. The realization she could have been killed as easily as Dorokhov made him sick to his stomach.

He grabbed Jon Regan by the collar. "Who ordered that initial surveillance?"

Regan bared his teeth. "I can't be here, Lazlo. If I'm called to testify on the stand then my TacOps career is finished."

Matt didn't let go. This was bigger than any of their careers. "Tell me who ordered it. Was it Branson?"

Regan shook his head. "It's fucking *classified*." Then his gaze shifted to the prostrate form on the concrete. "Shiiit."

He seemed to realize how big this thing had blown. "The request came from the WFO." Washington Field Office. "Guy Clarkson applied for the wire tap for eyes on Dorokhov."

"Wouldn't that sort of thing usually come from the counterespionage section?"

"Sure, but not always. Plus, Clarkson and Branson were always tight. Branson used to run requests through Clarkson all the time. Things he didn't want an official paper trail to."

Could Branson be using Clarkson as cover, or was it the other way around?

"There's no way it's him…" Suddenly Regan didn't sound so sure. Sirens started screaming all over the city. "I was never here." He took off back to the surveillance van and Matt let him go. They had nothing to lose by making this investigation official now. The spy already knew they were looking for him. He'd be set to run if he wasn't long gone already.

Frazer came back.

"We need someone to head over to the WFO to talk to Clarkson," said Matt. "Regan just told me that's who ordered the surveillance on Dorokhov. He also said Clarkson often does 'favors' for Branson. They're both still firmly in the frame."

Frazer nodded. "I'll have to stay here." He looked pissed.

Matt hauled Scarlett into his arms and just held her for a few more moments protected by solid concrete as she shook from the aftereffects of the assassination.

"Could they have been shooting at me?" she asked.

"They might have been."

"A vest wouldn't have been much good against that…" She nodded toward Dorokhov's corpse and started to cry. Brain matter oozed onto the sidewalk.

He hugged her closer as a chill ran through him. "Time to move."

Frazer was on his cell again. "Shot came from the National Art Gallery. Police have been dispatched. We need to get Scarlett back to the surveillance van and to safety."

Matt nodded. There was a lot of exposed ground between here and there, but chances were the shooter was long gone, assuming this wasn't a suicide mission. He kept his body between Scarlett and the direction from where the shot had come. Frazer on her other side.

"You could have filled me in on your plan," said Matt angrily to his boss.

"I didn't have time."

"Nice dreads," he muttered.

His boss's mouth curved. "The best I could come up with when every costume shop in North America was closed." He scratched his head. "I think it has fleas."

They reached the white van. Regan and his team were huddled inside looking at monitors for a potential sniper. Matt caught a blanket that Regan tossed him, then wrapped it around Scarlett as he sat her on the step of the van.

"It's not over, is it?" Her eyes were red-rimmed from fatigue, but her brain was turning again. "You lied to me about Angel."

He stared at her. Held that bottomless brown gaze. Nodded. Her gaze drifted away from his, and he felt a little twist in his gut. "I needed you to stop trying to go to the guy. To let the professionals handle it."

"You treated me like a suspect."

"I treated you like a civilian."

"You treated me like a criminal," she spat the words in his face.

"Not true." His voice got loud and suddenly he was yelling. "I don't make love to suspects, and I don't fall in love with criminals." Shit. He looked around and realized everyone had stopped what they were doing and were watching the show. He dragged his hand through his hair, surprised he wasn't bald from the stress of having this woman in his life. Thirty-six hours they'd known each other, and he was willing to sacrifice everything for her.

She didn't respond to his untimely declaration. Maybe she didn't believe him, or maybe she just didn't care. She was definitely in shock and considering what had just happened, he wasn't surprised. He was being an ass.

"How are we going to find Angel? What if she's dead?"

Guilt was a terrible thing. He put his hands on either side of her head and stared into her eyes, willing her to believe in him. "We'll find her. I promise."

Regan stuck his head out the door. "We're looking for her. We have people working on the metadata of both the image that was sent to Agent Lazlo of his mother, and the one of Angel LeMay that was sent to you. Both came from the same phone."

Police cruisers and cars were starting to fill up the Mall. It was still shadowy and dark. Just the glimmer of Christmas morning creeping into the sky. Frazer pulled off his wig and flung it on the ground before going to talk to the first responders.

A car pulled up on Maryland. A silver Mercedes. Angel LeMay's mother got out, eyes frantically searching the crowd until they found Scarlett.

The woman started running toward them. Matt braced himself for anger, but the woman just opened her arms, and Scarlett went into them willingly. More willingly than she'd accepted his recent comfort.

Because you lied to her, idiot, and then yelled your declaration of love like an insult.

Mrs. LeMay stroked Scarlett's hair, but looked at him. "Have you found her yet?" Her voice cracked.

"No, ma'am. Not yet."

She blinked away tears. "I can't find my husband. He went out an hour ago, said he was going to look for Angel as no one else seemed to be doing anything." She swallowed noisily. "I have two FBI agents sitting uselessly in my house when they could be out scouring the streets." She seemed to bite back her anger. "I'm taking Scarlett home with me."

Frazer shouted over to him. "Cops found the sniper over at NAG. Shot dead by the security guard. Let's go."

Matt didn't want to leave Scarlett, but he had a job to do. From the events of today alone there promised to be hours of debriefing and reports and God Almighty fallout to manage.

Scarlett looked at him, eyes wide and beseeching. There would be plenty of questioning for her too, but she was dead on her feet. She should be safe enough at the LeMay's with the FBI agents there.

Matt nodded. He wanted to touch her. Kiss her. "Get a few hours' sleep. You'll need to talk to investigators." He wanted to tell her he was sorry and that he loved her, but he'd already shouted it to the world. *Shit.* Maybe she wasn't interested. Maybe she'd never forgive him.

Mrs. LeMay kept her arm around Scarlett as she helped her back to the car. She tucked the blanket around Scarlett's knees and then hurried around to the driver's side. She slipped inside and drove quickly away.

The sight of Scarlett leaving dug a crater in his chest. He turned away and went back to the van to grab Parker's laptop and followed Frazer at a run across the Mall. It was time to find the real spy and shut the bastard down. Proving Richard Stone's innocence might be his only way into Scarlett's heart. It was certainly the only way he could get the man justice. He just hoped it was enough.

——

Scarlett had never felt so cold in her entire life. It was like her bones had been dipped in liquid Nitrogen.

"I am s-s-sorry about Angel, Mrs. LeMay." Her teeth chattered. "The FBI told me she'd been released. I never meant to get her inv-v-volved."

Angel's mother's lips tightened, but she nodded. "I know you didn't. You were just trying to help your father." She turned the heat up. They did a big loop around the Library of Congress, back onto Pennsylvania Avenue, headed north on 6th Street.

Scarlett huddled deeper into the blanket. Last she'd heard, her dad had been stable. She hoped he was still okay. Maybe they were lying about that too? No. She understood why Matt had told her Angel was free. She'd have gone to Dorokhov and probably wound up dead. He'd saved her life too many times to doubt him. He'd been right to stop her. Right to lie.

His lies had ironically helped start the process of redeeming her father, and rebuilding her faith in the system.

She wasn't all the way there yet, but at least some people in the FBI believed in her father and wanted the truth. She stopped shivering, the heater finally doing its job.

The look on Matt's face…She blinked as she realized he'd told her he loved her. Her throat got tight as emotion swelled. Matt Lazlo loved her. *Her.* The daughter of Richard Stone. It seemed too much to believe and yet, despite everything, she did believe him. She loved him back. It didn't make any sense, was founded on instinct rather than logic, but instinct had been around for a lot longer than either of them, so who was she to argue?

She sat up a little. She hadn't told him. In fact she had been too traumatized to even acknowledge his words. What if he thought she wasn't interested? What if he thought she'd just used him to get her father's case reopened?

She pulled out her cell phone.

"What are you doing?" Mrs. LeMay asked.

"Calling Matt. Agent Lazlo."

Mrs. LeMay pulled out her own cell and texted a message while driving. She left the cell in her lap.

"Lazlo." Matt answered straight away.

"It's Scarlett."

"You okay?" His voice was wary.

"Yes, I mean, not completely." She swallowed hard. "It isn't every day you see a man's head blown off." The words brought the image sharply back to life and she pressed her hand across her mouth. "But I'm okay."

"Good. We found the shooter. Remember the other guy from the party?"

Raminski? "Really?" What did that mean?

"I can't say any more right now."

"No, no of course not." The fact he'd told her anything at all showed he trusted her. She'd been a fool. "I wanted to say sorry for what happened. I should have listened to you. Trusted you." But some anger at his betrayal remained. "You should have trusted me. You shouldn't have lied about something so important." She swallowed. "Especially not after we..."

There was a long pause. "Look, Scarlett, when this is over, you and I need to talk. Please don't leave the LeMay residence." He sounded clipped and tense. Was he regretting his earlier declaration of love?

She opened her mouth to tell him how she felt, but lost her nerve. Maybe now wasn't the time. "Find the real spy, Matt. For my father."

"I intend to." He disconnected.

Had she screwed that up too? Had she ruined the best thing to happen to her in years by acting impulsively and not trusting Matt to do his job?

Mrs. LeMay turned right on New York Avenue.

"Aren't you going the wrong way?" Scarlett pointed out gently.

Mrs. LeMay blinked at her. "I want to check the cemetery. Adam's mother is buried there and we go every Christmas Eve normally. I thought he might have gone there..." Her voice trailed off.

"Where's Sarah?" Scarlett asked.

"We haven't told her yet. The FBI seemed so sure they'd get Angel back, and it's not like she can do anything to help." She bit her lip, clearly torn with the decision. "She'd insist on coming back, and she's probably safer in Utah."

Scarlett clenched her fists. Keeping her in the dark to protect her—just as Matt had done with her. This was all her fault. "I'm very sorry, Mrs. LeMay."

Valerie's brown eyes held hers for a moment before she looked away. "You should never have tried to bug him."

Scarlett winced. She wasn't going to argue about that with this woman. Not while her daughter was missing.

There was no traffic on the road. The whole city seemed deserted. It was only ten minutes from when they left the Mall until they were driving through the stone pillars that marked the Mt. Olivet Cemetery. Although dawn had begun to break along the horizon, it was still dark and creepy. "You really think he came out here? In the dark?"

"He's heartbroken, Scarlett." Mrs. LeMay headed north toward the mausoleum. "I'm worried he's going to do something stupid."

Oh, God. The idea that Angel's dad might harm himself made Scarlett shake off any remaining self-pity. She threw off the blanket and scanned the massive cemetery, frantically looking for Congressman LeMay. Finally she spotted the bulky shape of a car up ahead on the right. "Is that him there?"

Mrs. LeMay squinted ahead. "I think it is."

Scarlett' eyes bulged when the woman pulled out a pistol and pointed it right at her.

CHAPTER NINETEEN

Matt stared down at the body of Sergio Raminski. The guy had made a bloody mess of the art gallery. The poor old guard probably hadn't stood a chance. Something about the scene was niggling at him.

At the back of his mind something else was niggling at him too. Too many facts to chase down and clarify. Too many loose ends.

Matt stared at the single shot, bolt-action ArmaLite AR-50 sniper rifle. Functional, utilitarian, nothing too fancy, but in the right hands would get the job done. There was a pistol, a Glock on the floor. What was bothering him about the scene? "The rifle has a left-hand grip."

Frazer's eyes flashed to the rifle then the pistol. The pistol was a right-handed grip.

"It's possible he was ambidextrous."

Matt nodded. Good law enforcement officers always practiced with both hands, but they tended to have a preference and stick to it. He stared back at the guard.

There was a knock on the entry doors. A uniformed officer looked over at them. Frazer nodded and Rooney and Parker came in, careful of the blood spatter.

Distaste showed on both their faces. "Branson hasn't moved and doesn't look like he's going anywhere. Parker even managed to get inside Branson's private computer and there was no record of any of the banking transactions we discovered earlier."

"He could have gone to an internet café," suggested Matt.

"Except a guy in his position barely gets to piss on his own, let alone wander off to an internet café. We called the WFO." Parker looked like he had something to share. "An FBI agent name of Rosemary Fatima picked up. Said she was the only one in the office. I asked her to check Clarkson's office, and she said it was empty. His cell phone was there though, sitting right on his desk."

They'd been tracking his cell assuming it was with the man. Mistake.

"Clarkson is looking more and more like the culprit. I need to bring Branson in on this," said Frazer.

"Why not go straight to the head of Counterintelligence Division?" Rooney asked.

"Because Branson might be able to tell us something we can use to find Clarkson, especially if he discovers the guy has been setting him up for the fall all these years," said Frazer.

"Just like he set up Stone," said Matt.

Parker nodded. "The back-up, back-up plan." Then he pointed to the dead Russian. "Staged."

"How can you tell?" asked Frazer.

So fast?

"Shell casings." Parker pointed at the floor. "They're all congregated on the other side of the room. None behind this guy. You obviously spotted our man here was a southpaw." He pointed at Raminski.

Matt nodded, relieved he'd at least noticed that. "Good eyes. How'd you know so fast?"

Parker's expression closed down, and Matt didn't want to know why.

"Where's Scarlett?" Rooney asked.

"Angel's mother came to the Mall and took her home with…her." He stumbled to a stop as something odd hit him. "How the hell did she know we were gonna be there? With Scarlett?" He looked at Frazer, but suddenly knew they'd made a massive mistake. He called Scarlett's cell while Frazer dialed the FBI agents at the LeMay household.

Scarlett didn't answer. Fuck. Crap.

"Adam LeMay is there? You're certain?" Frazer asked, catching Matt's eye. She'd told them her husband was out searching for Angel. "Ask him where he thinks his wife went. He doesn't know? Fine. Give me her plates and vehicle type. Thanks." He called the local cops. "I need an APB out on one Valerie LeMay, driving a silver Mercedes." He reeled off the registration.

"Her phone is off." Parker was typing into his laptop one-handed. "Shit. I missed it. One Valerie *Jones* once worked as a secretary at FBI HQ—she kept her maiden name for work. She left about a year before Stone was arrested. I bet that's how the LeMays and Stones became friends. Families with kids of similar ages hanging out?"

"She could have taken the photograph from the home on the day of Stone's arrest." Frazer looked pissed. "She could have planted the ciphers and damning information the other agents found there."

"She can't have carried out the hit on Maidstone or taken that photograph of Lazlo's mother because the FBI were with her for most of the day. So she has an accomplice—probably Clarkson," said Rooney.

"Doesn't matter *how* she's involved, she's involved." Matt spoke with sudden clarity. "We need to find her." Because she'd just driven off with the woman he loved. "Scarlett's cell isn't working."

Parker nodded. "No signal visible. Either disabled or jammed."

"Scarlett had a second bug in her jacket pocket. Can you trace it?"

Parker grimaced. "I can try, but we don't know the transmission frequency—she says it jumps on a cell signal? And if they are using a signal jammer we won't find anything anyway. Not until they turn it off."

Matt thought frantically. "Can you see the areas in the city where signals are being jammed?"

Parker's eyes lit up. "Yeah. Should be easy to see depending on the radius of the jammer, but it might take a little while." He began typing again.

They didn't have time.

Rooney was on her cell. "Cops got traffic-cam hits on the plates, heading north on New York Avenue. Let's go."

"No sirens. Let Parker drive," Frazer ordered.

Matt started to argue that Parker was working his magic on the computer, but his boss was adamant. "Trust me. It'll be faster."

———

"Mrs. LeMay?" All the moisture in Scarlett's mouth dried up. "Why do you have a gun?"

293

The woman pulled the car to a stop, turned off the lights, and pointed the gun straight at her chest. "Give me your cell phone."

"I don't understand."

"You don't have to understand, dear. You just have to *do it*," she hissed.

Scarlett reached into her pocket, touching the transmitter. Her heart thumped crazily as she saw a figure near the car. A man. Dark clothing. Wooly hat. She dug out her cell.

"Take out the battery." Mrs. LeMay waved the gun at her, and Scarlett's pulse skipped a few beats. There were some buildings ahead. A mausoleum and some storage sheds, hard to make out in the gray light. The sound of the occasional car suggested they weren't far from the highway.

She still wore the Kevlar vest beneath her jacket and sweater. Her biggest chance might be keeping that information a secret. She took out the battery and laid it on the dash.

"And the other one."

Scarlett turned toward Valerie, and her mouth dropped open.

"I know you have a burner. Just bring it out carefully and take the battery out of that too. I'm not going to hurt you. That man has Angel." Scarlett's eyes whipped around as the figure opened the trunk. "He wants to swap you for Angel because he's worried what you might know."

Dread squeezed her from the inside. She'd told Dorokhov that Maidstone had told her something before he died. Had someone passed that information on to this man? Had Raminski betrayed his Russian boss before shooting him dead?

Was this the man who'd set up her father all those years ago? Was she finally close to figuring out the truth? This wasn't quite how she'd expected it to go down.

Scarlett put her burner phone on the dash, but also clicked the switch of her transmitter to activate it. Then she saw the signal jammer Valerie drew out of her pocket and placed on the dashboard alongside the cells. Crap. Her bug would record, but not transmit until it found a cell phone signal. Then the digital audio file would beam directly to her email account. The truth would come out eventually, but until the jammer was disabled there was no way anyone could trace her location. Mrs. LeMay removed the keys from the ignition and eased out of the car. She went around the back before coming up and opening Scarlett's door. Scarlett sat there thinking frantically, but coming up with nothing. Then it was too late. Valerie waved the gun to indicate she get out. Scarlett did so, the cold bite of the air at least making her feel more awake.

"Walk toward him. This is a straight swap. You for Angel. You said yourself this was all your fault. I just want my daughter back. She hasn't done anything."

Scarlett nodded and breathed lightly. "I want her back too." But she did not want to die and this did not seem like a situation where an abductor would let his captives walk away. "What makes you think you can trust him to keep his word?"

"Oh, he'll do as I tell him." The woman sounded confident. Too confident.

Scarlett half-turned to look at her face, but was captivated by a blonde-haired figure climbing out of the trunk of the car. The figure wobbled.

"Angel, honey. Are you okay?" Mrs. LeMay called out.

"Mom?"

Scarlett swallowed back a cry of relief that her friend was still alive. Then Valerie prodded her forward with the gun. Angel was alive, but Scarlett doubted it would be for much longer. This man wouldn't want any witnesses.

To think she'd shied away from telling Matt how she really felt. How foolishly optimistic to think she'd get a second chance.

Scarlett had to keep them talking. She wanted that second chance. She wanted a future with him. Matt would find her. He and Parker and Rooney and Frazer. They were smart and brilliant and they would find her. She just hoped it wouldn't be too late.

"Let her go, Guy." *Guy? Clarkson?* "I brought Scarlett. For the love of God let my little girl go."

"I told you I'd get her back for you." The man eased the blindfold up over Angel's forehead. Even in the dim light Scarlett could see a cut on Angel's cheek, and her eyes were almost swollen closed from an obvious beating. Angel's arms were secured behind her back, and she staggered as if she couldn't hold herself up properly. The man grabbed her from behind, and she cried out in pain.

"Oh, God, Oh, baby. What did they do to you?" Valerie sobbed.

"I think she might have a broken rib. The drugs are wearing off. She'll be fine."

"Thank you. I can't thank you enough." Valerie was sobbing.

"Send me the girl," Guy ordered. "That's all I want."

"You first." Valerie grabbed Scarlett's arm and dug in her nails. *Ouch.*

The man smiled sadly. He was unremarkable, nondescript—someone easily overlooked. "After all these years you don't trust me? All those afternoons we spent together naked? All those promises you made me?"

"Mom?" Angel said uncertainly.

"Be quiet, Guy," Valerie snapped.

"You always were dominant, Valerie. I dug it in bed. Didn't much care for it the rest of the time." His voice became harder.

Things were clicking into place in Scarlett's head. "You two were lovers?"

"What the hell, Mom?"

"Wow—no wonder everyone says you're so smart, Scarlett Stone." Guy's gasp was mocking. "Your daddy used to sing your praises like you were the only kid to ever learn the alphabet. Heard he wasn't doing so well…"

Rage rose up inside Scarlett, but she controlled it.

"Stop talking, Guy. You're going to ruin everything." Valerie was edging closer. Trying to get to her daughter.

"No, Valerie." His voice rose. "You don't get to tell me what to do. Not anymore. I believed you. I *loved* you. You said you were going to leave him, but you never did."

"Oh, my God, Mom. How could you do that to Dad?" asked Angel.

This was a nightmare.

Valerie's fingers on her arm grew even more painful, but Scarlett had figured it out. "Dorokhov found out you were having an affair, didn't he? Blackmailed you into spying for him. You're Marlon, both of you."

Clarkson sneered. "He said it would be a one-time deal and then photographed us doing that too. Had us by the balls."

"You persuaded Raminski to shoot him." Scarlett didn't know how, but she knew it was true.

"Dorokhov deserved to die."

"Shut up, Guy!"

He put his pistol to Angel's head, and Scarlett heard Mrs. LeMay's breath seize. These two people had destroyed so many lives simply because they'd refused to own up to having an affair.

Scarlett refused to stay quiet. She had to stall for time. For some sort of chance to get away. She eyed the gloomy tombstones, mist clinging to the ground. It was dark enough they might be able to run and hide. Maybe. "And you two decided to set up my father to take the fall. You destroyed my family." She half-turned to Valerie. "Then acted like you were doing us a favor to even talk to us." She felt sick. The betrayal was beyond anything she'd imagined. "You planted that evidence in our house." It all made sense suddenly.

"You set up Scarlett's father? He really is innocent?" Angel asked on a whisper. "Oh, Scarlett, I'm so sorry. All these years and I never believed you."

Scarlett's heart ached for her friend. She couldn't imagine what this would do to their family. God knew what hers had suffered had been bad enough, but a spy sex scandal involving a congressman's wife, and a rogue FBI agent? Combined with the wrongful conviction of an innocent man and the assassination of the Russian Ambassador? It would make the press coverage from fourteen years ago look like a community picnic.

Assuming the truth came out.

Angel's expression held a touch of madness. "This is actually all my fault. I should never have made you go to that party, Scar." She started to laugh, but the sound was awful, full of the knowledge she was about to die. "Next year we'll stay home and watch old movies, I promise. Is it still Christmas?"

Scarlett nodded. "You're the best friend a girl could ever have, you know that?"

Guy Clarkson gave a harsh laugh. "Without your friendship, your dear, old daddy would never have gone to jail."

"Maybe, maybe not. You and Valerie are the ones who set him up." She couldn't keep the revulsion out of her voice.

Valerie LeMay shoved her forward. "Send Angel to me. Now. Take this one and do what you have to."

Angel staggered forward as Clarkson pushed her. "You mean kill her, right, Mom?"

"Shut up, Angelina."

"Why? Because you're my mother?" Angel spat at her mother's feet. "You disgust me." Angel took a step toward her, and Scarlett locked her arms around her friend, making sure Angel felt the stiff vest she wore beneath her clothes.

Over Angel's head she watched the man, Guy Clarkson. His eyes glittered and never left Valerie.

A noise in the darkness had him glancing quickly around. Was that the cavalry?

Think fast. "I lied," Scarlett said quickly, "when I said Maidstone told me something. The FBI used it as bait to see what the people under their surveillance did. They'll be here any minute." She edged Angel a little sideways. Hugged her again and whispered in her ear, "We need to run."

Clarkson's mouth thinned. "There's no way they'll link this to me."

"They were watching Branson all night. They know it isn't him."

He lifted the gun, aiming not at her but at Angel's mother, the woman who'd ultimately betrayed him—the only person left alive who knew the true extent of his crimes. Valerie was the true reason he'd brought them all here.

Angel's mother seemed to figure it out in the same moment. Her hand shook as she pointed the gun at Guy. They stared into one another's eyes. "Please," she said. And then she pulled the trigger.

———

Parker drove like the getaway man from a bank heist. Rooney was in the back, strapped in, laptop on her knees as she and Matt poured over satellite imagery. Scarlett had been out of his sight for twenty-five minutes and was probably in mortal danger, and it was his fault. He'd been blind because of some outdated notion of what...that American housewives didn't commit espionage, or weren't dangerous? How stupid could he get?

Had he lost Scarlett forever? Even if he found her alive would she forgive the fact he'd lied to her about her best friend? Right now, he could only think about getting her to safety. Everything else would wait.

He had Rooney's phone to his ear as the traffic cops fed him information.

"Camera has her as far as Fenwick Street North." Which they were just passing. "But they didn't pass Bladensburgh Road." He repeated what the operator told him.

"Big intersection ahead," Parker stated, not slowing down. "Left or right?"

Matt was staring at a map of the area. Industrial plots and residential houses. He zoomed in on a big green space. There were two big crosses on the ground visible from the air. What the hell was that?

"Left or right?" Parker demanded.

"Left," Frazer ordered.

Matt stared harder. It was a cemetery. "Right."

Parker went right. They took the corner hard, and Matt cushioned Rooney as she was pressed against him from the g-force. They were traveling too fast to take the first right again and ended up on Montana Avenue. "Mount Olivet Cemetery on the right-hand side."

The dispatcher was talking him through more negative sightings on the traffic cams. Suddenly the phone went dead. "Shit. I lost the signal."

Parker pulled over so fast Matt thought he'd get whiplash. "Then they're here." Parker pointed to the iron railings that surrounded the cemetery.

"How can you be so sure?" Matt asked. Then he spotted it. A big ass cell tower fifty feet away, which should have provided crystal-clear service, but didn't. "Bingo." They got out of the car, and he vaulted the railing. Rooney was pissed that she needed help to get over the high metal fence.

"Everyone is wearing a vest, yes?" They all nodded, weapons drawn. Frazer pointed Parker and Rooney north behind the building to circle around from one side while they went the other.

———

Scarlett didn't wait to see whether or not Valerie hit Clarkson. She pushed Angel ahead of her. "Run!" There was another shot behind her. And then another. Scarlett risked a look, and

Valerie was down on the ground, hands outstretched above her head.

"Mom?" Angel tried to turn around.

Scarlett grabbed her arm and shoved her along. "Run, dammit."

She heard footsteps behind them and knew Clarkson was in pursuit. They were almost at the side of the nearest storage shed when a fourth shot rang out. The force of the bullet hit just beneath her right shoulder blade, punching hard enough to drop her to her knees. Angel stopped and whirled, but then a dark figure—Matt—stepped out from behind the wall. Another man dove on top of her friend as a bullet whizzed over her head and smashed into the wall. Matt took aim and fired two shots.

The silence that followed seemed to swallow up sound. All she could hear was her breath rasping in her chest as she sank to the icy grass.

Arms rolled her over. "Scarlett? Are you okay?"

Matt. He'd found her.

Hands kept searching her body, icy cold seeping in when he ripped up her sweater and scanned every inch of flesh. "It's okay." She tried to grab his hands. "I'm not hit. Just winded." Holy hell, it *hurt.*

"I'm so fucking sorry I let them get their hands on you." Matt closed his eyes. "When I saw you go down…" His voice cracked. "I thought I'd lost you."

She touched his cheek and smiled. "You *found* me."

His arms closed around her. "I should never have let you go in the first place."

"I love you." It came out as if she'd said it a million times, rather than being the first time. "I should have told you on the phone earlier, but I was scared you didn't mean it, or you'd changed your mind."

Matt kissed her. Not a polite peck on the lips, but a toe-curling, lip searing, take-me-to-Heaven smacker. Immediately her heart started beating faster and her blood heated. She wrapped her arms around him and never wanted to let go.

Then Angel's forlorn cry of "Mom!" shattered her happiness and her relief. She clung to Matt as she listened to her friend scream out her grief. And although Scarlett was glad they'd finally found the real traitors, she hurt too. All those years she'd been taking comfort from the person who'd been responsible for setting up her father. She felt so stupid. So used. Matt helped her up out of the damp grass and tucked her under his arm.

Their footsteps crunched as they walked across to where Guy Clarkson lay dead. Matt handed his weapon to Frazer who took it with a nod. Scarlett knew that anyone involved in this type of shooting had to go through all sorts of questioning, but there could be little doubt it was justified.

Angel was bent over her mother's body, holding her hand. Someone had released her bonds. "Mom," she sobbed. "Don't die. Please don't die."

Parker met Scarlett's gaze and shook his head.

After a couple of minutes of listening to Angel cry, Rooney put her arms gently around her and moved her away. Scarlett wanted to go to her friend, but Matt wouldn't let her. "Not until after you've both made official statements." The area was a crime scene. Everything had to be left as untouched as possible.

It was over.

It was finally over.

Bright, pink sunlight streaked the horizon.

Scarlett turned to face Matt. "I need to go to Mom and Dad. I have to see them. I have to tell them the truth about everything that happened." Tears burned. She also wanted to stay here with Matt, to make sure he was safe and didn't get into trouble for helping her.

His eyes shone as his hand smoothed back her hair. He kissed her, and she rose up to meet him. Then he pulled back and rested his forehead against hers. "You have to go. But I have to stay. For now."

She grabbed his hand. "Promise we aren't over? Promise this wasn't one of those adrenaline-based flings that burns out as soon as the danger is over?"

He kissed her again. "I fell for you when I thought you were a politician's daughter. I fell for you again when I thought you were the daughter of a spy. I don't think I'm going to have a problem staying in love with a super-smart scientist. Trust me."

She did trust him. Had almost from the start. "I still owe you a boat." Emotion made it hard to talk. "Will you come meet my father? As soon as you're able?"

Matt glanced at his boss. "I'd be delighted and humbled to meet your father, Scarlett."

Frazer nodded. In the distance sirens droned through the air. "I'm sending Rooney and Parker with you to Colorado, Scarlett. I'll have a jet at Andrews waiting for you in thirty minutes."

"Good," Matt said firmly.

"Rooney can take your statement on the way."

Scarlett knew she should feel great. She was alive and she'd done everything she'd set out to do. Proved her father wasn't the spy he'd been convicted of being. She started to walk away from Matt and Angel, but a well of sadness started opening up inside her with every step she took. She stopped moving. Parker turned and looked at her expectantly. "Actually," she said to him. "You and Rooney should head back to West Virginia as planned. I'm going to wait for Matt. We'll go to Colorado together."

Matt's eyes looked suspiciously damp when she turned around.

She ran and threw her arms around his neck and hung on tight. She'd already waited a lifetime. She could wait a few more hours.

Parker checked his cell, then reached into Mrs. LeMay's Mercedes to switch off the signal jammer, using his shirt sleeve over his hand, presumably not to disturb fingerprint evidence. A moment later, Frazer was on the phone, talking to someone high up if his posture was anything to go by.

"Give me your phone," she urged Matt.

He handed it over. She dialed a number and closed her eyes as Susan Stone answered.

"Hi, Mom? Is Dad okay?" She sagged a little against Matt as her mother told her that her father had woken up and even said a few words. "We did it, Mom. We found the real spy." She caught Frazer's gaze. "I think Dad's going to be exonerated."

Frazer nodded.

"We're going to make sure he gets the best treatment possible," Matt said into her hair.

Scarlett spoke for a few minutes, then said goodbye and hung up. "I don't think she really believes me."

Frazer squeezed her arm. "She'll believe it when the Attorney General turns up this afternoon to offer his sincere apologies and a presidential pardon."

Scarlett nodded. "Good. Thanks. We need to get the questioning over with as soon as possible. Matt needs to go see his mother before we both head to Colorado tonight." She held Frazer's blue eyes. "It has to be tonight. Please, the FBI can come with us and question us en route." Her hand dipped into her pocket and brushed against the transmitter. She held it out. "I almost forgot…Hopefully it recorded Clarkson's and Valerie's confessions. They were lovers, and Dorokhov blackmailed them into working for him when he found out." She shuddered and Matt's arms wrapped tightly around her. Frazer took the bug and tossed it to Parker.

"Now Valerie's signal jammer is turned off the audio file should have jumped on the cell phone signals and been sent to my email account. At least that's the theory."

The cops came screaming along the lanes of the quiet cemetery. She tensed as they got out, hands on weapons. Frazer, Rooney, and Matt had their gold shields out and were trying to explain the two dead bodies.

Scarlett couldn't believe the weight of sadness that had lifted from her chest.

Matt glanced over at her and smiled. Even as grim sadness surrounded them, she knew with sudden clarity that everything was going to work out. She'd asked for one miracle and gotten two.

"How much are sailboats?" she asked Parker, who'd come to stand beside her as the cops tried to figure out jurisdiction.

"One like Lazlo's? About ten grand."

Oh, boy. Thankfully she had some savings.

Parker looked over to where Rooney was comforting Angel. "Tell Lazlo he owes me a twenty, by the way. I cracked his password."

Scarlett huffed out a laugh. "Really? While everything else was going on, you took the time to hack his password?"

"TOEDWY—all uppercase." His grin made his face come alive.

"TOEDWY? I don't get it." Scarlett's teeth chattered.

"The Only Easy Day Was Yesterday. SEAL motto." Parker winked, then walked away as a bunch of FBI agents arrived, Ridley Branson amongst them. He stood in front of her, and Matt was suddenly miraculously back at her side.

The chief of counterespionage hung his head. "I don't know what to say, Dr. Stone. I am beyond shamed by my own personal failures."

"Don't say it to me." All the anger that had kept her going for the last fourteen long years hit her hard again. "Go say it to my father, right now. Today. Beg *him* for forgiveness. Not me."

Branson nodded and walked away. Emotions she'd thought she'd controlled started fizzing inside her again.

Matt took her hand and squeezed her fingers. "Did I tell you I loved you, without yelling at you, yet?"

She blinked away all the stupid tears that wanted to come. She wouldn't let them. "I could get used to you saying that, you know."

"You better." He turned so they were face-to-face. "This is it, Scarlett. That whole love at first sight cliché? We're it. Living proof." The gold in his hazel eyes glowed. "It's going to take a while to figure out the mechanics of us being together, but don't doubt the sentiment. I love you. That isn't going to stop. *Ever.*"

"I know." She looked up at him. Touched his cheek. "I think I've been waiting for you my whole life."

"Promise me one thing." His eyes scanned her face. She spotted an agent over his shoulder who was obviously waiting to take him in for questioning or debriefing or whatever they called it.

"What?"

"No more taking the law into your own hands."

"That's an easy promise to make." She laughed. "You have to promise me something too." She rose up on tiptoe and whispered in his ear. "It involves having sex in the shower at every possible opportunity for the next twenty years."

"Only twenty?" He pulled back.

"I didn't want to scare you with too long a commitment."

He narrowed his gaze. "Okay. We can reassess in twenty years."

The FBI agent stepped closer.

Matt's eyes got serious. "You should go to your dad, you know. I promise I'll get there as soon as I can." He threw a look over his shoulder. "This could take a while."

Scarlett nodded. "I want you with me."

"I am with you, Scarlett." He touched his heart and was finally led away.

She found herself pulled against another male chest offering comfort.

"Come on." Alex Parker took her hand and led her through the patrol cars and uniformed officers. "It's almost over. And then the good stuff begins."

EPILOGUE

One month later.

Scarlett stood in the living room of her childhood home, waiting for the car to arrive. She'd cleaned the house literally from top to bottom. People crowded the streets outside; the press was camped out ten-deep.

"Relax." Matt pulled her into his arms for a kiss. She savored the taste, the warmth, the solid reassurance of the man. He was everything she'd imagined when she'd first seen him, and more.

His mother was still in a coma, which had been the only thing that hadn't changed over the last few weeks. It was heartbreaking, but Scarlett tried to keep him company as much as possible when he went to visit. It was all they could do. Congressman LeMay had stepped down. Scarlett had been to see Angel, and they'd talked for hours about everything that had happened. Angel wasn't the same person she'd been before the kidnapping, but Scarlett no longer held herself completely responsible—Dorokhov had kidnapped her in an attempt to control Valerie. Angel was getting help. Scarlett would be there if she needed her.

The feds were still trying to figure it all out.

The fact Raminski had been the one to shoot Dorokhov didn't seem to be in doubt. It had stopped a major incident turning into all-out war. As far as the rest of the investigation went, none of them were really sure what was happening. They'd all been excluded from it; reprimanded for not following protocol on one hand, applauded for solving the case on the other. Frazer had told them it was bureaucracy versus politics, and for once politics was working in their favor.

She'd been back at work for the last two weeks as her father had continued to recover and receive treatment at one of the top hospitals in the country. Today he was finally coming home.

"I have something for you." Matt held out a jeweler's box—too big to be for a ring, though her heart sped up at the thought. She chided herself.

Matt had spent three full days being questioned by the FBI. Even Frazer's clout hadn't been able to make the wheels turn any faster. They'd missed their first Christmas together.

"What is it?" She grinned, taking it from him. She had a present for him too, but it wouldn't fit in a box.

He'd met her father and they seemed to like each other. Easier now that her father had been given a public, presidential pardon and his conviction quashed, which Matt had helped make happen.

She opened the box and inside was a key on a silver chain. She frowned. "What's it for? Did you buy me a Ferrari?"

"It's for my house."

"But you don't have a house."

"I do now, or rather, *we* do. In Arlington, assuming you want to, you know…live together?" His confidence slipped as he took in her expression. "Oh, crap. I moved too fast, or too slow, I—"

She caught his hands. "No. No! I just…" She bit her lip. "I had Alex help me find you a boat. We had it delivered to the marina yesterday."

He grinned. "You were gonna live with me on a boat?"

She nodded tentatively. "Assuming you wanted me to."

"Of course I'd want you to, but trust me, a house will be easier." He crushed her lips to his and by the time they came up for air she'd forgotten there were a thousand people outside the door. "I can teach you to sail." His grin turned wicked. "I can teach you all sorts of things."

She shivered with anticipation. Then she heard the sound of a car pulling into the drive. Matt heard it too and took a step back.

Scarlett grabbed his hand and opened the door. A motorcade worthy of a president lined up along the driveway and down the street. FBI agents held back the press and crowd as everyone tried to get a look at the man who'd been the victim of a terrible miscarriage of justice. Ridley Branson himself opened the door for her father to climb out of the limousine. Her dad looked pale, but much better than the last time she'd seen him in the hospital a week ago. He'd gained weight and could move around without wincing in pain. Scarlett almost couldn't believe the sight. Her mother walked around the car and took her husband's arm. Scarlett noted the tilt of both their chins, high and proud. Ignoring the blinding cameras, she ran down the steps and hugged her father tightly, careful not to knock him over in her enthusiasm. Matt came out too and they stood aside to watch Richard Stone walk back into the house he'd left fourteen years ago, thinking it was just another ordinary day at the office.

"Welcome home, Agent Stone," Ridley Branson said, loud enough for the crowd to hear.

Her father nodded, graciously in Scarlett's opinion, and began to climb the steps without anyone's help. Emotion expanded in her throat until she couldn't speak. Matt rubbed his hand down her back. "Breathe. You did it, Scarlett. You cleared his name."

She smiled and kissed him, in front of the entire world. "*We* did it. We cleared his name. Together."

A COLD DARK PLACE

Cold Justice Series Book 1

Former CIA assassin Alex Parker works for The Gateway Project, a clandestine government organization hell-bent on taking out serial killers and pedophiles before they enter the justice system. Alex doesn't enjoy killing, but he's damn good at it. He's good at dodging the law, too—until a beautiful rookie agent has him wondering what it might be like to get caught.

FBI Special Agent Mallory Rooney has spent years hunting the lowlife who abducted her identical twin sister eighteen years ago. Now, during an on-going serial killer investigation, Mallory begins to suspect there's a vigilante operating outside the law. She has no choice but to take him down, because murder isn't justice. Is it?

When Mallory starts asking questions, The Gateway Project management starts to sweat, and orders Alex to watch her. As soon as they meet, the two begin to fall in love. But the lies and betrayals that define Alex's life threaten to destroy them both—especially when the man who stole her sister all those years ago makes Mallory his next target, and Alex must reveal his true identity to save the woman he loves.

COLD PURSUIT

Cold Justice Series Book 2

Single mom Vivi Vincent is thrust into her worst nightmare when she's trapped inside a mall during a terror attack along with her eight-year-old son. With the help of Jed Brennan, an FBI special agent on enforced leave, Vivi and her son survive the assault. But the danger is far from over.

Vivi's son may have witnessed critical details of the terrorists' future plans and is targeted for death, but he's mute, and he's traumatized. Still someone launches a strike against the FBI's safe house, and Jed fears the bad guys have an inside man. No longer knowing who to trust, he hides mother and son in a log cabin deep in the heart of the Wisconsin Northwoods. There Jed and Vivi try to figure out how to unlock the information inside her son's head. What they don't bargain for is the red-hot attraction that flares between them, or the extent of the sinister plot that threatens to rip apart not only any chance of happiness they might have together, but also the very fabric of American society.

COLD FEAR

Cold Justice Series Book 4

When old evidence turns up on a fresh corpse, ASAC Lincoln Frazer is determined it won't delay the execution of a convicted serial killer. But when more young women are brutally slain, it becomes clear—this new killer is intimately familiar with the old murders.

Former Army Captain Dr. Isadora Campbell helped her mother conceal a terrible crime. After her mother's death, Izzy resigned her commission and returned to the Outer Banks to raise her rebellious teenage sister. But it doesn't take long for Izzy to suspect that someone knows exactly what she did, all those years ago.

With pressure mounting to reopen the old case, Frazer will use any means possible to catch the killer. Thrust together during the investigation, he and Izzy find themselves reluctantly attracted to one another, and begin an affair. Meanwhile the killer is much closer than they think. Izzy's confession of her secret drives Frazer away as he struggles with her deception. By the time he realizes he's fallen in love with the stubborn woman, the killer has her. Now the race is on to save Izzy, and any chance of a future they might have together.

ACKNOWLEDGMENTS

I want to thank Angela Knight's husband Lieutenant Michael G. Woodcock for detailed information on how polygraph results are stored, and other associated matters. I probably shocked him when I yelled out of the elevator in San Antonio, asking if I could email him with questions. Big thanks for understanding the crazy minds of authors. Also, Angela Bell, Office of Public Affairs, Federal Bureau of Investigation, for answering my many and varied queries about evidence storage, and procedure—thanks for your patience. And author, Saranna DeWylde, who generously talked me through various prison details. The writing community never fails to amaze me with their varied experience and willingness to share. Needless to say, I used artistic license with the information they provided and any errors are mine.

As always, biggest thanks go to my amazing critique partner Kathy Altman—she rocks! Also editors, Alicia Dean, and Joan at JRT Editing, who helped get this manuscript into shape. I'm very grateful to Syd Gill for interpreting my vision and creating the awesome covers for the *Cold Justice Series*.

Thanks to my fabulous family, near and far. And also to my readers and friends, both in real life and online—especially the other authors from the Dangerous Attraction box set, Not Your Usual Suspects blog, and the Montlake Romance authors. It's great to have such beautiful support.

DEAR READER

Thank you for reading *Cold Light Of Day*. I hope you enjoyed it. If you did, please help other readers find this book:

1. If you have time to leave a review, I appreciate it. Thanks.
2. To keep up-to-date with releases and find out about exclusive offers check out my website (http://www.toniandersonauthor.com) and sign up for my Newsletter/ Mailing List.
3. Come "like" my Facebook Page: https://www.facebook.com/pages/Toni-Anderson-Author-Page/153356538022559?ref=hl
4. Interested in a writer's life? All my web links are on my website www.toniandersonauthor.com. I love chatting to readers!

Thanks again!

REVIEWS

COLD LIGHT OF DAY
(Cold Justice Book #3)
(2015 Holt Medallion Finalist)

"This has easily cruised into my top ten
romances…in the history of EVER."
—Heroes and Heartbreakers

TOP PICK "*Cold Light of Day* has all the elements of a
great romantic suspense…danger, romance, action, and
intrigue. I'd recommend *Cold Light of Day* to any romantic
suspense reader looking for a thrilling adventure!"
—Harlequin Junkie

COLD PURSUIT
(Cold Justice Book #2)
(Finalist in 2015 Gayle Wilson Award of Excellence,
National Readers Choice Awards, and National Excellence
in Romance Fiction Award for Romantic Suspense.)

THE KILLING GAME
(2014 RITA® Finalist, and National
Readers Choice Awards Finalist)

"I'd recommend this to any romantic suspense
reader looking for a unique, intricately woven
story that will really touch you."
—Peaces of Me (5 Stars)

"This is a smart story. This is a sexy story.
This is a well written story. This is one of my favorite
romantic suspense stories I've read all year.
I wish there was more!"
—Love Affair With An e-Reader (5 Stars)

DARK WATERS
(International bestseller. National
Readers Choice Awards Finalist)

"In this action-packed contemporary, Anderson
(*Dangerous Waters*) weaves together a tapestry
of powerful suspense and sizzling romance."
—*Publishers Weekly*

"The pacing in this book is superb. The tension
really never lets up…I never felt there was
a good 'stopping point' in this book, which is
probably why I was reading all night."
—Smart Bitches, Trashy Books

pleasure of reading this year and I will definitely
be looking for more by Toni Anderson."
—Blithely Bookish (5 Stars)

"Sensual, different; romance with a bit of
angst, just how I like them; *Edge of Survival* is
a romantic suspense not to be missed."
—Maldivian Book Reviewer's Realm of Romance (5 Stars)

STORM WARNING
(Best Book of 2010 Nominee
—The Romance Reviews)

"*Storm Warning* is an intense, provocative paranormal
romance with a suspenseful twist…This is a book that
I am unquestionably adding to my keeper collection."
—Night Owl Reviews (TOP PICK)

"It is exactly the way I like my romantic
suspense novels to be."
—The Romance Reviews

"The plot is full of suspense and some pretty incredible
plot twists.…will have you on the edge of your seat."
—Coffee Time Romance & More

SEA OF SUSPICION
(Best Book of 2010 Nominee
—The Romance Reviews. National bestseller)

"Deeply atmospheric and filled with twists and turns, *Sea of Suspicion* kept me flying eagerly through the pages."
—All About Romance

"*Sea of Suspicion* is one heck of a book! The twists, turns, passion, and many colorful characters give Ms. Anderson's novel a delightful edge."
—Coffee Time Romance

"Set along the coast of Scotland, *Sea of Suspicion* is a riveting story of suspense and the depths and heights of human character."
—The Romance Reviews

HER LAST CHANCE
(2014 Daphne du Maurier finalist)

"A high intensity story, with action from the first page on, an intricate suspense tale with twists and turns that are surprising and a conclusion that is as near to closure as is possible to come. The characters are deep and rather brooding, but manage to lose themselves in each other. And the writing is clever, hot and altogether fabulous!"
—Ripe for Reader

"From the opening scene I was turning the pages totally entranced in the story. I've loved all this authors books but at this moment this has to be my favorite."
—SnS Reviews

HER SANCTUARY
(National bestseller)

"*Her Sanctuary* is a riveting fast-paced
suspense story, filled with twists, turns, and danger. As
the story flows seamlessly between the protagonists
and antagonists, the tension rises to fever pitch. Just
when you think you know the good guys from the
bad, Anderson provides a surprising twist, or two."
—Night Owl Romance (TOP PICK)

"Suspenseful, riveting and explosive, this
reader absolutely loved this story."
—Fallen Angel Reviews (5 Angels)

"Ms. Anderson presents us with one fantastic
story that has me wanting more."
—Romance Junkies (4.5 Blue Ribbons)

ABOUT THE AUTHOR

New York Times and *USA Today* international bestselling author, Toni Anderson, writes dark, gritty Romantic Suspense. Her novels have been nominated for the prestigious Romance Writers of America® RITA® Award, Gayle Wilson Award of Excellence, Holt Medallion, Daphne du Maurier Awards for Excellence, and National Readers' Choice Awards in Romantic Suspense. *A Cold Dark Place* won the 2014 New England Readers' Choice Award for Romantic Suspense.

A graduate of Marine Biology from the University of Liverpool, and the University of St. Andrews, Toni was a Post-doctoral Research Scientist for several years, and travelled the world with her work. After living in seven different countries, she finally settled in the Canadian prairies with her Irish husband and two children. Now she spends her time talking to the voices in her head and making things up. Toni has no explanation for her oft-times dark imagination, and only hopes the romance makes up for it. She's addicted to reading, dogs, tea (never travels without it), and chocolate. She loves to hear from readers.

Toni donates 15% of her royalties from *Edge of Survival* to diabetes research. Find out more on her website at www.toniandersonauthor.com.

9/16-1

CPSIA information can be obtained at www.ICGtesting.com
Printed in the USA
LVOW11s1306031115

460913LV00001B/46/P

9 780993 908927